PRAISE FOR *HOROSCOPE*

"Frontiere grabs you immediately with her lucid prose and engaging style. Kelly York is a flawed but beautiful character whose dedication to helping people through the use of astrology, psychology, and wisdom is deeply touching and affecting. *Horoscope* is truly out of this world. A must-read."
> —David Assael, writer/producer (*Northern Exposure, St. Elsewhere, Picket Fences, Star Trek: The Next Generation, Evan's Crime*)

"The story hooked me from the very start. I couldn't wait to see what would happen next as Kelly York gets more and more deeply involved in a murder case that draws her out of her comfortable existence and into a dangerous mystery."
> —Andrew Tennenbaum, President, Flashpoint Entertainment, and producer (*The Bourne Identity* and *Water for Elephants)*

"Frontiere has created a thoroughly believable character, and we know it's only a matter of time before we enter her nightmare. An absorbing read."
> —Phyllis Naylor, best-selling author of *Shiloh*, *Faces in the Water*, and *Jade Green*

"*Horoscope* grabs your attention and keeps it. Better check your sign before reading this one!"
> —Dylan Ratigan, best-selling author of *Greedy Bastards* and sustainability entrepreneur

"A taut psychological thriller, *Horoscope* combines the best of literary fiction with heart-pounding suspense. With its compelling characters and rich, multilayered plot, *Horoscope* is mystery writing at its best."
> —Lori Andrews, author of the Alexandra Blake mysteries (*Sequence, The Silent Assassin*, and *Immunity*)

"Put a log on the fire, lock the doors and windows, and settle in for a good read."

—Scott Wilson, actor (*The Walking Dead* and *In Cold Blood*)

"A real page-turner. I was totally engrossed in the mystery and captivated by the characters. Dr. Kelly York is the new leading lady of mystery thrillers."

—Robert Levy, producer and partner, Tapestry Films (*Wedding Crashers*, *Serendipity*, the Mary-Kate and Ashley series)

"Frontiere has created an intelligent, sympathetic, and compelling character in Kelly York. I can hardly wait to read the Kelly York mysteries to come."

—Sara Risher, CEO, Chick Flicks Productions, and former Chair of Production, New Line Cinema

"The *Da Vinci Code* meets *Rear Window*. Like Robert Langdon unravels mysteries utilizing a fascinating expertise, symbology, Kelly York solves crimes with an equally intriguing specialty, astrology. And just as Jimmy Stewart's character faces thrills and murder while unable to leave his apartment, Kelly York encounters a killer and an ingenious whodunnit as she's confined to her Manhattan brownstone. This exciting combo of Dan Brown and Alfred Hitchcock made Georgia Frontiere's novel one of the most exciting reads I've had in a long time."

—Michael Davis, writer/director/artist (*Shoot 'Em Up*, *Eight Days a Week*)

"*Horoscope* is an exceptionally well-written and engrossing thriller. The suspense will keep you on the edge of your seat until the last page."

—Chris McGurk, Chairman and CEO, Cinedigm; former President, Walt Disney Motion Pictures; and former President, Universal Pictures

"With its intriguing use of astrology as a repeating element and the touching backstory about its author, with an engaging and sympathetic heroine and its bonus supply of FBI lore, *Horoscope* is an absorbing and most satisfying read."
    —Jamie Wolf, Vice President, PEN Center USA

"A great read. A total page-turner with characters that pop off the page and a plot that keeps you guessing."
    —Richard Arlook, producer/manager (*Turn It Up, Rodham*)

"James Patterson, watch out—here comes Georgia Frontiere's *Horoscope*. Enjoy this book. You won't be able to put it down."
    —Richard Krevolin, best-selling author of *Screenwriting from the Soul* and *King Levine*

"A true page-turner. Kelly York is a terrific heroine—vulnerable, intelligent, and in real trouble. The combination of astrology and psychology is quite a twosome."
    —Julian Schlossberg, theatrical producer (*Bullets over Broadway, Sly Fox*)

"I loved this book! A page-turner and a great mystery. Kelly York is a great character!"
    —Andrew Jenks, best-selling author of *My Adventures as a Young Filmmaker* and filmmaker (*World of Jenks, The Zen of Bobby V*)

"Frontiere has penned a mystery thriller worthy of the best Agatha Christie novel, and she clearly has a Hitchcockian instinct for relentless suspense. *Horoscope* will have your mind racing and your heart pumping! I can't wait to go on Kelly York's next adventure!"
    —Steve Bratter, filmmaker (*Demolition Man*), host of *Talking Movies*, and author of *The Bratter Breakdown*

"Who knew that Georgia could write such a powerful thriller?"
—John Shaw, former President, St. Louis Rams

"*Horoscope* had me sitting on the edge of my seat from the first chapter throughout the entire read. A powerfully exciting storyline that's impossible to put down. Bravo!"
—Vicki Escarra, CEO, Opportunity International, and former
CEO, Feeding America

"*Horoscope* is fast-paced, colorful, and compelling . . . just like Georgia herself."
—Sandy Tung, filmmaker (*Across the Tracks, Saving Shiloh*)

"From the first chapter, *Horoscope* captivates with its original characters and clever plots twists. I couldn't put it down. I kept wishing it wouldn't end."
—Bruce Taylor, writer/producer (*The Brave One, The Equalizer*)

"Georgia Frontiere's creation of the character Kelly York is inventive and unique. Frontiere's mastery lies in her incredible attention to details. I look forward to seeing Kelly York in a movie or television series based on this enjoyable and well-crafted read. "
—Carl Borack, producer (*Shiloh, The Big Fix, Bienvenue à Cannes*);
US Olympian; and former Captain, US fencing team

"*Horoscope* is not simply a compelling mystery but so much more. It is visceral, original, intelligent storytelling in the tradition of great contemporary mystery writers from John le Carré to Dan Brown; I actually did not want to put it down."
—Arthur Joseph, best-selling author of *Vocal Leadership*, creator of
Vocal Awareness, and motivational speaker/educator

HOROSCOPE

The Astrology Murders

A Novel

GEORGIA FRONTIERE

Violet Mountain Press

Violet Mountain Press
9595 Wilshire Blvd., #201
Beverly Hills, CA 90212

Ordering Information

Quantity sales. Special discounts are available on quantity purchases by corporations, associations, and others. For details, contact the "Special Sales Department" at the address above.

Orders by US trade bookstores and wholesalers. Please contact BCH: (800) 431-1579 or visit www.bookch.com for details.

Publisher's Note: This is a work of fiction. It is a product of the author's imagination. Any resemblance to people, living or dead is purely coincidental. Occasionally, real places or institutions are used novelistically for atmosphere and are employed in a fictional manner. There is no connection between the characters or events in this novel to any real-life people, places, organizations, or companies of any kind.

Printed in the United States of America

Cataloging-in-Publication Data

Frontiere, Georgia.
  Horoscope : the astrology murders : a novel / Georgia
Frontiere.
    pages cm
    ISBN 978-0-9903101-3-6 (pbk)
    ISBN 978-0-9903101-4-3 (ebook)

    1. Serial murders—Fiction. 2. Detective and mystery
  stories. I. Title.
  PS3606.R64H67 2014   813'.6
  QBI14-600103

First Edition

18 17 16 15 14   10 9 8 7 6 5 4 3 2 1

Note to Reader

Our mother was known as the first prominent woman to own an American sports team. But her background was very different from what sports fans believe. Born at the dawn of the Depression, she was raised in a show business home. By the time she was eighteen, she had travelled the country with her mother and her brother and had toured as a singer with Bob Hope and other major entertainers. Singing was one of her creative passions. The other was writing. She wrote hundreds of poems and kept notebooks filled with her thoughts, sometimes just her anticipation of what the day might bring. A limited edition book of her poetry was published in 2002, and she was very proud of it.

Our mother died in 2008. In the last decade of her life, she had several offers to write an autobiography. She refused to do it on the grounds that she wouldn't write anything negative about anybody else and publishers weren't interested in a book that would have no negative gossip. She was compiling a book of anecdotes, photographs, and drawings that would tell her life story, and she contemplated publishing that at some point.

She told those closest to her that she had started writing a thriller about an astrologer and psychologist named Dr. Kelly Elizabeth York who lives in New York City. She loved the character and enjoyed talking about what was happening in her book. She had ideas for Kelly to solve lots of mysteries.

The initial book she was writing was to be called *Horoscope*. Our mother was so fascinated with astrology and psychology, she thought what better way to explore these fields than to come up with a character who was in both. Kelly and our mom shared another trait in common: the desire to help those around them. This became a core quality of Kelly's and a way for our mom to relate even more to her creation.

We had heard sections of the book read aloud over the phone or at dinner in the last couple of years before our mother died. We didn't know what there was of the novel until we went through her papers. What we found was the almost completed novel along with several outlines for other adventures for Kelly and many notes about Kelly and the other characters that our mother created as part of Kelly's life.

We reached out to Mark Bruce Rosin, who not only is a friend of the family's (including our mother) but is an accomplished writer and editor. We asked Mark to work on the manuscript as an editor and, in some ways, a collaborator. He read our mother's draft and notes and saw that the book was essentially there; all it needed was a fresh pair of eyes and an expert editor to bring it into shape. He did a tremendous job of doing just that while honoring the book and characters our mom created.

So, here is our mom's book, *Horoscope: The Astrology Murders*. We hope that the other Kelly Elizabeth York stories will be told in the future too.

Lucia Rodriguez
Chip Rosenbloom

Acknowledgments

We would like to thank the following people who were both personally inspiring to and caring of our mother during the writing of this book and her wonderful life: her six grandchildren—William, Stuart, Andrew, Lauren, Alexander, and Olivia; Kathleen Rosenbloom, her daughter-in-law; Lupe Rodriguez, her son-in-law; Earle Weatherwax, her adored companion of nineteen years; Ken Irwin, her brother; her ten nieces and nephews; John Shaw, her dear friend and confidant; Tom Guthrie, her close friend; Mike Moyneur; Lance Ferguson, her personal astrologer; Margie Baldwin, our spectacular cousin; Father Sal Polizzi, Marshall Klein, and Paul Mason, her dear friends; and Mark Bruce Rosin, who made this book possible through his dedication, experience, and talent. We would also like to thank Jane Rosenman and Dr. Leana F. Melat, Jungian psychotherapist and student of astrology, for their valuable support.

Prologue

HE COULD JUST SEE the moon through the fog. It was a weak, round glow. If you didn't know better, you might've thought it was full, but of course he did know better. It was only seven-eighths full.

He'd also known to expect Long Beach to be foggy. After all, it was a beach town, and a light fog had just begun to settle in on the night he'd driven there to get a look at the house and plan for tonight.

Tonight's fog was heavier. As he walked, he could see only a few feet in any direction. Looking down, he could make out the asphalt driveway under his feet. Looking straight ahead, he couldn't see any sign of the house, but he knew it was there, fifteen or twenty yards up the driveway. Most people preferred staying in on a night like this, but a night like this made his job easier. That's how he'd thought about it at first, as a job, a job he loved, a job he was born for. Then he'd realized that it wasn't just his job; it was his vocation. He had been called to it; it was his destiny.

Earlier tonight, at home, in the special room he had made, he had dressed himself in black: black jeans, black sweater, black jacket, black running shoes. Black was his favorite color. Wearing black was like hiding. It was like being in a black hole—you could just disappear in it and stay lost forever.

He heard the waves hitting the beach, and he knew he was nearing the house. He kept walking, and sure enough, through the fog, he began to see the outline of the house in the moonlight. Soon he arrived at the steps leading up to the porch. The house was dark, just as he knew it would be. It was 3:10 a.m. He knew she'd be asleep. She'd said she could sleep twelve hours at a go, and she had trouble waking up.

He reached into his back pocket, took out a pair of surgical gloves, and put them on. When he'd pulled them snugly over his hands, he tried the door in case she hadn't locked it. It didn't budge. No worries; he'd worked it all out ahead of time. He was a born planner.

He took the key from the front pocket of his jeans and slipped it into the lock. It went in easily, just as it was supposed to. He let himself in, noiselessly closing the door. He was enmeshed in darkness now, as if he'd disappeared into a real black hole. He took his black ski mask from his jacket and put it over his head. It was new, and it didn't have as much give as it would have later, after he'd used it more. He could feel it constraining his hair and his face, but it had slits for his eyes so he could see and for his nose and mouth so he could breathe.

For a while he just stood there, feeling his excitement as his eyes became used to the darkness. He saw that a sliver of moonlight was entering the house through the narrow space between the top of the door and the doorframe. Through the soles of his running shoes he could feel the plush carpet beneath his feet. No wooden floors to creak under his weight as he walked. Another sign that tonight's work would go well.

In front of him was a small living room, barely visible in the darkness; to his left, an even smaller room—a den or a study— almost as dark; to his right, an ink-black hallway that he thought must lead to the bedrooms. He took his first silent steps on the carpet into the hallway.

Almost immediately, he could hear her breathing in her sleep. He followed the sounds of her inhalations and exhalations. They were rhythmic and regular; soon they would cease altogether.

But not quite yet. There was more to his job than just that.

He stopped at the open door of her bedroom and looked inside. The drapes were open, and the moonlit fog came right up to her bare windows, casting the room in a silver light. He could see her torso as she slept, one of her arms dangling over the side of the mattress. She was still breathing deeply, unaware that he was in her house, unaware that he could be. That was part of what made him so excited: the element of surprise. The other part was the element of justice.

He passed a closet, a small closet, the kind they used to build in houses like this. The door was closed, but he didn't need to see inside to know what it was like in there: dark and close. If you sat on the floor of a closed closet like that, under the clothes, some of them hanging down and touching you, surrounding you, you would feel scared and you would think that you couldn't breathe. But gradually, you would realize that you were breathing, because otherwise you would be dead. You would still be scared, but after a while, a long while, you would begin to feel safe. Safe and private because you were alone.

He found himself thinking about the needles. His mother's needles. Then he thought about his mother. He pushed the thoughts away, burying them in the out-of-the-way corner of his mind where he stored all the things he didn't want to think about. The black corner was even better than a closed closet; it was like a black hole.

He looked again at the sleeping woman and walked toward

her bed. He could see her pale, pretty face, her short black hair. She was twenty-nine years old. Twenty-nine years old, three months, and four days. She had not had a long life.

He slipped his hand into his jacket and found the leather cord. The surgical gloves were so thin that as he stretched the cord tightly between both hands, he could feel the slightly rough texture of the leather. Whoever invented surgical gloves deserved some sort of prize, he thought. They were like an extra layer of skin, but better, because they would leave no prints.

He climbed onto the bed, turned her on her back, and straddled her sleeping body, kneeling with a bent leg on either side of her. Holding the cord in his left hand, he opened the button on his jeans and pulled down his zipper with his right. He wasn't wearing any underwear. He never did. It made him excited to feel his stiffness pushing against his pants, aching to get out. Or should he say to get in?

Aroused to the point of pain, he slipped on a condom and looked down at her. She was still asleep.

"You're making this too easy," he said.

Reaching down between his legs, he pulled up her nightgown and gathered it around her abdomen.

Her eyes opened. Seeing him above her, feeling the press of his knees against her body, holding her there, she gasped.

He stretched the leather cord between both hands again and lowered it onto her neck, applying just enough pressure to let her know how easy it would be for him to kill her with it.

Staring up at him, her eyes bulged with fear.

"The more scared you are, the hotter I get," he said.

Her mouth opened, but she was too frightened to scream.

Still pressing the cord across her throat, he lowered himself on top of her.

"The astrological aspects are good for this. They really are. At least mine are."

She felt him working his way inside her and started to cry. Unable to look at him, she closed her eyes. She never opened them again.

When he was through, he thought about how simple it had been. All the planning he'd put into it was worth it. For a moment he regretted that he'd decided on her first, because her house was so isolated. That had its advantages, of course, which was why he'd picked her, but now he realized it would take a while before someone found out what he'd done, and he wasn't sure he was happy about that. He consoled himself by thinking that someone would find her eventually. As invisible as he was that night, soon, through her, he would be very visible.

One

A SAFE PLACE? MARRIAGE is not. At least not for me, Kelly thought. I don't even know why I would wake up thinking about it.

But maybe it wasn't really marriage her dreaming mind had been thinking about, she reflected; maybe it was feeling safe. She felt cozy in her bed. Yet warm and comfortable as she felt ensconced under her duvet, maybe her dreaming mind, like her waking mind, was preoccupied with the fact that suddenly everything about her life had changed, and feeling safe was something she could no longer take for granted.

She looked around her room. It was filled with things she liked, things she'd inherited from her grandmother and parents and things that she'd collected herself. Old things mostly and things from faraway places. A tall, graceful, yellow and violet art nouveau vase; a squat blue, green, and white rosewood pot; a one-hundred-year-old wooden mask from the Himalayas; a lavender piano shawl embroidered with pastel-colored flowers; a 1920s wicker child's chair that she used as a plant stand. All of them were as familiar and comfortable to her as her bed, and she loved being surrounded by them.

Kelly felt the sudden pressure of her red cat, Meow, pushing against her leg, stretching in her sleep. She glanced down next to her bed at King, her white Siberian husky, awake in his dog bed, waiting for her to get up. His bright blue eyes met her dark blue eyes, and he gave her a good morning howl. Often he and the cat got up in the middle of the night and went downstairs; King would scratch on the inside door to her housekeeper Emma's garden apartment on the basement level of the brownstone, and Emma, good soul, would wake up and let them stay with her. But today, King and Meow had remained with Kelly. She smiled, glad to have them close to her; it made her feel secure, a feeling that she cherished more and more because recently she had experienced it less and less.

She turned to the clock on her night table. It was 8:25.

"You must be famished," she said to King.

He howled again, as if to agree.

Kelly got out of bed, pushed her blond, curly hair out of her eyes, and walked to the windows. Opening the curtains, she looked out at the treetops on West 85th Street. It was the third week in October, and, despite ten days of Indian summer, the leaves were changing color. She'd had a view of the same trees for most of her life, ever since she was nine years old and had moved into the brownstone to live with her grandmother following her parents' accident. The only time she'd lived anywhere else was for the two years she'd been at Northwestern and the three years she'd been married to Jack and they'd lived in Kings Point. When she and Jack had separated, her grandmother had asked if Kelly wanted to move back into the brownstone on 85th with her children, Jeffrey, who had been one and a half, and Julie, who had been four months old. Kelly had been grateful for the offer, as grateful as she'd been as a child when her grandmother had taken her in after her parents' death. The brownstone had become her refuge after she'd lost her parents, it had become her refuge again when she'd left Jack, and it was her refuge now.

Turning away from the window, she focused on the carved table that held her family photographs: a snapshot of her grandmother, Irene, her white hair in a not-very-neat bun, her open, friendly face virtually unlined; her parents' wedding photo: her mother slim and beautiful in her wedding gown, her hair short and cut like a French movie star from the 1950s, her father in a tuxedo, looking more severe than Kelly remembered him, his hair brushed back flat, his usually playful eyes hidden behind wire-rimmed glasses; a photo of herself at eight, tall for her age and looking very much as she did today. In the photo, she was smiling a big, toothy smile, the smile of a child whose parents were loving and alive and seemed as if they would live forever.

Her eyes settled on her photos of her own children. They were both tall like her and her ex-husband, and they had inherited Jack's black hair and strong features. Kelly had taken the photo of Julie in June, right after Julie's high school graduation. Julie, in her cap and gown, was grinning proudly. Her black hair, usually as unruly as Kelly's, was pinned up neatly under her cap, and her brown eyes shone with excitement about her future. Jack had been there that day, too, and taken his own photos of Julie. That was how it was; she and Jack saw and communicated with each other when they had to, but they were very separate, even when they were in the same place.

Jeff's photo was taken last spring, during his freshman year at USC. Kelly had gone to Los Angeles to visit him, and Jeff's roommate had snapped a picture of her with Jeff. Jeff's arm was around her, and he and Kelly were both laughing. Every time his roommate had gotten ready to snap a picture, Kelly had sneezed, and when she finally managed to stop, she and Jeff couldn't stop laughing.

Looking at her children, she felt a profound sense of longing.

Julie was at UCLA now, close to Jeff at USC, but three thousand miles from Kelly. She missed them so deeply that at times she felt bereft, as if she would never see them again. She knew it was nonsense, of course. She had encouraged them to go; she wanted them to have their own lives. She wanted them to be free of burdens, most of all any sense that she was a burden. She would never tell them how she felt, because she knew it was irrational. Gazing at their photos, she realized that not only did she miss them, she also missed the sense of freedom she had felt at the time when the photographs were taken.

Despite missing them, she was aware that she was a very fortunate person, and she was grateful for it. She felt grateful for her home and grateful that she worked at home. In fact, she didn't know what she would do if she had to work somewhere else.

✻

Emma was at the kitchen stove when she heard Kelly's footsteps and King's loud tromping on the staircase. She was sixty-eight, generous, and oversized in every way: large boned, ample bodied, with a heart almost as big as her broad chest. She had come to New York from Ireland when she was nineteen to work as a housekeeper for Kelly's grandmother, who had been confined to a wheelchair. Growing up, Emma had helped take care of her eleven younger siblings, and by the time she was nineteen, taking care of people was second nature to her, as it still was. As she often did lately, Emma felt relieved knowing that Kelly was out of bed, ready to start her day. Things might not be as they should be, but at least in some ways Kelly was going about her routine.

Kelly walked into the kitchen, accompanied by King and Meow. She'd pinned her hair back with two barrettes and was wearing the green blouse she'd found in a thrift shop, her long black skirt, and an enameled necklace from India. Emma thought she looked lovely.

"Good morning," Kelly said on the way to the cabinet over the sink to get her coffee cup.

Emma looked at King and Meow. "I see you brought the army." She addressed them directly now: "Don't fret, you two. I've got breakfast all prepared."

While Kelly poured herself a cup of coffee, Emma took the pets' bowls of food from the counter and placed them on the floor. King and Meow immediately began eating, slurping their food and chewing it noisily.

"Look at them!" Emma complained good-naturedly. "They eat like animals!"

"They can't help it," Kelly said, spooning the oatmeal Emma had made into a bowl. "They're Tauruses. You know how much Tauruses love their food."

"I know how much *these* Tauruses love their food. You may think they're a dog and a cat, but they're both pigs!"

Kelly laughed, poured milk into her oatmeal and brought it with her coffee to the oak table that dominated the kitchen. She had just begun to eat when her assistant, Sarah, appeared in the doorway with a fretting look on her pretty face.

"You've got only fifteen minutes," Sarah said, her eyes on the wall clock, its hands indicating that it was 8:45. "Your first client is coming at nine, and after that you've got a full day." Without waiting for a response, she started back toward her office.

"Good morning!" Kelly called after her.

"Good morning to you, too!" Sarah called from the hallway. "Hurry up!"

"Looks like I'm going to have to eat fast, too," Kelly said to

Emma. "And I'm not even a Taurus."

"Just make sure you don't eat too fast," Emma admonished her. "You've got to take better care of yourself, Kelly."

Kelly shook her head and said dismissively, "Oh, Emma!"

She hated that Emma had begun to worry and that she'd given her a reason to worry. She hoped that soon everything would be normal again, and in the meantime, she wanted to pretend that it already was and for Emma to pretend it was, too. She could tell by the look in Emma's gentle gray eyes that she knew this, and that, for the moment, at least, she was willing to go along with Kelly's wishes.

But Kelly couldn't pretend to herself that things were normal now. Even in the moments during the day when she felt all right, she knew the only reason she did was that she was home. Her home was the only place she felt safe. One morning she'd woken up and had been about to go out to walk King, as she'd done most mornings since she'd gotten him. But that morning she'd stood in the front doorway, terrified to step over the threshold into the outside world. She'd felt that if she went out, something horrible would happen to her. She'd stood there, sweating, trembling, her heart beating hard, certain that if she went out, she would die. That had been weeks ago, and ever since then, she'd lived with the fear that the only way to stay alive was not to go out beyond the confines of her house and walled-in garden.

As an astrologer, she knew that Pluto was conjuncting—almost on top of—her Mars in the tenth house, the house of reputation and status, a difficult aspect that heightened her anxiety about public exposure, but this didn't fully explain the abrupt onset of the new fear she had developed. Why had she suddenly become anxious about leaving the house, something she had always enjoyed doing?

Besides the astrological influence, she deeply felt there was a psychological component to it, too. As a psychologist, she knew there was a term for her condition—she had a panic disorder: agoraphobia. She didn't know what part of her psyche had brought this on, and, although she recognized that Pluto conjuncting her Mars was increasing the emotional sensitivity that was always part of her makeup as a Pisces, no matter how much she talked to herself and told herself that her fear of leaving the house made no rational sense, it did no good. She felt as if she'd lost control of herself, and until she could understand the psychological component of what was causing her fear, all she could do was to keep hoping that one morning her agoraphobia would go away just as one morning it had appeared.

*

Sarah sat in her office and addressed an envelope to a client Kelly had seen the week before, a woman who had come to Kelly wanting to know if she should move to Chicago to live near her daughter. But Sarah wasn't thinking about the client or even the numbers and letters in the address she was copying from the form the client had filled out. She was thinking about Janáček's String Quartet no. 1, the piece she was practicing for a concert, thinking about the rehearsal schedule and wondering about whether she'd need to get one of the strings on her violin replaced. She was thinking about her mother in the convalescent home in Sheepshead Bay and wondering how she was feeling today. She was thinking about Kevin Stockman and what it would be like to see him again after the three months he'd been away, singing with opera companies in other parts of the world.

She was thinking about Kelly, whom she'd known since Kelly was eleven and she was six. Even when they were children,

Kelly had never treated Sarah condescendingly because she was younger, just as now she never pulled rank because she was Sarah's boss. Though employer and employee, they were equals, which is what made it possible for Sarah to work for Kelly while she pursued her musical career and what made her care for Kelly so much.

Sarah loved that Kelly appreciated her intensity, her tendency to be precise and organized; indeed, Kelly understood these qualities and loved Sarah for them. Kelly also understood and loved the compassion and emotion that were sometimes hidden beneath Sarah's well-ordered exterior. Sarah was a Virgo, with Virgo rising and a moon in Cancer, and Sarah knew that for Kelly, this meant Sarah was exactly as she was supposed to be.

Sarah's office was just off the entry hall, to the left of the front door when clients came in. It led directly into Kelly's office, which was at the front of the brownstone and had a street-level view of the same trees Kelly saw from her bedroom. Originally, both offices had formed a front parlor.

Many years ago, Kelly's grandmother Irene had converted the parlor into a library and a den so that when she was downstairs and wanted to look through her books or to watch television, she wouldn't have to go upstairs. Besides Emma, Irene had also had a nurse, Sarah's mother, Rose. But during her whole long life Irene had been independent by nature, and even though she'd had an elevator installed at the rear of the house, once she had gone down to the first floor for breakfast, she had preferred to remain there rather than cause Rose or Emma to follow her from floor to floor as she pursued various activities.

As Rose's daughter, Sarah had visited the brownstone often when she'd been a child, and she liked working there now for Kelly, but she knew that one day she would be leaving, when her violin began demanding more of her time. She looked forward to that, and she knew Kelly did, too. They both hoped it would happen soon, as a result of Sarah's upcoming concert. That was another thing Sarah was thinking about. She hoped that by the time she was ready to leave her job, Kelly would be all right again. She didn't know what was wrong; she just knew that Kelly wasn't as spontaneous as she usually was, that something was worrying her that she didn't want to talk about, and that she seemed never to want to go out of the house.

The phone rang. She answered it as Kelly entered.

"Dr. Kelly Elizabeth York's office," Sarah said. "Oh, hello, Mr. Winokur . . ."

She looked up at Kelly, ready to hand her the phone, but Kelly indicated that Sarah should handle it and continued into her own office. "She's in the middle of something at the moment," Sarah said into the receiver. She listened for a while and then said, "Hold on a second. I'll ask her."

Sarah put the receiver on her desk and stuck her head into Kelly's office. Kelly was already at her desk. "He wants to remind you about the fund-raising dinner at the beginning of next month. He said you haven't RSVP'd yet."

"Tell him I'll send a check, but I'm sorry, I can't go. Julie might be coming home."

"I thought she wasn't coming until Thanksgiving—"

"No. She changed her mind." Kelly couldn't quite look at Sarah when she said this, so instead she concentrated on taking the pencils from the top drawer and putting them in an old pewter mug on her desk. She didn't like to lie, especially to the people closest to her, but she was just too ashamed to tell the truth.

Sarah saw that Kelly was avoiding her eyes. She thought of saying something to her, but Kelly continued busying herself with arranging the pencils in the mug, so she returned to her office and picked up the receiver.

"She's very sorry, Mr. Winokur, but her daughter will be coming home from school. She'll send a contribution. . . . Yes, of course I'll tell her, but I don't think she'll be able to."

As Sarah was hanging up the phone, a nervous-looking man with light red hair stood on the steps of the brownstone and rang the bell. The day was warm and he was wearing a white business shirt and khaki pants. He carried the rolled-up copy of *Luminary World* magazine that he'd read on the subway on his way uptown. He rang the bell again, but before he even took his finger off it, a small, trim woman with fair skin, hazel eyes, and black hair down to her shoulders opened the door.

He looked her over and said, "You're not Kelly York."

"No, I'm her assistant, Sarah Stein."

"I'm Lewis Farrell. I'm here to see Dr. York."

Sarah moved out of the doorway so he could come in. "She's expecting you."

Sarah led him through her office into Kelly's and then left, closing the door behind her.

Kelly rose from her chair and shook her new client's hand. "Nice to meet you, Mr. Farrell."

"Nice to meet you, too."

He looked around Kelly's office. A painting of the signs of the zodiac in vivid colors hung on the wall to his right; on the opposite wall were three filing cabinets. On top of the one nearest him was Kelly's book: *Aspects for the New Millennium* by Kelly Elizabeth York, PhD. He glanced at her shyly. He'd seen her on a television interview show and he'd seen her photograph in *Luminary World* magazine, next to her column, but in person she was taller than he'd thought and the intelligence of her dark blue eyes made him feel intimidated.

Finally, he spoke. "I read your column every week."

She smiled warmly. "Thank you." She let her blue eyes rest on him. They were nice eyes, accepting eyes, and they made him feel calmer.

"I have a question for you—"

"Good," she said. "But first, please write down the time, date, and place of your birth. That's the information I'll need. And write down your address and e-mail address, too."

"Sure," he responded.

She handed a legal pad and pencil to him across the desk.

He placed his rolled-up copy of *Luminary World* on the desktop. She noticed that it was opened to her column. Across the top of the page was the name of the column, "The Stars," and her byline, Kelly Elizabeth York, PhD, Intuitive Astrologer. Below that was the airbrushed photo of her that she hated.

She observed him as he wrote on the sheet of yellow paper. He was in his late twenties; judging from his manner, he was self-conscious and earnest. She watched as he erased the word *February* and wrote it over, this time more neatly. She wondered if he was obsessive-compulsive or just overly careful. When he finished writing, he gave her back the pad and pencil. He glanced at her only momentarily and then gazed again at the painting of the zodiac signs.

She read the information he'd written aloud. "Born 10:30 a.m., February 4, 1986, Greensboro, North Carolina." She looked up at him, but he was still gazing at the painting. "You're sure of the time and place? It makes a difference in determining the positions of the planets in your chart."

He looked at her now and nodded. "Yes, I'm sure."

"So you're an Aquarius . . ."

"Yes."

She noticed that he was clasping his hands tightly on his lap, like a child who wanted to make sure the adults around him knew that he was well behaved.

"Please, Lewis. Relax. There's nothing to be anxious about."

He looked down at his lap, unclasped his hands, and laughed at himself. It was the first spontaneous moment he'd had since coming into her office. Kelly felt it was a hopeful sign, the fact that he could laugh at himself. And he was looking at her directly now, another hopeful sign that he was capable, with some guidance and support, at least, of enjoying himself.

She breathed a deep sigh. "That's better."

He laughed again. "Yeah, it is. I've never had a chart done before. I guess I just don't know what to expect, and I'm a little uptight."

"Today I'm just gathering information. Then I'll do your natal chart and send it to you with a written explanation. I'll also tell you what the transits indicate for you for the next twelve months." She saw the blank look in his eyes and continued. "Transits are the way the movement of the planets at a given time will affect you, because of the placement of the planets in your chart. It's why astrologers say that a particular time is propitious for a certain activity and not for another." She smiled warmly at him again. "You said you had a question—"

"It has to do with my girlfriend. We've been dating for two years. I'm thinking about asking her to move in with me."

"I'll need her date, time, and place of birth, too. Do you know it?"

"I saw it on her birth certificate when she applied for her passport. She was born in Forest Hills on December 26, 1989, at three p.m."

"In Queens?" Kelly asked as she took notes.

"Yes. Her parents still live there."

"She's a Capricorn, but of course you know that. I'll have to check her rising sign, her moon, and her other planets, especially where her Venus is located, and compare them with yours. I'm sure you care for each other a lot or you wouldn't be considering living together."

She watched to see how he'd react to this and saw his face break into a smile; just thinking about her seemed to make him happy. "We do . . . At least I do. I'm not sure how Laura feels. She's very quiet."

"That's not unusual with Capricorns," she said reassuringly. "They're not always big on talking about their feelings."

He nodded again.

"It seems to me you may not really be wondering whether you want Laura to move in with you. You may just be anxious about asking her because you don't know how she'll answer you. And you're anxious that even if she says yes, it may not work out."

Now it was Lewis Farrell's turn to sigh deeply. "That about sums it up."

"I'm not going to tell you that you should ask her or that you shouldn't. I'll tell you what your charts tell me about your personality, character, and needs, and Laura's. I'll tell you about the areas where you're most compatible and the areas that will be challenging. And I'll tell you approaches for resolving those challenges. If that's all right with you, I'll do your charts. If not, we'll just say goodbye and wish each other well."

Her dark blue eyes were still on him. They didn't display the least suggestion of judgment or impatience. He wondered why he had found her intimidating.

"I'd like you to do the charts," he said.

"Fine. I'd like that, too."

She stood up and shook his hand again before showing him into the waiting room, where Sarah would have him write a check for $550 for the two charts she would be preparing.

Alone in her office, she wrote down her impressions of him on the same sheet on which he'd written the information she'd asked for. She had a feeling that she could help him. While she was studying psychology, she'd read that the psychoanalyst C. G. Jung, one of Freud's disciples, had used astrology as well as psychology to help his patients. Jung had said that astrology contained all that the ancient world had learned about human psychology and behavior. She'd already learned astrology from her grandmother, and she believed that Jung was right; there was wisdom in astrology just as there was in contemporary psychology.

A true astrologer didn't focus only on identifying the influence of the planets' positions at a given time on the different parts of a person's life—love and work, to use Freud's famous words—or on looking at future potentialities in those areas; a true astrologer used the positions of the planets and moon at the time of a person's birth as a tool to analyze personality and character, to learn about that person's potential talents, strengths, and weaknesses. As Jung had put it, "We are born at a given moment in a given place, and like vintage years of wine, we have the qualities of the year and of the season in which we are born."

Astrology and psychology were both means of helping people. And that was what Kelly loved doing; helping people gave her life purpose, and she needed purpose, especially now. Reflecting on this, she asked herself for the millionth time why Kelly Elizabeth York—KEY—whom so many people considered the key to solving their problems, couldn't solve her own.

Two

IT WAS JUST BEFORE six o'clock and the end of Kelly's workday. She'd seen five clients after Lewis Farrell and had repeated the same process with all of them. It wasn't quite sunset yet, but the sky was already darkening. She felt a little tired, but in a good way, a productive way. She was taking notes on her last client, a woman of fifty who was thinking about embarking on a new career, when Sarah knocked and came into her office. Kelly looked up.

"I've got an extra ticket to the opera tonight, and I'd like you to come. They're doing *Faust*. My father was supposed to go, but he's visiting my mother, and he wants to stay with her for the whole evening."

"How is she?" Kelly asked.

"Her doctor says she's doing well. She's gotten back more movement in her left arm. But she's still not able to talk yet."

"Please tell your father to send her my love."

"I will. How about going to *Faust* with me? Kevin's singing the title role."

"I wish I could, but—" she looked at the pages with her clients' information spread out on her desk—"I've got too much work to do."

"You've been at it all day. Why not just take the night off?"

Kelly picked up her pen again. "I can't. I don't want to fall behind. Congratulate Kevin for me."

The way Kelly said this, Sarah knew the subject was closed. She watched, concerned, as Kelly began to write again on the sheet of yellow paper in front of her. Sarah sighed, went back to her office, and put on her coat. Emma was standing at the rear of the hallway, outside the kitchen, drying her hands on her apron when Sarah emerged from her office.

"She's not going," Sarah told her.

"But she loves opera! And not even to see Kevin?"

"She didn't even consider it."

Emma's face was as despondent as Sarah's voice had been when she delivered the news. For a moment they just looked at each other; then Sarah shrugged sadly and left for the night.

In her office, Kelly sat at her desk, miserable. She was ashamed of lying, of pretending it was her work that kept her from going to the opera and from visiting Sarah's mother, Rose. She'd known Rose most of her life, and she loved her—Rose had been as important a part of her growing up as Emma had been—yet in the weeks since Rose had had a stroke, all Kelly had been able to do was to write her a letter telling her how much she loved her and wanted her to get well and to send flowers with Sarah when Sarah visited her. Kelly was sure Sarah knew, just as Emma knew, that it was something other than the demands of her schedule that was making her act as she did, but so far they hadn't forced her to talk about the problem.

She looked at herself in the mirror on the wall opposite her desk. The satisfaction she'd felt from her work moments before had vanished. She looked as miserable as she felt.

Three

HE'D NEVER BEEN TO New Kent but he'd driven through it several times on his way to somewhere else. Tonight it was his destination. He parked in the upscale neighborhood where she lived, a block from her house, under a large evergreen that all but hid his car. Not that he was worried about anyone remembering what kind of car it was anyway; it was a fawn-beige Toyota, like millions of others you saw on the road. There was no reason to look at it twice.

He'd lucked out again. The streetlamps on the block she lived on were spaced far apart, and there were so many trees blocking their light that they didn't do much good anyway. The moon, blocked by the trees, too, was just a glimmering, ineffectual presence on the street. He was wearing his black clothes again, and he felt like he blended into the night.

He walked up the driveway to her house. Unlike the last woman he had visited, she had left the porch light on. He didn't wait until he got to the porch to put on the surgical gloves. He slipped them on and took the keys from his pocket—two of them this time—before he left the shadowed driveway. When he got to the front door, he felt exposed. He knew that someone passing by might see him there under the porch light. But he forced himself not to look over his shoulder as he unlocked the door. He just did it quickly, and did it as if he belonged there. He did, after all, didn't he? It was part of his job, his vocation, his destiny.

Once inside, he put on the ski mask and stared through the eye slits into the darkness until he could see the staircase that he knew would be there. It wasn't until he was on the first step that he realized the stairs were uncarpeted. He ascended slowly, carefully, mentally reducing his body mass so that he was just the phantom, weightless essence of himself, making sure she could not hear him on the stairs.

He reached the second floor and stepped onto a rug. For a while, he just stood there and waited. When his eyes got used to seeing in the small amount of light that came through a window at the end of the hall, he saw that the door across from him was open. He walked slowly to the wall on the left side of the doorway and listened. Nothing. No breathing. No turning in her sleep. Just silence. It reminded him of how his mother had slept. At least that was how she slept when she wasn't having nightmares. When she had nightmares, she would scream in her sleep, and then she would get up, she would come into his room, and scream at him, and that's when she would punish him.

With a surge of anger, he made his way toward another open doorway down the hall. Again all he heard was silence. His eyes focused on a third doorway at the end of the hall. Even before he reached it, he could hear her breathing in her sleep inside the room.

Her bedroom floor was covered with a thick white carpet. He knew it was white because of the tiny night-light she'd plugged into the wall just inside the doorway. He walked over to the bed, savoring each soundless step as it brought him closer to her. Taking out his leather cord, he saw her naked shoulders and realized that she was nude under the cover.

He peeled back the blanket and straddled her. A moment

later, he was undoing his pants and pulling on the condom. Suddenly, she was awake, and he saw the terror in her face as she stared up at him. She picked up her head, and her long brown hair spilled onto the pillow.

"No, please!" Her voice came out as a hoarse cry.

He stretched the cord across her throat. "Say one more word and I'll kill you."

She grabbed his arm and tried to push him away with a strength that momentarily surprised him, but it only made him more excited. He applied more pressure on the cord across her throat until she was so scared she stopped fighting.

He was hard as he lowered himself down on top of her.

"The transits aren't too good for you right now. I guess that's not a surprise, though, is it?"

Four

KELLY HAD BARELY EATEN anything for dinner. She'd spent the evening doing charts for clients and had become so engrossed that she hadn't even thought about food. When she'd finally remembered that she hadn't eaten anything since lunch, she'd gone into the kitchen and picked at leftovers from the refrigerator. Emma had been out all evening with Donald, whom she still referred to as her "friend," although it was clear to Kelly and Sarah and anyone else who might have met Donald and Emma together that he was her boyfriend. Kelly was glad that Emma had someone, and she was glad that Emma hadn't been home to see how little she'd eaten and worry even more about her.

It had been almost twelve-thirty when she'd finally stopped working and gone to bed. First she'd taken a bath, to relax her body and try to relax her mind. The hot water had begun to make her feel sleepy, and as she'd put on her nightgown, she knew it wouldn't be long before she fell asleep. She'd gotten under the covers and had immediately felt Meow jump onto the bed and nestle in the crook of her leg. King, already in his dog bed, had looked up at her to make sure she was all right before he'd closed his eyes. She had listened to Meow's steady purring and seamlessly drifted into asleep.

She heard a loud bell—like a kitchen timer—or an alarm clock. Or maybe the phone. Was she dreaming about a phone ringing? Or was someone calling her? Was it one of her children? Did Jeff or Julie have an emergency?

The panic that ran through her system instantly awakened her. She looked at the phone next to her bed and realized that it wasn't ringing. The house was silent. She looked at the alarm clock. It was 2:10 a.m. She closed her eyes again, hoping she wouldn't be awakened by the same disconcerting sound.

The moment her eyes closed, the ringing started again. She opened her eyes and got out of bed. The ringing, she realized, was coming from her study next to her bedroom, where she had an extension of the phone line that she had in her downstairs office. Maybe for some reason one of her children was calling on that line instead. Not bothering to put on her slippers, she ran into her study and answered her business phone.

"What's wrong?" she said anxiously.

She heard a man's whispered voice. "Kelly York . . . Kelly Elizabeth York . . ."

He said her name playfully, teasingly, as if he knew her very well.

"Who is this?" she asked.

He just laughed.

"Don't you know what time it is?" she asked, annoyed now.

"You're the one who doesn't know what time it is," he said to her, still whispering. His voice was no longer teasing. He spewed out his words like poison with the burning sting of dry ice. She had no idea that a whisper could be so ugly and so full of hate. It made her shiver and sweat along her spine.

"Who is this?" she asked again.

"Who is this?" he mocked in that whisper of his. Then the line went dead.

She stood there, holding the receiver, absorbing what had just taken place before slowly setting it back in its cradle. She saw that King had come into the room and was looking up at her with his electric-blue eyes, as if wondering why she had gotten up so suddenly from her nice, warm bed. She rubbed his nose, reassuring him that she was okay even though she felt queasy and shaky. He seemed to sense this, and when she sat down at the desk, he lay at her feet, his strong, furry body pressed against her bare legs, to show her that he was there to protect her from whatever was frightening her.

She opened the middle drawer of the desk and took out the chart she'd done for herself. Like all the charts she did, it showed a circle divided into the twelve houses, each house corresponding to a sign of the zodiac and revealing the astrological influences on a particular area of a person's life, which depended on the timing of that individual's birth. It also delineated which planets, if any, are in each house, revealing additional details about the influences on that person. The chart was a circle because it has no beginning and no end.

Kelly stared at her chart. To someone unfamiliar with astrology, it would appear to be a drawing of a wheel with a rim around it and twelve spokes. In the middle was what seemed to be the wheel's hub, containing more lines and symbols. It looked ancient, mystical, and even scientific, but the uninitiated would not understand what it meant.

To Kelly, of course, every line, symbol, and number had meaning, and in the chart she'd drawn using her birth date and time, she saw a picture of herself and every aspect of her life—material, emotional, intellectual, and spiritual—from her physical being to her personality, her values, her family, her friends, her romantic life, her career, her public self and her private self, what she allowed others to see and what she kept hidden. Her chart told her story: who she was and the challenges she faced in the present, who she had been and what had happened to her in the past, and who she could be and what could happen to her in the future.

The lines that looked like spokes were the dividing lines between the twelve houses; the symbols represented the astrological signs and the planets; the numbers were the degrees of the planets' exact locations, determined by date and time of birth. They showed how the planets interact with each other and revealed the blessings and challenges that are likely to appear in an individual's life.

Kelly ran her finger around the circle of the houses of her chart. The houses followed the seasons, starting with Aries, spring; progressing through Taurus and Gemini to Cancer, summer; moving through Leo and Virgo to Libra, fall; continuing through Scorpio and Sagittarius to Capricorn, winter; and progressing through Aquarius and Pisces to spring again. Kelly's chart showed the positions of her natal planets in these houses. It showed that her sun sign, Pisces, was in the twelfth house, the house of hidden matters; that her ascendant was Aries, making Mars the ruler of her chart; and that her moon was in Capricorn. It was, as she'd said to herself many times in the last weeks, the current planetary aspect of transiting Pluto conjuncting her Mars that made this a time when she felt so emotionally sensitive to her fear.

But what about the phone call? Pluto conjuncting her Mars seemed to have attracted an external threatening force. She needed to find out if there were other astrological aspects that had contributed to this.

Knowing that the aspects that were about to occur were affecting her experience even before they happened, she picked up a pencil and began to check her aspects for the coming weeks.

Her eyes focused on the planet that ruled her chart, Mars—named after the Roman god of war—a planet of energy that can be used for either good or ill. She felt her stomach tighten as she saw that Mars was about to square her natal Pluto. This alignment of these planets meant that she could be in imminent danger; it would require her to be extremely cautious for the next three weeks. It was compounded, of course, by what she already knew—that Pluto was conjuncting her Mars in the tenth house, which for her was ruled by Capricorn, heightening her anxiety about public exposure.

Seeing that transiting Mars was about to square her Pluto, she felt her body start to shake. She knew that when these two aspects coincide, there could be a life-or-death event. She had to be very careful of dark places, of secrets, hidden matters, anger, and angry people from the past. But no matter how careful she was, she knew that she might have to confront darkness, an energy so black that it could challenge everything positive she believed in.

Below the circle containing the twelve houses in her chart, she wrote *Mars squaring Pluto and Pluto conjuncting Mars.*

Mars, she knew, represented the body. Her body.

She was facing bodily harm.

Under what she had already written, she wrote the word *danger.*

Five

EMMA LOOKED AT THE clock. It was 9:20 a.m. King was lying on the floor beside his empty bowl and Meow was curled up on top of the refrigerator. They had scratched on her door at 4:00 a.m. and spent the rest of the night in her apartment before she'd woken up for good at 8:00 and fed them. She'd been expecting Kelly to come down for breakfast any minute, but Kelly had yet to appear.

Sarah walked into the kitchen and looked at the empty table. "Where's Kelly?"

"Still upstairs. She must've stayed up late working." Emma didn't have to say she disapproved; it was in her voice and on her face.

Sarah refilled her coffee mug. "Her first client is at nine thirty. I'd better go up and—"

The sound of Kelly descending the stairs stopped her midsentence. Moments later Kelly came into the room. Despite the makeup she'd put under her eyes to cover the dark circles, it was clear to Sarah and Emma that she was tired and had spent a sleepless night.

Kelly noticed their evaluating stares and the uncomfortable silence and decided to make a joke of it. "Gossiping about me?"

"We were just surprised you slept in again," Sarah said lightly.

"Are you feeling all right?" Emma asked.

Kelly took her cup over to the coffeepot. "Never better."

Her hands were unsteady as she poured the coffee, and she hoped that Sarah and Emma didn't notice. All she could think about was the phone call.

"I've been planning what to serve the Dennisons for dinner," Emma said. "I thought I'd make wild salmon, rice, and asparagus."

"Fine," Kelly responded. She opened the refrigerator to take out the milk for her coffee and was just about to reach for the milk carton when suddenly she felt a heavy weight drop onto her shoulders and knifepoint pricks in the skin on her upper back. Her body jerked back as she gasped, and the cup and saucer dropped from her hand, splashing hot coffee onto her dress before they crashed to the floor, where they shattered amid a puddle of brown liquid. Meow, as frightened as Kelly, jumped from her shoulder to the floor and landed with a thud. Kelly realized what had happened, but it brought little relief from her anxiety. She stared at the shards of china, afraid to look up and let Sarah and Emma see her fear.

"Are you okay, Kelly?" Sarah asked.

Kelly went to the closet and took out the dustpan. "I'm fine," she snapped. "Meow scared me, that's all." She knelt on the floor and began picking up the wet, broken pieces of china and putting them in the dustpan.

Emma hurried over to her. "Let me do that—"

Kelly continued picking up the shards. "I'm not a child, Emma."

She kept her head down, her eyes focused on what she was doing. She still didn't want Emma and Sarah to see how upset she was. She'd decided not to tell them about the phone call; what was the point of frightening them on top of the concern she knew they already felt for her?

But as she gathered the fragments of china in the dustpan, she made another decision: she would call the police.

*

Kelly closed the door to her office before placing the call. In case Sarah heard her on the phone, she'd told her that she had to call an old client who had an emergency. Now that she was alone, she sat at her desk, called information, and quietly asked for the number of the nearest police station. Her hands were no longer shaking, but inside she felt as if her whole body was trembling.

She dialed the number of the 20th Precinct and immediately found herself talking to a man with a strongly confident voice who identified himself as Officer Nelson and asked how he could help her. Kelly hadn't considered until now exactly what she was going to say.

"This is Dr. Kelly York. I received a threatening phone call," she said, lowering her voice so that Sarah wouldn't hear what she was saying. "It was from a man."

"What time did he call?"

"Four fifteen a.m. I looked at the clock, so I know."

"You say he threatened you. How did he threaten you?"

"He . . . he didn't make a specific threat. He just—he knew my name, and he wouldn't tell me who he was or why he was calling. When I asked him, he just hung up."

"Do you have any ideas about who he is?"

Kelly shook her head and then realized that the officer couldn't see what she was doing. "No. I have no idea."

"Anyone you've been fighting with about anything? Someone with a grudge against you?"

Kelly had been asking herself the same questions since the call; she'd asked them as she'd lain awake in her bed while the sky had still been dark, and she had still been asking them as she'd watched the sun come up in the moments before she'd finally fallen asleep again.

"No," she said. "There's no one."

She heard an intermittent scratching sound on the other end of the phone and she realized that Officer Nelson must be taking notes. Finally, he said, "I've got it all down, Dr. York, but there's nothing we can do right now. Call us if he calls again. If he keeps calling, we'll get the phone company to monitor your line, and we'll find out who he is and tell him to stop."

Kelly didn't answer right away. She didn't want to get off the phone yet. Talking with this policeman, she felt safe; she didn't know how she'd feel when she hung up.

"Dr. York?"

"I'm sorry, Officer. I was just thinking. But I understand what you said. I'll call back if he calls again."

She figured he must have known she was scared when instead of just saying goodbye, he said, "Don't worry, Dr. York. You'll probably never hear from him again."

She tried to sound as confident as he did. "Thanks."

She waited for him to hang up before she did. She felt no better and no more reassured than she had before she'd placed the call. Through the bars her grandmother had installed on the first-floor windows so many years before, she looked out at the trees and realized how sunny the day was. But even that didn't improve her mood. She couldn't forget the vitriolic whisper of the man who had called her; she couldn't forget the words that he'd said to her; and she couldn't forget what her chart had told her. She felt the man would call again.

She forced herself to get out of her chair and go over to the door between her office and Sarah's. She took a moment to gather herself before opening it. When she did, she saw that Sarah was at her desk and a sophisticated middle-aged woman in a black suit was sitting on one of the chairs against the far wall. "Forgive me for keeping you waiting, Ms. Weston," she said, doing her best to smile. "Please, come in, and we'll get right to work."

Six

THAT NIGHT, KELLY LAY under the cover, staring at the ceiling, unable to sleep. Meow was at the foot of the bed, and Kelly could hear her snoring as she slept with her head on Kelly's ankle. She glanced down at King sleeping soundly in his bed on the floor. She looked at the clock. Its illuminated digits told her that it was 2:15. She looked at the silent phone beside it. Except for the subtle sounds of Meow's snoring and King's breathing, the whole house was silent.

She knew that if she just continued lying there, thinking about everything that was troubling her, she would be awake all night, and at some point she would see her room growing lighter with daybreak and be all the more depressed knowing that she hadn't slept. Rather than staying in bed and ruminating, she got up, put on her bathrobe and slippers, and went into her upstairs study to work on her column. It was due in the morning, and normally she would've started writing it before now, but after looking up the aspects for her own chart, she'd been avoiding it. She found it difficult to concentrate on writing her column when her own aspects were so difficult.

Doing her best to emerge from her somber thoughts, she sat at her library table in front of her laptop computer. At the top of the file on her screen, she typed the words that would appear on this week's column: "The Stars: Week of October 26th." The sun sign for the week, of course, was Scorpio, as it had been since October 23. In her previous column, she had written about the sun entering Scorpio and the opportunities this offered for deeper reflection. Now she would elaborate on this in the context of the aspects for the new week.

She picked up her ephemeris, the almanac she used to see the positions of the planets as they moved through the heavens throughout the years, and opened it to October 26. She already knew that in the coming week Mars would enter Capricorn, where it would eventually conjunct Pluto—an aspect that would affect everyone and that she had been concerned about.

As always, she would begin her column by telling her readers the exact time that a significant planetary movement would take place. She was glad to see that on October 26, Venus was traveling with the sun, an aspect that she could write about favorably.

Once she'd gotten the time from the ephemeris, she typed:

On October 26th, at 7:08 p.m. eastern standard time, Mars enters Capricorn and moves toward conjuncting Pluto. On that date, Venus is traveling with the sun in Scorpio, bringing out love and the feeling that the world and other people are beautiful.

This is in contrast to the influence of the planet Mars entering Capricorn, which is potentially very challenging. Mars powerfully affects our drives and desires; channeled properly, Mars energy can help us to be productive and constructive; channeled improperly, Mars energy can lead to destructiveness.

She consulted her ephemeris again and saw that Mars would conjunct Pluto on November 10. Aware that by the end of the coming week some of her readers would start feeling this influence, she stared at the screen as she thought about what she wanted to write next; it was a problematic aspect, and she wanted to write about it as positively and constructively as possible.

Finally, she began to type:

Mars will conjunct Pluto in two weeks. As this conjunction approaches, it is a time to be cautious, even wary, to strengthen yourself. It is a time to prepare to confront challenges, external events, which is why caution is so important.

Reading over what she had written, she realized once again that Mars conjuncting Pluto would add to the danger she had already seen in her own chart. She reviewed again what she'd written for her readers and thought about how she could write about these aspects in a way that was accurate but encouraging. After a few moments, she started typing:

This conjunction creates change. It can lead to a powerful transformation—as long as you are vigilant.

She stopped again and asked herself exactly how she could be vigilant about the man who had called her when she didn't know who he was or what he wanted. Of course she would do all she could to be vigilant. She wondered if maybe his phone call had really been a one-time occurrence, a vicious prank, if maybe the danger from anger that her chart indicated she would have to be careful about didn't have to do with the caller but with her own anger at being trapped in her home because she was afraid to leave it. Maybe the best way to apply her own advice was to become even more vigilant about her thoughts, to learn precisely what had suddenly made her so scared of the world beyond the threshold of her house that the brownstone was the only place she felt safe.

Or at least this was the only place she had felt safe. Until the phone call. She looked toward her business phone and wondered if the man would call again.

Seven

IT WAS A TUDOR-STYLE house on a picturesque block in one of New Kent, New Jersey's best neighborhoods. The houses were all four-, five-, and six-bedroom homes that had been built seventy or eighty years ago, and the massive trees were older than that. The police had gotten a call at one thirty p.m. from the woman's maid, who had just found the body. She'd let herself in to clean and had started downstairs. As soon as she'd gotten upstairs, she knew something was wrong. When she got to the master bedroom, she found out what it was.

Forty-five minutes later, George Rayburn, the medical examiner, was looking at the pallid white body sprawled naked on the bed, her brown hair draped over the side. He remarked to himself that in life the woman had been beautiful. He examined the deep red line gouged across her throat and thought she must have been strangled with something like a rope. Not a rope, though, or at least not a conventional one, because a rope would have shown the marks of its weave and this didn't seem to have a weave.

Rayburn had just turned sixty-two. He'd been ME for the New Kent PD for twenty-four years, and in that capacity he'd examined a lot of dead bodies. It was not something that he particularly liked to do, but he was good at it, and he did like when his work helped catch a murderer. "She's been dead ten to twelve hours. I'm not quite sure what she was strangled with," he said.

"But I'll find out."

Frank Giordano, the detective in charge of the investigation, stood next to the older man, watching him. The top of the woman's left thigh and the sheet under her were covered with blood, but before determining the source of the bleeding, Rayburn was carefully examining the inside of her thighs and her genitals.

"Signs of forced penetration," he told Giordano. "She was raped before she was killed."

On the second-floor landing outside the bedroom, Sergeant Lanie Warner was doing her best to comfort the crying cleaning woman, but the woman seemed inconsolable. Tom Hernandez, Giordano's partner, walked past them into the bedroom. He hated to see women crying; he felt so bad for them that it threw him off his game.

He went over to Giordano and summarized what he'd found from his investigation of the house. "No windows open or broken, no door locks busted. Either she let him in, or he had a key or some other way to let himself in."

Giordano glanced at him. "So what are we dealing with? Friend? Family member? Or fucking clever sadistic stranger?"

Before Hernandez could speculate, the ME interrupted. "Whoever it is, he has a penchant for astrology."

Giordano and Hernandez looked at the body. Rayburn had cleaned the blood from the woman's left thigh. He pointed to gashes that had been made in the flesh.

"These cuts," he said. "They were made as she was dying, while her heart was still pumping. That's why there was so much blood." He stopped a moment and swallowed the repulsion he felt before going on. "At first I thought they were random. But they form a pattern. It's an astrological sign. I've seen it in the astrology column in the newspaper." He held his index finger above the gashes and traced the design. "See? Here's an arrow. The symbol for Sagittarius."

Giordano stared at the murderer's handiwork. "What the hell?"

Hernandez stared, too. Then he turned to Giordano. "I'd say we're dealing with a sadistic stranger."

Giordano couldn't take his eyes off the arrow the murderer had carved into the woman's thigh. He didn't disagree with his partner. "Shit," he said after a while. "That's only going to make it harder to find him."

Eight

SARAH HAD HAD AN uneasy feeling all day. Kelly had been distant and preoccupied since this morning. Until lately, she'd been a woman who clearly enjoyed her life, who loved her children and her work, who wore her success casually and without pretension, and used the city like a playground. Even in the last several weeks, when Kelly had changed, she had made the effort to be cheerful. But today she hadn't even tried. Sarah wondered if Kelly had just become more depressed about the problem she was having or if it was something else.

The only bright spot in Sarah's gray day was that she'd gotten a call from Kevin, whom she'd seen the night before at the Met, and he'd made a dinner date with her for his night off. He'd sung the title role in *Faust*, and he'd sung it beautifully. When he'd embraced her backstage, she saw that he'd become warmer and more loving toward her in the time that he'd been away on tour, that he'd forgiven her for disappointing him. Seeing him last night, she'd begun falling in love with him all over again.

She opened the glass door at the rear of the kitchen and walked down the slate steps into the garden behind the brownstone. In the dusky light, she could see Kelly in the greenhouse reaching up to a climbing rosebush. Approaching, she saw that King was in the greenhouse, too, staying close to Kelly as she snipped off a pink rose and added it to the roses in her hand. He howled one of his friendly hello howls, and Kelly turned to see Sarah standing in the doorway.

"I'm about to leave," Sarah told her. "I'm going to visit my mother."

Kelly looked at the roses. "I picked these for her. I thought she'd like them better than roses from a flower store. I've just got to put a wet paper towel around the stems. They're Zephirine Drouhins. They smell wonderful, and they have no thorns. Tell her it's the first time I've been able to grow them."

"She'll love them."

Kelly glanced down at the greenhouse floor before looking at Sarah again. "I'm sorry I was short-tempered with you this morning. I have a lot on my mind."

"That's okay."

"No, it isn't. I shouldn't take it out on you and Emma."

"You don't usually," Sarah told her.

Kelly kept her eyes on her. "That's no excuse."

"It's all right. Really, Kelly."

Sarah moved out of the doorway. As Kelly led King into the garden, Sarah could see that Kelly was still preoccupied.

"Is there anything you want to talk about?" she asked her.

Kelly shrugged. "No, I'm fine. I'm just making something out of nothing."

Sarah looked at her, waiting for her to say more, but Kelly didn't. Instead, she started walking toward the kitchen.

"How was the opera?" she asked. "How was Kevin?"

Sarah walked alongside Kelly and King. "Wonderful. I was very proud of him."

"Are you still seeing each other?"

"We're going to have dinner tomorrow night."

Kelly's face relaxed into a genuine smile. "I'm glad."

They reached the glass door to the kitchen and Kelly turned to Sarah. "Tell your mother I'll come visit her when she's home."

Sarah knew that on one level Kelly meant this, but the hesitation and strain in the way she'd said it told Sarah it was more of an excuse than a promise. It confirmed to her that she and Emma were right about Kelly's problem. She wondered how long Kelly thought she could keep it a secret from them.

As Kelly walked with Sarah into the kitchen, she could tell from the expression on Sarah's face that Sarah realized she wasn't being honest with her, and she prayed that Sarah wouldn't confront her about it. She knew from her training as a psychologist that keeping a problem hidden only increased the stress surrounding it, but she wasn't ready to talk about it yet. Especially not after the phone call that despite her best efforts to rationalize, continued to replay in her head. She wasn't ready to talk about any of it right now. So she took the bouquet of roses to the sink and began preparing it for Sarah to take to her mother. That way her back was to Sarah, so Sarah couldn't see her face, and maybe she could go on pretending that she wasn't afraid to leave her home and that a man hadn't called her and terrified her.

Nine

IT HAD BEEN THE kind of day that made Frank Giordano wonder if he'd be better off in some other line of work. Maybe any other line of work. The victim's name was Jennifer McGraw. She'd been thirty-five years old and had been a freelance graphic artist who had worked in a studio behind her house. For five years she'd been married to a partner in a Wall Street brokerage firm, and she'd gotten the house in New Kent when they'd divorced two years before. Six months later, her ex-husband had died of a heart attack. They'd had no children.

The tech team hadn't found any fingerprints in the house except those of the victim, the maid, and the victim's parents and sister, who lived in Short Hills and who'd been there on Labor Day for a barbecue. According to the parents and sister, Jennifer had had no known enemies and not many friends, and, despite having lived in the house for seven years, she hadn't really known any of her neighbors. Going door to door on both sides of the street, Giordano had concluded it wasn't a very friendly neighborhood. None of Jennifer's neighbors had seen or heard anything unusual, and they'd been more concerned about what her murder might mean about their own safety and property values than they were about the fact that she was dead.

Now Giordano and Hernandez were in the morgue with Rayburn, standing over the victim's body, and the ME had just told them there were no traces of semen in her genitals, no pubic hair mixed with hers, no skin cells or saliva except hers, no traces of the man who had raped and strangled her that would allow them to identify him through DNA analysis.

"What other bad news do you have for me?" Giordano asked him.

"No more bad news; just inconclusive," Rayburn said. With his index finger, he pointed to the bow and arrow that had been gouged into the victim's left thigh. "These cuts weren't made with a knife. They were made with some other sharp-pointed instrument. Something like a needle or a nail. I'm not sure what yet."

"What did he strangle her with?" Hernandez asked.

Rayburn took off his glasses and cleaned them with a handkerchief. "I'm still working on that, too."

Giordano let out a deep sigh.

Hernandez saw his partner had fallen into one of his funks. He patted him on the shoulder and said, "Don't worry, Frank. The guy's not going to get away with it." As he led Giordano out of the morgue, he added, "Let's not release details to the media. Nothing about the astrology angle. Meanwhile we'll check if any other murder reports have come in with similar MOs."

Giordano let out another sigh. He'd learned that in situations like this one, the only thing you could do was to put one foot in front of the other and assume that maybe one day you would actually get somewhere.

Ten

Sarah's parents lived in the Bensonhurst section of Brooklyn in the same house in which she'd been raised. The rehabilitation facility to which her mother, Rose, had been moved from the hospital after her stroke was four miles away. The emotional distance between the two was vast: Sarah's childhood home was a cozy brown-shingled two-story house with a small garden; the rehabilitation facility was a nondescript box with cinder-block walls that fronted on a decaying sidewalk and was flanked by alleys. Walking toward it, Sarah gripped the handle of her violin case more tightly and moved the bouquet she was carrying closer to her chest in an unconscious effort to stave off the desolate feeling that she had begun to have the moment she'd caught sight of the ugly, sterile building. Her only consolation was that the doctors anticipated that Rose would be able to return home within the next ten days.

Sarah's father, Sam had been a contractor, but he'd retired two years before. He'd worked in Brooklyn, Queens, and Manhattan and had done everything from home repair to partial renovations to building homes. He'd loved his work, but he loved his wife more, and he'd decided to retire so they could spend the rest of their lives together, enjoying each other's company and traveling. Sarah had applauded his decision and been thrilled when he and Rose had taken a trip to Italy and then another trip to Greece,

Turkey, and Israel. Two months after they'd returned from Israel, Rose had had a stroke. She'd been in the garden, putting mulch in the flower beds to prepare for the autumn and winter weather. Sam may have retired, but Rose, although no longer a nurse, had found things to do from morning until night, and that day she'd been working in the garden for more than five hours.

When Sarah entered her mother's room in the convalescent home, Sam was sitting beside Rose's bed, talking to her about the World Series. He and Rose were both baseball fans, and since he had to carry on the conversation himself, he liked picking topics that he could expound on while looking into her attentive green eyes, which showed she understood everything even though she wasn't yet able to speak. His face brightened as Sarah came in carrying her violin case and the flowers.

Sarah put the violin case on the floor and kissed her father on the cheek. "Hi, Dad."

He smiled as he looked up at her. "Hi, sweetie."

She turned to her mother and showed her the bouquet of pink roses. "Kelly sent these to you. She grew them in the greenhouse." She placed the flowers in her mother's left hand and watched as her mother's fingers moved to hold them. She noticed that as Rose looked at the flowers, her mouth curved into a slight smile. It made Sarah happy. The doctor was right; her mother was making progress.

"The nurse said she'll bring in a vase."

Sarah saw her mother's eyes focus on the violin case.

"We've got a rehearsal tonight. I'm excited about the concert."

Rose glanced up at Sarah. She opened her mouth as if she wanted to say something, but no sound came out. After a moment, she closed her lips. In her mother's eyes, Sarah saw tears from the pain of not being able to talk.

"That's okay, Mom," she said. "I know you're proud of me. And I know you'll be able to talk soon. Three days ago you couldn't move your fingers on your left hand; now you can. You can even move your arm. And when I gave you the flowers, you smiled. Your smile has come back, too."

Rose looked at her daughter and, with great effort, nodded.

"You moved your head, Mom!"

Sam took hold of his wife's right hand and squeezed it. "That's great, Rose."

Rose looked at the flowers again.

"Roses for Rose," Sam said.

Sarah sat on the chair beside her father's and moved it closer to the bed. "Remember, Mom, when Kelly's granny had Dad build the greenhouse? I was eight. I remember the day Dad finished, you took me to work with you at Kelly's grandmother's because it was a school holiday. The only greenhouse I'd ever seen was at the Brooklyn Botanical Gardens. I'd never imagined someone could have one in their own backyard! I remember her sitting in her wheelchair in the garden, telling you all the flowers she was going to raise in that greenhouse, and she did!"

As she remembered the day Sarah was talking about, Rose's lips curved into a slight smile again, and her eyes looked wistful. She was thinking about Kelly's grandmother, Irene; Irene had been more than just a patient to Rose; she had been a close and dear friend.

As if reading her mind, Sarah said: "You really loved Kelly's granny. I bet she lived ten years longer because of you."

Sam squeezed his wife's hand again. "Your mother was the best damned nurse anybody ever had. Irene was lucky to have you."

Rose's eyes were full of tears again. So were Sam's and so were

Sarah's.

"I love you so much, Mama," Sarah told her. "I just know you're going to get well."

Rose looked at her daughter again and, with great concentration, slowly nodded her head.

Eleven

KELLY WAS GLAD TO see the Dennisons. Michelle Dennison was her closest friend. They'd met at NYU when Kelly had gone back to get her BA after her divorce from Jack. Michelle had been premed; Kelly had majored in psychology. They'd sat next to each other in a psychology class that had ended at noon, and they'd often spotted each other having a quick lunch between classes in the coffee shop on University Place, just north of Washington Square. One day they'd sat next to each other at the counter and begun talking, and that was that—they were friends for life. Whether this was despite their different backgrounds or because of them, Kelly couldn't say; all she knew was that at NYU she'd felt more comfortable with Michelle than she did with other women their age, and nearly two decades later she still felt the same way.

Kelly had been twenty-three and already had Jeff and Julie when she'd met Michelle. As a psychologist, she'd come to understand since then that it was because of her parents' deaths when she was a child that she'd married Jack and had children at such a young age. Unconsciously wanting to replace the family she'd lost, she'd been so eager to start her own family that she'd instantly accepted Jack's proposal. She'd been so moved that he loved her and wanted to marry her that she'd ignored the female fans she'd seen waiting for him outside the locker room when he'd played football at Northwestern, and then later when he'd joined the New York Jets.

At the time Kelly had become friends with Michelle, Michelle had been twenty-one, and, like most women at the college, hadn't yet been married or had children. Michelle had been brought up Jewish in a suburb of Duluth, Minnesota, and had lived in the NYU dormitory on Washington Square, in Greenwich Village. Kelly had been born Episcopalian and raised with a New Age spirituality that her grandmother had practiced long before people had begun calling it *New Age*. She'd lived on the Upper West Side of Manhattan most of her life, and she'd commuted from there to NYU on the subway. Manhattan had been a constant source of excitement for Michelle; Kelly had loved it but taken it for granted; she'd thought of it as just *home*. Michelle had brought Kelly out of herself and her sorrow about her divorce by encouraging her to go to the theater, museums, and concerts with her; she'd loved getting to know Kelly's children, her grandmother Irene, and Emma and Rose. It had been such a different household from the one that Michelle had grown up in, and as a future doctor, she had been inspired by Irene's positive attitude in dealing with the MS that had bound her to a wheelchair.

Michelle had also encouraged Kelly to go to graduate school to get her PhD in psychology, and the two of them compared notes about the massive amounts of work each of them had to do while Michelle was in medical school at Columbia and Kelly was in the doctoral program at NYU. When Michelle had started dating Mark Dennison, who'd been freelance writing for magazines at the time, she'd arranged for Kelly to meet him and give her approval, which Kelly had done, and the couple had soon gotten engaged. Michelle had tried fixing up Kelly with some of Mark's friends, and although Kelly had dutifully gone out on dates with them, even seeing some of them three or four times, nothing had ever worked out.

Michelle and Kelly had talked about it, and Michelle had accepted the fact that going to school full time and raising two small children, even with the help of Irene, Emma, and Rose to watch them while she was at class, was as much as Kelly could handle. And Kelly was still getting over her divorce from Jack. He'd been her first and only love. She'd thought they were married for life, and then she'd found out he'd been unfaithful to her repeatedly. She hadn't really been ready to trust men after that, and that included Mark's friends, however charming they'd been and however interested they'd been in Kelly.

It had taken her a while to understand this, too, and to heal from her divorce. Since then, she'd gradually begun to date, and she'd had three relationships over the last ten years. The most recent one was with a doctor friend of Michelle's. They'd broken up the year before because he'd wanted a relationship that was heading toward marriage and starting a family, and they both knew that theirs wasn't going in that direction. It had been a sad but amicable split.

As she'd looked at Michelle and Mark at the dinner table in the living room of the brownstone, Kelly had been tempted to tell them about her agoraphobia, but she couldn't bring herself to admit it, even to her best friend. She was also tempted to tell them about the phone call. Now they were in her upstairs study, finishing off a bottle of cabernet and taking turns looking through Kelly's telescope, which she'd set up at the window, angled over the low building next door.

At the moment, Mark was at the telescope. He'd taken off his blazer and loosened his tie and was bending his tall frame so that he could gaze through the eyepiece. "Jesus! The moon looks like it's next door. But it looks cold! Not the kind of place I'd like to live."

Michelle poured herself another half glass of wine. "No one's asking you to move there, silly!" She took a sip of the cabernet and then added teasingly: "On second thought, that might not be a bad idea. You're always saying the house is too noisy. It would be very quiet on the moon."

"I see a couple of stars, too," Mark said amiably. "Maybe it would be better if I moved to one of them."

Kelly laughed. "They're probably not stars. They're probably Venus and Saturn."

Mark continued looking through the telescope. "Well, whatever they are, I see them. But that doesn't mean I believe they influence my life."

Michelle gave him a gentle poke in the butt. "That's not very nice, Mark."

"That's okay, Mich," Kelly told her. "Sticks and stones may break my bones, but words will never harm me."

Mark straightened up his lanky body and turned to Kelly. "I don't believe that. Words are powerful, and they can hurt you. Not that I meant to hurt you with what I said about astrology."

"Of course not," Michelle said. "You're just a wiseass. He reads your column every week, Kelly."

"Just for entertainment," Mark corrected her. "I don't actually pay attention to it."

"Well, I do. In fact, I planned our vacation for the time Kelly said it would be good to travel. And we had a fabulous time, didn't we?"

"Yes, we did," Mark conceded.

Kelly heard her friends talking in the kidding way they always did, but she wasn't really paying attention. She was looking at the phone she'd answered in the early-morning darkness and remembering what she'd heard.

"And if I recall," Michelle told her husband, "you waited till Kelly said it was a good time to sign contracts before signing your last book contract."

Mark snorted dismissively. "That was a coincidence. I would've signed it right away, but I misplaced it, and—"

"The dog ate your homework, right?" Michelle countered. "He pays attention to every word you write." She looked at Kelly and noticed that her friend was preoccupied. "You're not taking him seriously, Kell, are you?"

Kelly attempted a smile. "Of course not."

"Good. Nobody should ever take him seriously."

"I concur," Mark said emphatically. "I don't even take myself seriously."

Michelle saw that Kelly had withdrawn into herself again. She walked over and took her hand. "What is it, Kelly?"

Kelly looked at her friends. "I was just thinking about what you said, Mark. About how words can hurt you." She felt her chest tighten and took a deep breath before continuing. "A man called me the other night. Four in the morning. I asked him if he knew what time it was, and he said, 'You're the one who doesn't know what time it is.' It wasn't just the words. It was the way he said it. It scared me."

Mark's ruddy face was serious now. "Did you call the police?"

Kelly nodded. "They said it was probably nothing. But if he calls again, they'll monitor my phone."

Michelle put her arms around her and hugged her tightly. She hadn't realized how thin Kelly was; it made her seem more fragile than she appeared. "Why didn't you tell us before?"

Kelly broke away from Michelle's embrace and looked at her

and Mark. "I keep trying to convince myself I'm overreacting." She saw the caring in her friends' eyes and knew that if she was ready to, she could tell them not just about the phone call, but about the fear that was confining her to her home. She felt her chest tighten again and took another deep breath. "Ever since Julie left for college, and with Jeff already away, I've been alone in the house, except for Emma downstairs in her apartment . . ." She was still looking at her friends. She wanted to tell them. She really did. But she couldn't. Instead, she took another breath and said: "I haven't been myself."

"Why don't you come home with us tonight?" Michelle asked.

There it was. The question that always came up. Why don't you leave your house like a normal person would? "No, I can't. I mean I don't need to. I'm sure I'll be fine."

"But what if he calls again?" Mark asked.

Kelly shook her head. "He won't. That's what I was trying to say. I've just been nervous lately, so everything puts me on edge."

As if to prove her point, Kelly practically jumped in response to the sudden knock on the study door. It was Emma.

"Sorry to startle you, Kelly. I'm about to close up the kitchen before I take King for a walk. Anybody want anything?"

Kelly turned to Mark and Michelle. Her look told them to drop the subject they'd been discussing.

"No, thanks," Mark responded.

Michelle smiled warmly at Emma. "It was a wonderful dinner, Emma. Thank you."

"My pleasure."

As Emma left the doorway and headed toward the elevator that would take her downstairs, Kelly called after her, "See you in the morning, Emma."

"See you in the morning," Emma's voice called back to her.

Mark glanced at his watch. "We have to go," he said apologetically. "We promised the babysitter we'd be home fifteen minutes ago."

Michelle turned to Kelly again. "You're sure you won't come home with us? It wouldn't be any trouble—"

Kelly shook her head. "No. Really. It was probably just some drunk who didn't like what I said in my column, looked up my office number, and called to spook me. I'll probably never hear from him again."

She couldn't tell from their faces whether Michelle and Mark believed what she was saying; she certainly didn't believe it herself. In an effort to convince them, she added, with more confidence than she felt, "I'll be fine."

Twelve

FIFTEEN MINUTES LATER, KELLY stood in the front doorway, her feet on the inside edge of the threshold, watching her friends walk down the steps of the brownstone toward the street. This was as far as she was able to go. She felt the anxiety rising within her and knew that if she tried to step out the door onto the front stoop, her mind and body would rebel in panic that she would die. Her toes just touching the portal, she pretended nothing was wrong, and she waved and did her best to smile when Michelle waved to her from the sidewalk.

"How about meeting for lunch on Wednesday?" Michelle offered. "I only have patients in the morning."

Kelly shook her head again. "No, I . . . I'm sorry. Wednesday's impossible."

Michelle looked disappointed. "I'll call you."

Kelly saw that Mark had already gotten a cab to stop, and he was about to open the passenger door. She couldn't wait for him and Michelle to get into the cab and go home; the stress of having to stand in the doorway without being able to move a millimeter farther outside was beginning to make her feel short of breath.

"If that man calls again," Michelle was saying, "come to our place, okay? It doesn't matter what time it is."

Kelly nodded. "Okay." She could feel her heart beating faster, and she was relieved when Michelle finally turned away from her and got into the cab. Mark gave her a final wave before he started getting into the cab, too. She stepped back into the house and closed the door before the cab even pulled away. She locked the top and bottom locks on the door and started up the stairs. She was happy that she'd had her friends over, but now that they were gone, she was aware once again of how lonely she felt and how helpless to deal with the terror of the outside world that was keeping her in her home, more a prisoner there than her grandmother in her wheelchair had been. She wished she didn't feel so ashamed of her condition, but she did, and even knowing that hiding it only contributed to her loneliness, she felt unable to do anything else. She couldn't talk about it with Emma or Sarah; now she'd avoided the opportunity to talk about it with Michelle and Mark.

She walked up to the second floor. When she reached the landing, she stopped and looked toward Jeff's and Julie's bedrooms. Their doors were open, but the rooms inside were dark, emphasizing her children's absence. The time they had all lived in the brownstone together had gone by so quickly. While it was happening, it seemed as if they would be children forever, but now they had embarked on their own lives and, except for school vacations, they might never live in the house with her again. She was still their mother, of course, but their relationship would change. It had already changed. They loved her, and she loved them, but they didn't need her on a daily basis as they once had. They were becoming independent. She was pleased about that; it was part of what every parent wanted for her children. But she hadn't realized until Julie had left for college how dependent she had become on at least one of them being there and needing her.

She went into Julie's bedroom and flipped the light switch

beside the door. The room was all Julie. Julie had picked out the peach paint for the walls, the oak bedroom set that she had spotted in an antique store in upstate New York the summer that she turned fourteen, and the white lace curtains. Her dresser held the trophies she'd won on Dalton's swimming team. Kelly's eyes went to the teddy bear that had fallen off the bed onto the blue and peach hook rug. She picked it up and placed it where it belonged, sitting against the pillows on the bed. Kelly had given the chubby brown bear to Julie after her first frightening trip to the dentist to have a cavity filled. Julie had hugged the bear, and it had made her stop crying.

Kelly left Julie's room and walked toward Jeff's. His bedroom was at the front of the brownstone, with windows looking out onto 85th Street, and the street lamp threw a large swath of light across the room. This had been Kelly's bedroom when she was a child, and when she'd moved back to the brownstone after her divorce, it had become her bedroom again. Jeff and Julie had been babies, and they'd shared the room that eventually became Julie's. The bedroom Kelly had now, one floor above, had been her grandmother's, and Kelly hadn't moved into it until a year after her grandmother had died. Jeff's windows looked out on the same trees that Kelly saw from her bedroom, but instead of just seeing the treetops, Jeff saw the trees' strong trunks and their graceful leaf-covered branches, which would soon be bare. Kelly remembered seeing the same view so many nights and days and mornings when she was younger.

She stood at the window and thought about the seasons, the seasons of the year and the seasons of life. This was her work as an astrologer—to see clearly the relationships between the seasons as expressed in the movements of the planets and the lives that were affected by these inevitable movements. She looked at Jeff's varsity football letter that he'd pinned to his bulletin board and the other souvenirs he'd collected: a trophy he'd won for being the football team's most outstanding player, an award that had made his father especially proud; a ceramic ashtray he'd made in eighth grade; a picture of the view from his window that he'd drawn with a pen and India ink; photos from his high school prom. Now he and Julie were in a new season of their lives.

She walked out of Jeff's room to the staircase and up to the door that led to the third-floor landing. Even before she reached it, she heard King running up the stairs to join her. As she opened the door, he leaped up on her and licked her hand affectionately. She petted the thick white fur on his head and said, "Good boy, King. Did you enjoy your walk with Emma tonight?" As if to answer *yes,* he gave her a short, bright howl and looked up at her with his light blue eyes. "Good," Kelly told him.

King followed her into the bedroom. She turned on the lamp on her bureau and saw Meow jump up onto her bed. She watched King pad over to his dog bed and lie down. As always, having King and Meow near her comforted her. She took off her dress and hung it in her closet; then she took off her necklace and earrings and placed them in the jewelry case in the top drawer of her bureau. In her bra and panties, she headed toward the bathroom, stepping into her slippers along the way. It was an unseasonably warm night, but she felt a shiver move through her body. She hadn't thought about the disturbing phone call since she'd talked about it with Michelle and Mark, but now it was almost midnight, and she wondered if the man would call her again tonight.

There were seasons, and there were seasons—and her chart told her that in this season, with the movements of Pluto and Mars, she was in mortal danger. She knew that meant she had to be cautious, but the question was, cautious about what? And cautious of whom?

She unhooked her bra and threw it in the hamper along with her panties. She looked at herself in the bathroom mirror. She'd lost four or five pounds since August, but she looked slender, not skinny. Her breasts were still full and her waist was slim, which emphasized the womanly curve of her hips. At forty-one, her body looked much the same as it had when she and Jack had gotten married. But so much had happened since then, and feeling as she did now, she wondered if she would ever share herself with a man again.

She opened her jar of makeup remover, lifted out a piece of the moist cotton, and began taking off her makeup. When she finished, she went over to the bathtub and turned on the water for a bath. She was about to get in when she heard the ringing. She stood at the tub, shivering, and listened as the phone rang again. She turned off the water and forced herself to walk back into her bedroom, where the phone was ringing on her night table. Her naked skin all over her body contracted into goose bumps as she answered it. Bringing the phone to her ear, she found that she couldn't speak.

After a moment, she heard her daughter's voice. "Hi, Mom."

Kelly almost laughed with relief. "Hello, darling. I was just thinking about you and Jeff."

"When you didn't answer right away, I thought maybe you were out on a hot date."

There was something in the way Julie said this that made Kelly wonder if her daughter was just making conversation or probing. It was unlike Julie to be indirect, and it made Kelly uncomfortable.

"I was about to take a bath," she said. "Michelle and Mark

were over for dinner. They just left."

"I'm glad you had company. Say hi to them for me next time you see them."

Kelly sat on the bed. "Is everything okay with you, honey?"

"More than okay," Julie said, a smile in her voice now. "I started seeing this guy who lives down the hall. His name is Roger Green. He's a junior and a history major. He's been telling me about the English Renaissance and the problems with succession to the throne. He's fascinating. And I wanted to thank you, Mom."

Kelly began to relax again. "I'm glad you want to thank me, but for what?"

"For supporting me when I wasn't sure if I should break up with Billy."

Kelly thought back to last spring and remembered Julie staying up late one night to talk with her about why she wanted to break up with the boyfriend she'd gone out with since her sophomore year in high school. She remembered how clear her daughter was about feeling that ultimately she and Billy didn't have enough in common and that she didn't want to be tied to him when they went off to college.

"Oh, you were sure," Kelly said. "You just needed me to tell you that you weren't a bad person if you broke up with him."

Julie laughed. She didn't speak right away. When she did, she said, "Are you all right, Mom?"

Kelly felt herself shiver again. She pulled the cover up around her and spoke into the receiver with an equanimity that she hoped would cover her true feelings. "Why shouldn't I be?"

"I don't know," Julie said. "You always used to go to the theater and out to dinner, but now every time I call, you're home."

Meow, who had already fallen asleep, had stirred when Kelly

first sat on the bed, and now she was awake and purring loudly. Kelly watched the fat red cat walk sleepily across the bed toward her; it helped her to keep the lightheartedness in her voice. "I'm busy, that's all. I've got the column to write and clients to see, and—"

Before Kelly could continue, Julie interrupted her. "How about coming out to Los Angeles for a long weekend?" she asked enthusiastically.

Kelly felt her face grow hot; she hated lying, and now she had to lie again to her daughter. "I'd love to, honey, but I couldn't. And you and Jeff will be home soon anyway. It's practically Thanksgiving."

"Thanksgiving is a month away! I'd love to show you around campus and introduce you to Roger and my other friends."

Kelly didn't say anything. Julie remained silent for a while, too. When Julie finally spoke, she was uncharacteristically quiet and serious. "I keep thinking about why you don't go places anymore. It's like you're . . . I don't know . . . afraid. You're not afraid to go out of the house, are you, Mom?"

It was the question Kelly had been dreading. Now her daughter was asking her directly. It shouldn't have surprised her that Julie would sense this; she and Julie were so close. She felt drops of perspiration forming on her forehead. Of all the people she didn't want to talk to about her problem, the two she most wanted to spare any worry about it were Julie and Jeffrey.

She made herself laugh. "Of course not!" She didn't know how much longer she could bear to be on the phone. "My goodness, darling, I've got to go! I just realized I left the water running in the tub and it's going to overflow. I'm glad you called."

"Me, too," Julie said. "Love you."

"Love you, too."

Kelly waited for Julie to hang up before she placed the receiver back on the phone on the night table. Meow was rubbing against her, waiting to be petted. She stroked the cat's soft red fur and hoped that her lies had convinced her daughter. Then she looked toward her study and remembered the voice of the man who had threatened her. The mere thought of it terrified her.

Thirteen

HE SAT AT HIS worktable, opening the surveillance equipment. There was something intriguing about the boxes that the miniature cameras came in. Perhaps it was the fact that equipment so technically advanced and so important could come in such tiny, nondescript cardboard containers. He tore open the first box, took out the camera, and held it in his hand. It was even tinier than the box and weighed almost nothing.

He glanced at the computer he had set up. He'd brought it with him when he moved, a gift from his old job in Silicon Valley. A gift of sorts. All his boss knew was that one day the computer, like the new surveillance equipment they'd bought but had yet to install, was missing. He'd liked working there. He'd liked knowing his boss had valued his skill at programming. He'd even thought his boss was about to promote him. Then he'd found out he had to leave. It was her fault, of course. Kelly Elizabeth York's. Everything was her fault.

He thought about his mother for a moment, but she really wasn't whom he wanted to think about. He wanted to think about Kelly Elizabeth York. As of tonight, he'd walked by her house twice. He'd figured out a plan for how he would get in, and he was pretty sure it would work. One way or another, he *would* get in. That was a given.

This last time he'd passed her house, he'd seen her in the

doorway, waving to a couple who were getting into a cab. Some people would've said she was beautiful. He didn't see her that way. The only thing he saw when he looked at her was that she deserved to die.

Fourteen

IT WAS SUNDAY. KELLY had opened her eyes briefly at nine thirty a.m.—just long enough to check the clock—and gone back to sleep until one fifteen. Keeping her eyes open this time, she noticed that Meow and King were no longer in the room.

She roused herself from her bed. The house was colder than it had been. Glancing out the window, she saw that the day was gray and sunless. Since it was her day off, she threw on her favorite jeans, a T-shirt, and an old cable-knit sweater she'd bought on a vacation with the kids in Cape Cod. She gathered her hair into a ponytail and fastened it with a rubber band. There was no point in wearing makeup, because there was no one to see her, except possibly Emma. As she walked down the stairs, she wondered if Emma was going somewhere with Donald today or if she was staying home in her apartment. Sometimes Emma liked to spend Sundays in front of the television, watching old movies.

Kelly was walking down the staircase from the second floor to the first when she heard the familiar two-note chime of the doorbell. She wasn't expecting any clients; there was no mail delivery on Sundays, and if Donald had come to see Emma, he would go to Emma's front door, not hers. She had no idea who would've come unexpectedly. Could it be Julie or Jeff paying her a surprise visit? It seemed unlikely; they had too much work to do for school. The doorbell chimed again, and she felt her body tense. Could it be the man who had made that phone call?

Her body remained tense as she slowly approached the front door. She was grateful that it had a peephole and two locks. Just as she reached the door, King bounded in from the kitchen and jumped up on her to announce that he was there. She rubbed his nose, reassured by his presence. He stayed close to her as she peered into the peephole and, through its distorting lens, saw a dark-haired man looking at the door, waiting. He was about her height, five foot ten, and he was wearing a leather jacket and jeans and carrying some kind of bulky equipment. She'd never seen him before in her life.

"Who is it?" she asked, making the effort to sound firm.

He glanced down to the peephole. She knew he couldn't see in, but the subtle movement of his head and eyes seemed intimate somehow, and feeling his presence so close to her increased her anxiety.

"Chris Palmer," he said from the other side of the door. "We have an appointment at two thirty to take new photos of you for your column. I'm a little early. If you want me to come back—"

That was why he was carrying equipment. He was a photographer. And it was true. She had made the appointment for the photo shoot. She'd scheduled it for her day off so that it wouldn't interfere with seeing clients. "No, that's okay," she told him. "Come in."

Kelly unlocked the bottom lock, then the top lock, and opened the door. She stepped back into the entry hall, a foot from the threshold, so that she wouldn't become scared and have to control her anxiety in front of the photographer.

He came in and deposited a large metal box and a tripod in the hall; then he turned around and headed out again. "I'll be back soon. I've got more in my truck."

As Kelly closed the front door, she heard Emma open the door near the kitchen that led up from her apartment.

When Emma saw Kelly, she said, "So you finally got up, Sleeping Beauty!"

Kelly laughed. "I guess it's about time."

Emma glanced at the metal box and the tripod, which King was circling and sniffing. "I thought I heard someone at the door."

"The photographer from *Luminary World* magazine. I forgot he was coming. I'm going upstairs to change. He'll be back in a few minutes. If you'd just let him in, I'd appreciate it."

"I put some coffee up for you," Emma said as Kelly started up the stairs.

Kelly climbed three steps when she heard King howl and gnash his teeth—the kind of sound that did not bode well. She turned around and saw that the front door was open and King was no longer in the entry hall. She ran down the stairs to the open doorway. Standing with her feet on the inside edge of the threshold, her right hand holding tightly onto the doorjamb, she looked up the block toward Central Park and didn't see King. She turned toward Columbus Avenue and saw him running west on 85th Street, chasing a white-and-brown terrier. Her heart palpitating, she forced herself to stick her head out of the doorway a little farther and scream out to him. "King! King!"

The dog paid no attention; he just kept running after the terrier.

Fear rose from Kelly's stomach and seized her body. She desperately wanted to run after him, but she couldn't move. Her heart beat even faster at the prospect of going out onto the street. Her face, her limbs, her torso broke out in perspiration, and she found it hard to breathe. She choked out, "Emma! Emma!"

Emma hurried out of the kitchen into the hall. "What's

wrong?"

"It's King," Kelly said between quick, labored breaths.

Emma looked at Kelly, and then she moved toward the open door as fast as her overweight body would let her. As Emma rushed toward her, Kelly met her eyes. She didn't know what she would say to Emma if she could catch her breath long enough to speak. Then she saw in Emma's gray eyes that she didn't have to say anything: Emma knew, and seeing Kelly in pain hurt her. She didn't waste a moment saying anything. She gently touched Kelly on the arm as she passed her and went down the steps.

Her feet on the inside edge of the threshold, Kelly watched as Emma reached the sidewalk and headed west to pursue King.

"King!" Emma shouted. "King! Come here!"

For a while, Kelly could see Emma running toward Columbus Avenue, but soon she was out of her line of vision. The only way she could continue watching her go after King was if she went onto the front stoop, and that was something that every cell in her body told her she couldn't do. Looking out the front door into the bleak October day, she was filled with dread that if she stepped outside, the world would just swallow her up. It made no rational sense, but she *couldn't* move beyond that threshold; she felt that if she did, she would die. Her feet were planted on the threshold; her hand was gripping the doorjamb for dear life; her body shook with terror, and she was permeated with shame that she was so scared. Tears streamed from her eyes down her cheeks. One thing she knew: this had nothing to do with that phone call. She'd experienced this for weeks every time she opened the front door. She had become powerless, and as much as she'd searched for an answer, she still didn't know why.

She stepped back into the hall and wiped the tears away with the back of her hand.

✳

Nearing Columbus Avenue, Emma was out of breath. She loved King, and she enjoyed walking him, but this was something else. Once again she told herself that she had to lose weight, and once again she admitted to herself that liking food as much as she did, she probably never would. She saw that King and the terrier he'd been chasing had stopped at the fire hydrant near the corner. Giving herself a mental pep talk, she picked up her pace and got to the hydrant while the dogs were sniffing each other. She grabbed King by the collar. While she caught her breath, he looked up at her with his blue eyes and voiced a forlorn howl in protest of her ruining his good time.

"I know. I'm a meanie," Emma told him. "But you've got to come home now." She looked at the terrier to see if he had a tag and found that he didn't even have a collar. "Be careful crossing streets, you hear?" she advised him.

As Emma pulled King back toward the brownstone, King gave his playmate a parting howl, and the smaller dog barked a bright goodbye.

"You shouldn't go running out like that, King," Emma chided him. "You don't want to upset Kelly, do you?"

King glanced up at her as if to apologize.

"You're a good dog," she said reassuringly. "I know you love her."

Emma found herself thinking about Kelly and what had just happened. It was the first time anything like that had occurred—the first time she had seen Kelly frozen in the doorway, the first time Emma had seen with her own eyes what she and Sarah had known intuitively was right: Kelly was afraid to leave the house.

Climbing the steps to the brownstone with King, Emma saw

that the door was open and Kelly was waiting for them in the entry hall. Emma brought the dog into the house and let go of his collar. He ran up to Kelly and licked her hand.

"Thank you, Emma," Kelly said. There were a hundred apologies in her voice. "Thank you."

Emma closed the door and then turned to Kelly. Kelly looked awful. Her eyes were pink, and she'd obviously been crying. The worst part was that she looked so ashamed of herself.

"Why don't you go wash your face and get dressed," Emma suggested. "That photographer's going to be back any minute."

Kelly stood there, looking at Emma. She wanted to explain herself, but the words wouldn't come. How could she make Emma understand her when she didn't understand herself? Instead she just said, "I love you, Emma."

Emma's eyes grew wet with tears, too. "Come on, now, darling," she scolded softly. "You don't want to keep him waiting."

Fifteen

HERNANDEZ WAS IN Jennifer McGraw's living room. He'd just about finished looking through the books in her bookcase, and he was feeling discouraged. He'd taken each book from the shelves and opened it, looking for an inscription or something that might have been placed between the pages. Most of the books had been purchased during Jennifer's college days, and she had written her name and dorm address on the inside covers. A scrap of paper fell out of the art history book he'd just pulled from the top shelf. He picked it up and read it. It was a long-ago note that Jennifer had written to herself; all it said was "library 7 p.m." Not too helpful. He wasn't eager to share his lack of progress with Giordano, who'd remained at the station, researching the database.

"Tom!" Hernandez heard Officer Allen Kim calling him from the den. He could always tell when Kim was excited because it was the only time Kim raised his voice. "Come here!"

Hernandez put the note back in the book and walked into the next room. Kim was holding an astrology magazine. He showed Hernandez the cover. Emblazoned across the top in large red letters were the words *You and Your Sign.*

"This could be a link to the killer," he said. "He wasn't the only one into astrology. So was the victim."

Sixteen

KELLY SAT ON THE living room sofa facing the camera. She'd taken Emma's advice and washed her face. She'd also used eyedrops to wash away the pinkness from her eyes and put on eye makeup and lipstick, brushed her blond, curly hair so that it fell more or less behind her shoulders, and changed into her favorite blue silk dress. The dress had a scoop neck, which showed off her Pisces necklace, with the two delicate silver fish that symbolized her sun sign, against the pale skin of her chest.

She reminded herself once again that the photographer's name was Chris Palmer. She was still ruminating on the fact that even if it had meant losing King, whom she dearly loved, she had not been able to go out of the brownstone onto the street.

Chris Palmer's camera was on the tripod, and he'd strategically placed two umbrellas and flash equipment on either side of it. Now he was looking through the camera lens at Kelly. She waited for him to snap a picture, but he didn't.

"Relax!" he told her from behind the camera. "You look like I'm putting you through a medieval torture."

She tried to smile.

"Now you look like you've traded the torture rack for the iron maiden. You're certainly not having fun with this." He emerged from behind the camera again. "Is it me?"

She laughed. She saw the light from the flash equipment and

realized that when she'd laughed, he'd taken a photograph by squeezing the ball in his hand that was attached to the camera by a cord.

"That was very clever," she said.

"I had to do something. You looked so gloomy."

She thought he had a pleasant voice. In fact, she thought Chris Palmer was pleasant altogether. She liked his attentive, dark brown eyes, his athletic body, and the small bump on his nose that she thought he'd gotten from playing sports. She liked the curve of his lips when he smiled and the masculine line of his jaw.

"I'm afraid you picked a bad day," she told him.

"The aspects aren't very good?" he asked.

"I wasn't talking about the aspects. I was talking about my frame of mind. But you're right; the aspects aren't good right now. Especially for Pisces like me."

"I'm a Pisces, too," he said. "That must be why I picked a bad day to photograph you. And that's why I have to be so clever."

She laughed again. He took another picture.

"That's better," he said. He got behind the camera again and looked through the lens. "You're the first celebrity astrologer I've ever photographed."

Kelly kept looking at the camera, and he snapped another photo. "I'm not a celebrity."

"You write a column, you wrote a book, and you were interviewed on television." As he talked, he took one picture after another.

"Oh, God! I hope you didn't see me. I was terrible!"

"You were not. You were charming and funny and you made me believe you knew what you were talking about."

He removed the camera from the tripod, held it up to his eye, and moved nearer to her as he continued shooting photos.

"I do know what I'm talking about," she told him.

He got down on one knee now and looked up at her with the camera. "That's why you're a celebrity astrologer."

She smiled. It wasn't so difficult now. He'd actually made her relax. "All right. You win. I'm a celebrity astrologer."

While they talked, he started taking pictures in rapid succession again. "I never realized your eyes were so blue."

"It's the blue dress. And the blue eyeliner. They make them look bluer."

"It's your eyes that make the dress and the eyeliner look bluer."

Kelly grinned. "Flatterer!"

"That's my job. But with you, it's easy." He lowered the camera. "Okay. That should do it."

Kelly got up from the sofa. "I'm glad. I hate being photographed."

"Why?" Chris asked, putting his camera back into the equipment box. "What's wrong with being photographed?"

"Actually, I don't always hate it. I just hate it at the moment."

"Why?"

He was looking at her as if he really wanted to know, but she wasn't about to tell him everything that was going on with her.

"I just don't think I look very good right now. I'm a bit tired."

"It's my job to make people look good." He started taking down one of the umbrellas. "But in your case—"

"I know," Kelly said. "In my case it's easy. You really are a flatterer!"

He laughed. "Well, it is." Then he added, looking at her with a smile. "You're a lot younger than I thought."

"I'm a lot younger than that line," she told him.

He laughed again. She liked the way his cheeks creased when

he laughed.

"How about going to dinner with me tonight?" he asked her.

She shook her head. "Sorry, but I can't."

"You've already got plans?" He started taking down the other umbrella.

"Yes."

He looked at her. "I don't believe you."

She glanced out the window into the garden. The day was still gray and sunless. "I just don't think it's a good idea."

He was still looking at her. "Why not?"

His brown eyes were no less attractive than they had been before, but now they were serious. Looking into them, she felt embarrassed. She rose from the sofa. "I told you. The aspects aren't good for me. Pluto is conjuncting my Mars in the tenth house and—"

He interrupted her. "What's the real reason?"

She walked over to the window and watched as the wind ruffled the trees that lined the garden walls. Usually she loved the fall, this mysterious transition between the fertility of summer and the stillness of winter that manifested in the changing colors and the shedding of leaves. But this year, so far she had experienced it only as a time of fear, and she realized that she was afraid now. Not just afraid of going out of her brownstone, and afraid that the man who had called her would call her again—or do something worse—but afraid of opening herself even to the possibility of a relationship again. She had sensed nothing wrong with Chris Palmer, but how could she let him or anyone near her when she didn't really know who she was anymore?

After a while, she turned away from the window. He was standing two yards from her with the folded umbrella in his hands, waiting for an answer.

"I haven't been out with anyone for a long time. And I don't think I'm ready."

"Why not see?" he asked her simply.

She looked at him and wondered if he might be right. He was about her age, maybe a year or two younger. He was smart. There was no doubt that he was good-looking. His eyes continued to meet hers, unfazed by her evasions and protests. He worked for the same magazine that she did. That meant that its editor, Wendy Storr, whom Kelly had known for five years and liked enormously, thought he was responsible.

"Why don't we have dinner here?" she said finally. "Say seven thirty."

He smiled. "I'm glad I broke down your resistance. Seven thirty it is."

Seventeen

GIORDANO WAS SITTING AT his computer, completing his search of rape and murder cases reported in the past five years. He'd started out looking in the metropolitan area, then broadened his search to include the entire Northeast and, eventually, the South, Midwest, and West, including Hawaii. So far he hadn't found a single rape/murder or rape or murder case in which the method matched that of Jennifer McGraw's killer. Many victims had been strangled, but none with the singular, thin cord—not rope or wire—that her killer had used. More important, none of them had been marked with a sign of the zodiac—in Jennifer McGraw's case not, in fact, just *a* sign of the zodiac, but her sign. As Giordano had found out from Jennifer's parents, she was born on November 28, which made her a Sagittarius, and the man who had raped and murdered her had gouged that sign into her flesh.

Giordano looked through the last of the rape and murder cases in the database. It had occurred last night in Honolulu, a young woman walking alone on the beach just after midnight. She'd been raped and stabbed, and the drunken tourist who had done it had already been caught.

The accumulation of details of brutality and violence that he'd taken in as he'd read about the crimes made Giordano sick to his stomach. He picked up his coffee and threw it back like a shot of bourbon, hoping to wash the disgust from his mouth and gut and mind, but the coffee was old and stale, and it only made him feel worse. He was just about to get up and pour himself a new cup when the phone rang. It was the ME.

"Glad you're still there," Rayburn said from the morgue in the bowels of the building. "I thought you'd be home by now."

"I can outlast you, old man, any day," Giordano growled.

Rayburn, as usual, remained unperturbed. "Not much luck on the McGraw case, I guess."

Giordano was the only one in the office. He took advantage of the situation to light up a cigarette. "Did you just call to make me more depressed, or do you have something to tell me?"

"You're smoking, aren't you?" Rayburn asked.

"Don't drive me crazy, Ray. Do you have something to tell me or not?"

"As a matter of fact, I do have something to tell you," Rayburn said with self-satisfaction in his voice. "It's about what the victim was strangled with."

Giordano continued to smoke as he listened.

"I found microscopic bits of leather in the strangulation marks. It was a leather cord. Maybe something used in handicrafts. Like a piece of rawhide. Sturdy enough that it wouldn't break when force was applied to it."

Giordano felt slightly less despondent. But only slightly. "At least that gives us something to go on."

"You've been hitting a wall until now, Frank?"

Giordano took a drag on the cigarette. "Four of them."

"Sorry," Rayburn told him. "But put out that damned cigarette before somebody sees you. They're going to be pissed off anyway when they smell you've been smoking."

Giordano stubbed the cigarette out on the bottom of his shoe and put the stub in his pocket. "I'll deny it was me."

"Start looking at leather cords."

"Thanks, old man."

Giordano hung up the phone and walked over to the coffee machine. He'd just begun swigging down a hot mug of the vile stuff when Hernandez walked in. Giordano knew that Hernandez and Kim had been talking to the clients Jennifer McGraw had worked for as a freelance artist. He didn't know they'd also stopped at Jennifer McGraw's house and what they'd found there.

Hernandez sniffed the air and made a face. "It smells like an ashtray in here, Giordano. You been smoking again?"

Giordano stared his partner straight in the eye and lied. "Not me."

Hernandez didn't pursue it.

"You got anything from your interviews?" Giordano asked.

"She did good work. Turned it in on time. None of her employers knew anything about her personal life. They hired her because they were impressed with her portfolio. They got a sense that she was lonely. Maybe that was why the killer chose her."

Giordano nodded, disappointed. He'd been hoping for more. Before he could say anything, Hernandez was talking again. "But look what Kim found." He smiled and showed Giordano the copy of *You and Your Sign* that Kim had discovered in her den. "Some of the corners on the pages are turned down and sentences are underlined. It looks like the victim spent a lot of time reading it."

Giordano stared at the magazine. His dismal feeling about the case began to lift. He decided it wasn't impossible that they would find the man who had raped and strangled Jennifer McGraw.

Eighteen

THERE WERE SEVERAL TYPES of occasions for which Sarah always got dressed up: when she was giving a concert, when she was attending a concert or opera, and when Kevin was in town and they were going out to dinner someplace special. Tonight she was wearing a new green sheath dress. It was more sophisticated than the suits and dresses with A-line skirts that she usually wore. She'd bought it because it showed off her trim figure and because green had become her favorite color. Wearing green, she felt that her shoulder-length black hair seemed to shine, and it brought out glints of green in her hazel eyes.

Tonight she and Kevin were definitely having dinner someplace special. He had brought her to the Four Seasons Restaurant, and their table was next to the pool, which was the focal point of the elegant, high-ceilinged room. Four paintings in somber colors and coarse textures hung on the similarly colored brown and black walls of the Pool Room. There were also beautiful live trees. It was like being in a midcentury modern palace.

After turning to look at the paintings, Sarah turned to Kevin again.

"What a lovely place," she said. "I've never been here before."

"Neither have I," he told her. "That's why I thought it was time we tried it." He broke off a piece of the bread on his bread plate. Then he looked around the room. "It really is lovely, isn't it?"

The way Kevin was acting made Sarah feel he had something on his mind. He was often like this: He didn't like to just come out and say things; he liked to build up to them.

He smiled at her. "I'm glad you liked my *Faust*."

"I have to admit, it was a bit frightening. Seeing you condemned to hell."

He laughed. "Don't worry. It's only an opera."

"Your aria, 'Salut, demeure chaste et pure.' It was gorgeous."

"It means a lot to me that you liked it. Now tell me about your quartet."

It was her turn to smile. "We're performing at Merkin Hall at the end of next month."

"Congratulations."

"I hope you'll be able to come."

"If I've got the night off, I wouldn't miss it. You know that."

"I know."

He reached across the table for her hand and took it in his. "I have something to tell you, Sarah."

So she was right; he did have something on his mind. She felt the warmth of his hand holding hers and smiled at him again. "Tell me."

"This is even harder for me than I thought it would be—"

Sarah had never seen him look so worried. "What is it?"

It took him a long time to speak. "When you turned down my proposal," he said finally, "I thought I'd never find anybody else . . ."

Sarah felt herself tense up, but she didn't say anything. She just kept looking at Kevin and trying to act as if she didn't feel the earth was about to give way right under her.

"But I have found someone. Lisa Golden, the soprano who's singing Marguerite."

Sarah willed herself to keep letting Kevin hold her hand. "I'm happy for you, Kevin."

"I know it's a bit of a shock. There's never really been anyone that either of us has been close to except each other. I don't know how wise it was that we kept sleeping together after, well, you know . . ."

"We never made each other any promises," she said, trying to continue looking into his eyes, knowing that this would be the last time they would ever have a dinner alone together, or at least the last time that she could ever dream on the way to dinner that they would always be having dinners together alone. "I'm happy for you," she repeated.

"Thank you, Sarah."

She waited as long as she could and then withdrew her hand from his. "Excuse me. I have to go to the ladies' room."

As she got to her feet, Kevin rose from his chair, too. "Are you all right?"

She laughed. "Of course I'm all right. I'll be right back."

She smiled just long enough to turn away from him. As she took her first step toward the restrooms, she was already silently crying.

*

Kelly, an apron over a white silk blouse and jeans, her long hair fastened into a ponytail with a barrette, stood at the kitchen counter, cutting fresh basil for her favorite tomato sauce. It was a recipe she'd concocted when Jeff and Julie were little. Fortunately, she had all the ingredients in the house. Her eyes were still wet from peeling onions, and she dried them with a tissue before picking up another piece of basil.

Emma hovered over her shoulder. "I wish you'd let me do that for you before I go. No need to tire yourself out doing all this for the photographer."

"His name is Chris, and I'm not tiring myself out, and you're going to be late for the movie."

Emma sighed. "Are you sure you're okay?"

Kelly turned to her and looked into her kind gray eyes. "Yes, I'm sure."

Emma's face was still filled with concern.

Kelly couldn't pretend she didn't know why Emma was worried. She smiled and put her hands affectionately on the older woman's shoulders. "Thank you for going after King. And thank you for being so loving to me."

"There's nothing I wouldn't do for you, Kelly. I just—I just want to make sure you're all right."

Kelly continued to meet her gaze. "I am all right. I promise."

Emma sighed again. "Well, I can't say I'm not glad you've met a man that you're interested in. And from what I saw when he was photographing you, he is cute."

Kelly laughed and took her hands off Emma's shoulders. "Please, Emma, go. You're going to keep Donald waiting."

The doorbell rang, and Emma looked toward the hallway as if she was going to answer it.

"I mean it," Kelly said. "Go!"

"I'm going. I'm going," Emma assured her. She picked up her coat and scarf from the back of a chair, putting them on as she followed Kelly out of the kitchen and toward the front door.

By the time they reached the hall, King, who had been napping in the living room, joined them and started howling. Kelly grabbed his collar as she opened the front door. The bleak day had turned into a cool, damp night, and Chris Palmer, wearing a black turtleneck under a leather jacket, was standing on the stoop, carrying a bottle of wine.

"Don't mind King," Kelly told him, pulling the dog with her as she stepped back into the foyer. "He'll calm down in a minute."

As Chris walked into the brownstone, King continued howling.

"I think you should tell him that," Chris suggested.

Kelly gave the dog a reassuring look. "It's okay, King. He's a friend."

Emma thrust herself between Chris and Kelly. "I don't think we've been introduced. I'm Emma O'Brian, Kelly's housekeeper and cook. But she's making the dinner tonight herself."

"I'm Chris Palmer." His dark eyes shone at Emma as he extended his hand to shake hers. "Pleased to meet you."

"Pleased to meet you," Emma responded. She gave Kelly an approving nod before heading out the door and telling them to have a good time.

Once Emma was gone, Kelly let go of King's collar. He kept howling as she walked to the guest closet under the stairs and opened it for Chris. "Let him smell you while you hang your jacket up. Then he'll stop. If he gets to be too much, I'll put him upstairs. I've just got a few things to do for dinner."

As Kelly started toward the kitchen, Chris was hanging up his leather jacket and King was sniffing him and still howling.

"I really am a friend," he was telling the dog. "So you don't have to protect her. You can just hang out and have a good time. All right?"

Kelly liked the way Chris talked to King. She was glad she'd invited him to dinner. She only wished King would stop howling.

✳

Sarah and Kevin exited through the imposing doors of the Four Seasons onto East 52nd Street. The temperature had dropped since they'd entered the restaurant, and Sarah buttoned her coat all the way up. Kevin was next to her, wearing only his blazer and a scarf. She was avoiding his eyes, as she had for most of the evening, ever since he'd told her about his engagement.

"I didn't ask about Kelly," he said as they emerged onto the sidewalk. "How is she?"

"She's fine," Sarah responded. Even under normal circumstances, she wouldn't have allowed herself to discuss the problem she believed Kelly was having, but these circumstances were anything but normal.

She suddenly felt his hand gently take hold of her arm.

"I'll walk you home," he said.

"I think I'll take a cab."

She could feel him looking at her, feel him thinking how strange it was that she didn't want to walk. She loved walking; she usually walked the thirty blocks from her apartment near Carnegie Hall to Kelly's brownstone every morning and sometimes walked back again at night. Her apartment was only a fifteen-minute walk from the restaurant; of course she could walk. But tonight she was going to take a cab. She could feel Kevin about to protest and then decide not to. She could feel everything about him, and she knew he could feel everything about her. And that was why she wanted to escape from him as quickly as she could. He must've known that, too.

"I'll hail one for you," he told her, moving toward the street.

She watched him as he looked west on 52nd toward Park Avenue. "I don't see any," he said after a few moments. "You wait here. I'll go to Park and catch one coming north."

He ran toward Park. When he got to the corner, she saw him

looking south, waving his hand in the air for a cab.

She didn't know how she got through the last few moments when Kevin put her into the cab. She knew she must've said something, but she had no idea what it was. She didn't even remember giving the cabbie her address. She remained in a fog as the taxi took her to 57th Street and 8th Avenue. She didn't know if the trip was fast or slow; time had become meaningless. She got out at the entrance of the apartment building, unlocked the door, somehow got into the elevator and pressed the button for her floor. When the doors opened, she drifted across the hall, fumbled with her keys, and finally managed to open the door to her small apartment. All she could think about was that this was probably the last time that she would ever see Kevin.

Ultimately, Kelly had had to take King upstairs and leave him in her bedroom with the door to the third floor closed so that she and Chris could have dinner in peace. They ate at the dining table in her living room, looking out on the moonlit garden behind the brownstone. She'd set the table with her grandmother's red damask tablecloth, matching napkins, flowers from the greenhouse in a crystal vase, and four candles in cranberry glass candleholders. The Dennisons had shared dinner with her at the same table, but tonight was very different. Michelle and Mark were her closest friends, like family, really, and having them over was so comfortable for her that it required no effort. With Chris, she was aware of the way his brown eyes looked at her, not with the interest of a photographer, but with the interest of a man looking at a woman he was attracted to. When he'd asked her out, she'd told him it had been a while since she'd dated; she hadn't realized then how unused she'd gotten to being looked at as a date. She also hadn't realized how much she would enjoy it again.

"I guess you could call me a sweetaholic," Chris observed, savoring his second butter cookie. "You really made this?"

"Pastry is my specialty," Kelly told him. She was on her second cookie, too. Once again she felt grateful for being tall. She didn't have to watch what she ate like Sarah or Michelle, who were more petite and never ate more than one portion of anything.

Chris sat back in his chair and kept his eyes on her. "I thought astrology was your specialty."

Kelly was looking at him, too. She liked the fair skin on his handsome face and the dark beard that had begun to show on his cheeks and along his jaw since that afternoon when he'd come clean shaven to photograph her. And of course she liked his brown eyes.

"Astrology is my professional specialty. But I also love cooking."

"If you love cooking, why do you have a cook?"

"Emma used to cook for my grandmother. This was my grandmother's house. She raised me after my parents died. When she passed away, she left the brownstone to me. Emma lived downstairs. I didn't want her to have to look for another home or another job."

"That was generous of you."

"Emma's been generous to me, too. I was twenty-five when my grandmother died. I was a single mother with two children and starting graduate school in psychology. Emma took care of my children when I was at school. She cooked and she helped clean. For years I couldn't pay her what she deserved. It took everything I had to keep the house, feed us, and pay for school."

Chris glanced over his shoulder, into the hallway. "Where are your children?"

"Actually, they're not children anymore. They're in college."

His eyes returned to Kelly. "I won't say you look too young to have children that age because you'll say that line's been around since Adam left the Garden of Eden."

She laughed. "Not this time I won't."

"Good. Because it's true."

The way he looked at her, she believed him. She also believed that if she let herself, before the end of the evening they'd be in bed, making love.

Smiling, he got to his feet. "Why don't I help you clear the table?"

"You don't have to—"

"I know. I want to."

She watched as he rolled up the sleeves of his black sweater and started gathering the dessert dishes. Suddenly, a chill pierced through her body with the sharpness of an ice pick. Ingrained into the skin under the dark hairs on his forearm was the tattoo of a skull.

He must have seen that she was staring at it because he said: "A remnant of my Goth days. When I was young and grim and obsessed with death."

He headed toward the kitchen with the dishes, but she didn't go with him. She just stood there, thinking about the black, blue, and red skull, with black holes where the eyes and nose should be and its mouth grinning with the rictus of death. For the first time that night she realized that she was alone in her house—the one place she felt safe—with a man she did not know. What did it matter that she'd liked the way he looked? Or that he'd been so charming and clever when he'd photographed her? Or that he worked for *Luminary World* magazine and that Wendy had assigned him to take her pictures? Had she called Wendy to ask about him? No. She'd called no one. Chris Palmer was a stranger.

All evening he'd asked her questions and she'd told him about herself. The first thing he'd told her about himself all night was that he had a sweet tooth. Now he'd told her that the skull on his arm was a relic from years ago. But she had no idea if he was telling the truth. Maybe it wasn't left over from the past; maybe it was very much a part of his current life. Maybe the black, blue, and red skull, five inches long and the width of his muscular forearm, meant that Chris Palmer was violent and sadistic. Maybe King had sensed this about him and that was why he'd kept howling at him. Maybe Chris Palmer was the man who had—

She didn't finish the thought. She didn't need to. She didn't care if he was any of the things that she feared or if she was needlessly frightening herself. She wasn't going to take a chance; she wanted him out of her house.

All night he'd been as pleasant and flirtatious with her as he'd been that afternoon. Obviously, he wanted her to like him; he wanted her to let him into her life. The best way to get him to leave, she reasoned, was to act as if he'd succeeded. That meant she had to continue to seem as interested in him and as relaxed as she'd been during dinner.

As she walked toward the kitchen, she forced a smile onto her face and steeled herself not to allow her fear to show. She found him at the sink, washing a dinner plate. Despite herself, she couldn't take her eyes off the skull on his exposed forearm.

She stood next to him and touched his arm with her fingertips. "That's sweet of you, Chris. But please, leave the dishes for me."

He ran the soapy sponge over the plate. "It's the least I can do to pay for my supper. When I'm finished, we can sit and talk in front of a nice fire."

She kept the smile on her face and tried to sound as pleasant as he did. "That sounds great for next time. But it's late."

"It's not that late," he said, not turning to look at her. "You just don't know what time it is."

You're the one who doesn't know what time it is. Those were the words with which the man had menaced her on the phone. Now Chris Palmer had used almost the same words. Her smile disintegrated as fear knotted her stomach.

He looked at her. "What's the matter? I just said if you think it's late, you don't know what time it is. It's only ten." He looked at the clock. "See?"

She glanced at the clock. He was right; it was ten. But how did she know that all he'd been referring to was the time? That he hadn't been deliberately echoing the words she'd been threatened with in the whispered phone call? How did she know that her fear about him wasn't the truth—that he was the man who had made the call?

She told herself again that it didn't matter if she was right to be afraid of him or not; someone had made the call and Chris Palmer was a stranger and she didn't want him in her house. And if he really was dangerous and wanted to insinuate himself into her life, her greatest chance of getting him to go right now was to let him think that she wanted to see him again.

She put on her smile. "I just meant I had a long day. And I get moody when I'm tired. No use putting you through that. I've got to go to sleep."

He smiled, too. "Party pooper." He turned off the faucet, then turned to face her. They were standing very close; she could feel his breath on her face. "I hope we can get together again soon."

It took all of her will to remain so close to him. "I'd like that, too."

"I hope you mean it."

She made herself lean forward and kiss him on the lips. "Of course I mean it."

"Good."

He returned her kiss, not forcefully, just enough to part her lips and touch her tongue with his. She didn't flinch. In a moment, he stepped back, smiled at her again, and told her that he'd call her tomorrow.

It wasn't until she'd stood at the inner edge of her front doorway and watched him descend the steps and walk toward Central Park West that she began to shudder. She closed the front door and locked both locks. She was shivering as she ran up the stairs to get King. If Chris Palmer came back, she wanted the Siberian husky to be with her.

The moment she opened the door to the third floor hallway, King ran to greet her, howling a brief hello and licking her hands as Meow circled her feet. Kelly let the animals precede her onto the stairs before closing the door to the third floor behind her and joining them on the staircase. Although the furnace had been on since dinner, she was still shivering, and she decided that she'd light a fire in the fireplace and stay down in the living room reading. She knew it would be impossible for her to fall asleep.

She pulled the living room drapes closed, kneeled down in front of the fireplace, took three pieces of wood from the pile on the flat stone hearth, and arranged them on the andirons. Then she took a long match out of the matchbox, turned on the gas jet, and lit the gas under the wood. As the flames rose into the wood, she took the coffee cups and saucers from the table and brought them into the kitchen.

Perpetually hungry, Meow and King were waiting in front of their bowls for a snack. She put dry food into their bowls and went over to the sink to finish washing the dishes. She had a dishwasher, but although Emma used it, Kelly never did. She preferred doing the dishes by hand, especially now that Jeff and Julie were away and she used fewer dishes. She liked the feel of the hot water on her hands and the process of starting off with a dirty plate and making it clean. As she washed the dinner dishes, she thought about Chris Palmer and wondered if she'd been right to be afraid of him or if she'd made a fool of herself and only imagined that she had anything to fear from him, let alone that he had been the man whose whispered voice had terrified her.

Meow had gone to her spot on top of the refrigerator and King was lying at her feet when she started to smell a dry, bitter smell, like something burning. She turned around, half expecting to see that she'd inadvertently left something cooking on the stove that had burned down to the pot, and instead saw black smoke coming into the kitchen. She ran into the hallway and saw that the smoke was coming from the living room. That instant, the smoke alarms began to scream, bleating like dying animals on speed. Her heart beating fast, the skin hot all over her body, she looked toward the front door and knew that no matter what, she couldn't run out into the street. King stood next to her, voicing his dismay; Meow was in the kitchen doorway, mewing.

As the smoke continued pouring in from the living room, Kelly ran back into the kitchen and opened the glass door and ushered the animals out into the garden. Once they'd gotten outside, she closed the door and, coughing, ran into the smoke-filled hall again toward the front of the house. Her eyes stinging, she made her way through Sarah's office and into her own, grabbed her cell phone from her desk, and ran out into the hall, closing the doors behind her. By the time she got to the kitchen again, she was coughing and could barely see. She reached the garden door and started choking so convulsively she couldn't breathe. She leaned against the door, wheezing, choking, her eyes tearing. Finally, she was able to turn the doorknob, open the door, and, holding on to the knob, stumble out onto the slate steps to the garden. She closed the door behind her and, between fits of choking, slowly began to breathe the cold air; then she went to the nearer of the two stone benches in the garden and sat down. King was at her feet. Meow was cringing in front of the greenhouse. She dialed 911 on her cell phone. Still coughing, she told the operator that she needed the fire department.

*

Sirens braying, a fire engine turned the corner onto 85th Street from Columbus Avenue, sped up the block, and stopped in the middle of the street in front of the brownstone. Walt Metzger, the first officer, a fifteen-year veteran of the FDNY, jumped out of the front passenger seat and fastened his fire mask as he ran up the steps, leading the three other firemen who were putting on their masks. Metzger rang the bell, knocked loudly on the door, and then tried to open the door, but it didn't budge.

"She said she'd be in the yard. She probably can't hear us," he told the other men.

He didn't wait long, just a few seconds, before he inserted the hydraulic wedge he'd carried with him and started the process of forcing the door open. Seeing bars on the first-floor windows, he glanced up to the unbarred windows above and called over his shoulder to the rookie who prided himself on his skill with the ladder, "Ferguson, see if you can get in through one of those windows up there!"

While Ferguson went back to the engine and raised the

ladder, Metzger kept working on the front door until he got it open and smoke streamed out of the house onto him and the other two firemen. They raced into the black haze and split up to search the brownstone for the fire. The woman who'd called in said she'd made a fire in the fireplace, but she neglected to say where the fireplace was located. They figured that was the most likely source of the fire.

As Metzger headed through the smoke-filled hall, he called on his portable radio to the battalion chief, the two trucks, and the ambulance that he knew were on their way from more distant locations. "Lots of smoke, but so far I don't see anything burning!"

The two firemen who charged into Sarah's and Kelly's offices at the front of the brownstone quickly found that neither room was the source of the smoke, and they closed the doors to prevent further smoke damage. Just as they were running up the staircase to the second floor, they heard Metzger yell from the living room, "The chimney's stopped up! I got it under control!"

When they joined him in the smoky room, they found that Metzger had already doused the logs in the fireplace with his fire extinguisher and turned off the gas jet. Now he was opening the door to the garden where the woman who'd made the call was sitting on a stone bench with a red cat in her lap and a big white dog at her feet.

"Get those damned smoke alarms turned off," he told them. "Then open the windows and get the blowers. I'll go see how she's doing."

Removing his smoke mask, he walked down into the garden, followed by a billow of smoke from the house. As he neared the bench, he noticed the woman looked dazed.

"Are you okay?" he asked gently.

Kelly turned to him and told him that she was. Then she started to cough.

"Sorry, but we've got to leave the door open. Let the smoke clear out."

"I understand." Stifling another cough, she covered her mouth with her hand and watched the smoke float out of the house and up into the sky.

"I got an ambulance coming. The medics can see about that cough."

She answered adamantly: "It's nothing. I got out of the house right away. As soon as the smoke started."

"Well, the medics'll be here in a minute or two if you decide you need them."

She ignored his suggestion. "Did sparks jump from the fireplace and start the fire?"

"There was no fire. Your chimney was stopped up. Sent the smoke right back into the living room and everywhere else."

Kelly looked at him, puzzled. "How did it get stopped up?"

"Maybe the flue was closed."

She shook her head. "I've never closed the flue. I always leave it open. Could it have blown shut?"

"Depends. I'll find out and tell you. That's part of my job." He looked at her. She was a beautiful woman, but she looked so drained that he felt sorry for her. It was a shock, and a frightening one, to go through what had happened to her. "Why don't you go to a neighbor's or to a coffee shop and wait till we get the smoke out? You can even wait in the engine if you want."

"I appreciate it, but I'll just wait here."

"Okay. If that's what you want." He waited a moment to see if she'd change her mind, but she didn't. She just sat on the bench, petting the cat, looking at the ivy on the garden wall. "I'll come for you when I've looked at the chimney," he told her.

She looked up at him, the whites of her blue eyes bloodshot from the smoke. "Thank you."

"I know the place is a mess," he said to her. "But at least it's not burned down."

"No, it's not burned down. I'm grateful for that."

She watched him go back into the house as the smoke continued to spill out and disappear into the night.

Nineteen

TWO HOURS LATER, THE brownstone was sufficiently aired out for Kelly to come back inside. The first- and second-floor walls and furnishings were stained with black where the smoke had left its imprint, but because the door to the third floor had been closed, her bedroom, bathroom, and upstairs study had suffered no damage. The smell of smoke pervaded these rooms, too, but not as badly as it did the rest of the house, and everything in them was unharmed.

Kelly was sitting on the sofa in her upstairs study, Meow clinging to her leg, King on the floor in front of her, while Metzger sat in the chair opposite her, reporting to her what he'd found.

"The chimney was clogged with debris. That's why the smoke backed up like that."

Kelly looked at him a moment before she asked, "What kind of debris?"

"Just plastic bags, newspapers, leaves—the kind of stuff the wind carries. Happens every fall to somebody when they make their first fire in the fireplace and they don't have a screen across the top to keep the debris out."

Kelly looked at him but didn't say anything.

Her silence made him continue.

"It was a cold night. Was it your first fire in the fireplace in a while?"

"Yes. I haven't made one since last March or April."

Metzger was satisfied. "Okay, then. That's it." He got up from the chair. "I'm afraid you're going to have to get the place cleaned and painted and all and get the chimney cleaned out. New smoke alarms. And a new front door. But we'll make sure this one's closed safe for the night."

Kelly stood up, too. "Thank you again."

"Sorry it happened," he told her sympathetically. "Just remember, it could've been a lot worse."

Kelly nodded; she knew he was right.

She saw him out, ignoring as best she could the soot-stained walls on her way to the front hall, where two firemen stood on the stoop, working on the front door. She waited until they had rehung the patched-up door on its hinges and closed it. Then she went back upstairs to her study. Earlier in the night she had felt scared; now she just felt numb.

✳

Emma walked home from where the bus had let her off on 86th and Columbus. She and Donald had enjoyed the movie and gone out for a snack afterward. He'd wanted to see her home, but she liked being on her own. She'd been on her own since she'd come to New York, and even though she and Donald had been going out together for the past four years, she liked maintaining her independence. Apparently, this must have been fine with him, she reflected, since he'd never proposed changing their living arrangements. She didn't know what she would do if he suggested it, but with Kelly's recent fear of leaving the house, she was glad that up till now it hadn't come up.

As she approached the brownstone, the arthritis in her hip started to hurt a little. She wasn't surprised: cold, wet weather always made her hip hurt. She was just about to walk down the steps from the sidewalk to the door to her apartment when, by habit, she glanced up to see which lights were on in Kelly's part of the house. She was surprised to see that although the lights were out on the first floor, behind the bars on the first-floor windows Kelly's office windows were open. She looked up and saw that the windows were open on the darkened second floor as well and on the third floor, where the lights were on in Kelly's study.

Why would all those windows be open on such a cold night? She was suddenly afraid. And as her gaze moved to the front door and she noticed that it was now patched with plywood, she became even more afraid.

Moving as quickly as she could, she went down the steps and unlocked the door to her apartment. Even before she entered, she smelled smoke. She turned on the lights, but her apartment looked just as she'd left it—white walls, comfortable gray furniture, a tiny Pullman kitchen. She hurried through the apartment and up the stairs that led to the first floor of the brownstone. Out of breath and anxious, she opened the door to the first-floor hall outside the kitchen, and in the light from her apartment, saw the blackened walls as she smelled the stale smell of the vanished smoke.

"Kelly!" she screamed.

Without waiting for a response, she got into the elevator and pressed the button for the third floor. It felt to her as if this time it was taking hours, not minutes, to get there, but eventually the door opened and she rushed out into the third-floor hall.

"Kelly!"

Kelly was in her bathrobe, at the desk in her upstairs study, with her ephemeris and her chart, the chart on which she'd written the word *danger* right after she'd gotten the phone call. She was focused on the ephemeris when she heard Emma's voice and rose to her feet.

"In here, Emma—" She was already at the door when Emma came in and threw her arms around her.

"Thank God!" Emma said, hugging her tightly.

Kelly put her arms around Emma. "I'm okay. Really, I'm okay. You don't have to worry. I should've left you a note. I'm sorry. I just forgot."

Emma held her for a long time. Then she let go and looked at Kelly assessingly. "You didn't stay inside the house during the fire, did you?"

"No. I went into the garden. But it wasn't a fire. It was—"

Emma felt her face grow hot. "I don't care what it was! You should've been outside on the street, well away from it! It's not right, Kelly. You have to do something about being afraid to leave home!" Looking at Kelly, who had been so strong for so long and now seemed so fragile, she felt heartsick. "You didn't used to be like this," she said tenderly. "Don't you want to be able to go out again?"

Emma looked into Kelly's eyes as she used to when Kelly was a little girl, to make sure that Kelly was going to tell her the truth. Kelly met her gaze, pained to see the anguish that she had brought to this woman whom she knew loved her as much as she would if Kelly were her own child.

"I will do something about it," Kelly told her.

"And when will that be?"

"That's what I was working out when you came in. But it won't be forever. I promise, Emma. I really do."

Emma continued looking into Kelly's eyes. When she was sure she saw in them that Kelly had not given up, she nodded and hugged her again.

In Emma's maternal embrace, Kelly was acutely aware that she'd given Emma her word. But although she'd meant what she said, she had no idea how she would accomplish it.

Twenty

THE MOON WAS FINALLY full tonight. Of course, he'd expected it to be. And he expected to have luck; the aspects favored him. They favored him for his vocation, and they favored him tonight. And as always, he had planned everything. Everything.

But when he got to her street, he saw a man walking a dog, and his insides liquefied as they used to when he was a child and his mother caught him doing what she didn't like and punished him with her needles. Despite the paroxysm in his gut, he forced himself to keep driving, knowing that if he made a U-turn, the man would be more likely to notice him. He continued driving until he got out of her neighborhood and then he drove for half an hour in a state of nerves. When he drove back to her block, the streets were empty, and he was full of rage again. He parked on the street around the corner from hers. It was three forty-five a.m.

She lived in a colonial-style house in the middle of the block. She hadn't left any lights on outside, but as he approached, the full moon enabled him to see the path he would take from her driveway to her front door. Fifteen-foot bushes lined the far side of the driveway, separating it from the house next door, so he walked next to the bushes until he reached the garage; then he cut over to the front door.

When he got to the door, he stretched the surgical gloves

onto his hands and took a key out of his jeans pocket. Slipping it into the top lock, he was not surprised when it fit perfectly and turned with no effort. The second key he'd brought with him slipped into the bottom lock and opened it easily. He congratulated himself on how well he'd worked everything out. This pleasure only sharpened his anger.

A moment later and he was in the house. No lights left on inside, either. But the full moon, shining through the windows, allowed him to see all that he needed to: the staircase he silently mounted in his black running shoes, the upstairs hall he quietly walked across, the doors of the bedrooms where she might have been sleeping, and the bedroom where he soon found her. The sound of her turning over in bed gave her away even before he reached her door.

He hadn't stopped to look around much downstairs, but now that he was in the curtainless bedroom, he surveyed the furnishings. It had once been expensive and elegant, but now it was shabby: a Native American blanket thrown over worn upholstery, flat patches in the light blue rug, a tear in the lampshade on the night table lamp. Soon, none of it would matter to her.

He looked at the woman on the bed, sleeping soundly in a white nightgown that looked as if it was silk. She was in her late forties and still very beautiful. Her fine blond hair fell on the pillow, framing her face. She had once been an actress, and she had high cheekbones. With her eyes closed, her long lashes fell on her white skin.

Soon he was on her bed, straddling her, opening his zipper and pulling on his condom. She stirred in her sleep but didn't wake up.

"You've got company, Sheryl," he whispered.

The blond woman opened her eyes, looked up at this man in

a black ski mask, felt him pinning her down on the bed between his legs, and saw that he was stiff and ready to rape her. She screamed.

He stretched the leather cord across her neck. "You scream again and you're dead!"

Her frightened eyes stared up at him, and he thought she was going to just surrender, but she screamed again and started flailing her arms, legs, and head so wildly that he became disoriented and lost his grip on the leather cord. Taking advantage of the opportunity, she raised her head and tried to bite his arm, but her teeth didn't penetrate his thick black sweater. Furious, he punched her in the jaw, and as her head fell back against her pillow, he pressed the cord down on her neck hard enough to make her gag on her fear.

"You wanted love, Sheryl? This is love!" he told her.

Frozen in terror, she watched as he lowered himself on top of her, and then she felt him enter her. After that, she didn't know what happened.

Twenty-One

KELLY SAT AT HER desk in the upstairs study, examining her chart. Although the smoke was long gone, its acrid smell remained, even on the third floor. She'd closed the windows in the study because it was too cold; now she glanced at them, wondering if she should reopen them to air out the room. The smell of smoke made her think of death, and she didn't need to think about death any more than she was already thinking about it. She'd begun looking at her chart, focusing on her moon in Capricorn, which could make her inclined to melancholy reflection. But since early September, when she'd started to be afraid of leaving the house, she hadn't just been melancholy; she'd been afraid. And she realized now that it hadn't just been a vague sense of fear; when she'd stood frozen at the threshold of the front door, unable to run after King, she'd been afraid of dying. The prospect of going out onto the street was like a death sentence to her.

Now her home had been marked by the smoke that had backed up from the fireplace. As she'd walked from the garden through the kitchen into the hall and up the staircase to the third floor, she'd been stunned by the black stains on the walls of the first two floors; the smoke had traveled like a dark manifestation of her fear and left its imprint everywhere. She'd been afraid of Chris Palmer and, right or wrong, had made him leave her house, and then she'd lit the fire and—

She was startled from her thoughts by the ringing of the phone. She looked at the clock; it was 4:35 in the morning. Her heart was beating fast, and she could feel the blood pulsating through her arteries and veins. She knew who it was.

The phone rang again. She looked at the two phones on the desk, her business phone and her personal phone. She wasn't sure which one was ringing. She picked up the receiver of her business phone. That was the line he had called on last time. When she brought the receiver to her ear, she heard a dial tone.

The ringing continued; it was her personal phone. She replaced the receiver on her business phone and picked up her personal line.

Silence.

For a while she didn't say anything. Then she quietly said, "Hello."

"You think you know everything, don't you?"

It was the same man, the same whispered voice taut with hatred.

"Who is this?" Her voice rose in fear.

"That's one thing you don't know, isn't it?"

"Please tell me! Is it you, Chris?"

"You don't know, do you? There's another thing you don't know. You don't know what I'm going to do to you."

All night Kelly had been so cold; now she was sweating. "Why are you calling me like this? Why do you hate me?"

"I hate you because you made her leave me. You made her go and never come back."

"No, I didn't! I wouldn't—I . . ."

She heard him hang up. Her hand trembled as she placed the receiver back on the phone. Then she picked it up again and called the 20th Precinct. When an officer answered, she gave him her name, told him the man who had called her before had called again and that this time he'd said he was going to do something to her. The officer asked her to come to the station to file a report. Unable to tell him the truth about what bound her to her home, she told him that she couldn't leave the house because it had been flooded with smoke, the fire department had just left, and there was a lot of damage. Her voice shaking, she asked if he could please send someone to her and she gave the address. She was told that an officer would be there, but that it would probably be in the morning.

As Kelly hung up the phone, she reconciled herself to the fact that she would be up for the rest of the night.

Twenty-Two

AT EIGHT A.M. KELLY called Sarah to tell her about what had happened with the fireplace and to ask her to cancel the day's appointments and ask her father, who had taken care of all the contracting work on Kelly's house until his retirement, to recommend workmen he knew personally to do the cleanup, painting, and repairs. By ten thirty, carpenters were replacing the front door, the electrician was taking down the old smoke alarms, the paint crew had washed down the walls and were already painting, and the upholstery and carpet cleaners were on their way.

Still, standing in the front hall, looking at all that needed to be done, surrounded by workmen, drop cloths, ladders, and paint buckets, and hearing the sounds of hammers and saws, Sarah was impatient. She felt the tension in her fingers and hands; as a violinist, that was the last place she wanted to feel it. She wished she could just close her eyes and open them again to find that the house was back to normal. But it was never that way; not with learning a piece on the violin, and not with knowing how she would look at the world and at life now that she knew Kevin was getting married. Maybe it was good that she had all this work to do; it would take her mind off him.

Since Kelly wanted the walls painted the same butter yellow as they had been with the same eggshell white for the molding, Sarah had been able to order the paint when she'd called the painters and begged them to come right away, and she'd authorized Ed Murrin and Peter Heath at Ace Painting to hire extra men so the painting would go quickly. But seeing the walls still mottled with smoke residue even after washing, she wondered how fast that could be.

She looked up at Peter, who stood on a ladder as he painted the wall outside her office with a roller. He'd arrived forty-five minutes after she'd called, ready and eager to work. He'd brought along Ace's whole painting crew and several of its part-timers, and they'd started right away, while his partner, Ed, finished another job in Queens by himself.

"How long are we talking about, Peter?" Sarah asked.

Peter was tall and gangly and, with his bushy blond hair, Sarah thought he looked like an overgrown child. He rolled on the yellow paint in a smooth, straight line as he answered her: "We've got eight men, so it's possible we can finish tonight. It's only the two floors. If not tonight, definitely by noon tomorrow."

Sarah felt the tension in her hands begin to relax. She thanked him and approached the ladder that held the electrician, a two-hundred-fifty-pound man wearing an unflattering red toupee who looked precariously balanced on the next-to-the-top rung as he installed a new smoke alarm. "How are you doing, Ivan?"

Without looking down, he replied, "Don't worry, Miss Stein. I'm not going to fall. I've been doing this a long time."

Embarrassed that she'd been so transparent, Sarah felt her face heat up. "I know. I just meant—"

"You meant I should probably lose some weight, right?"

Sarah was still blushing. "I guess so."

The older man laughed. "My wife tells me the same thing. So do my kids. So join the crowd. Like I said, don't worry."

"Okay, I won't," she responded.

Recognizing that if she stayed in the hall and continued exercising her nerves, she would do more harm than good, Sarah headed toward her office. She'd already canceled the day's appointments; now she had to cancel the appointments for the remainder of the week. Entering her office, she was relieved again to see that Kelly's having closed the office door so soon after the smoke had started had kept Sarah's office walls almost free of smoke. They looked like all they needed was touching up. And the walls in Kelly's office would only need touching up, too. That is, unless the touch-ups contrasted too starkly with the old paint; as a contractor's daughter, she knew that if that happened, the office walls would need to be painted just like the other walls.

She sat at her desk and looked at the closed door to Kelly's office. Kelly was inside, talking with a police detective. Sarah assumed he was talking with her about the chimney backing up, but she wondered why the police would be involved with something that Kelly had told her the fire investigator had said was an accident.

She knew that if she moved her chair close to Kelly's office door, she could hear what they were saying. But no matter how curious and concerned she felt, she believed in privacy too much to ever do that. Instead, she turned on the classical radio station and opened her calendar to the appointments scheduled for the next day so she could start making calls. Pavarotti was singing "Nessun Dorma" from *Turandot*. She found herself thinking of Kevin; he'd sung the haunting aria for her last year when he'd been preparing to perform it in *Turandot* for an opera company in Germany. Regardless of the amount of work she had to occupy her, she felt heartsick. As she lifted the receiver to make a call, she wondered if she would ever feel another way.

✳

Detective Mike Stevens sat in one of the chairs Kelly usually used for clients. The chair was a little too small for Stevens, who was six foot five, but he made the best of it. He crossed his long legs and sat back as if there were actually room for his big frame. At forty-five years old, that's how Stevens was; he tended to make the best of inconsequential things. Things of consequence were another matter. With his investigations, he tended to be relentless. He also tended to read people well. Sitting across the desk from Kelly, he could see that she was not a woman who would call the police for attention; she was a woman who would rather not call the police at all. And that made him take the threatening phone call she had reported all the more seriously.

"You said he told you that you made her leave him. Why would he say that?" he asked her.

Kelly had spent the six hours that had passed between the phone call and the detective's arrival pondering that very question herself. "Maybe his wife or girlfriend came to see me, and he thinks I told her to end the relationship. But I don't do that." She kept her eyes on his to make sure he understood what she was telling him. "The reason I call myself an intuitive astrologer is that besides being an astrologer, I'm a trained psychologist. The psychoanalyst C. G. Jung used astrology when he saw patients. I do the same thing in reverse. When I interpret people's charts, I use my background in psychology to add to what their charts tell me about the disposition of their planets. I never tell someone to leave a relationship. I help the person to understand himself or herself and the other person and the kinds of adjustments that he or she would have to make if they stay together. Then it's up to the person."

"But like you said, he may *think* you told her to go. That's why he might say that to you." Stevens unbuttoned his brown sports jacket and tried to make himself more comfortable in the chair. "Do you remember any woman in the last six months who came to you wondering if she should break it off with a husband or a boyfriend?"

"I remember at least two. I'll check my records for their names and see if there were others."

"Might as well go back a year. It may have taken this guy time to work up the steam to call you after she left."

"I will," Kelly told him.

Stevens noticed that she was no longer looking at him; her dark blue eyes were looking at nothing in particular; she was preoccupied with something she was thinking about.

He leaned forward. "What is it?"

"The night I got the first call, I looked at the transiting planets and how they were aspecting my chart. The aspects create the influences at a specific time." She was looking at him again, making sure he understood. "The movements of Mars and Pluto mean that this is a time of danger for me. My chart says the danger may be coming from something hidden, from the dark or the past. I think it's from someone I know directly or indirectly from the past and that it has to do with something that's been hidden."

Stevens continued looking at her, but he didn't say anything.

"You don't believe in astrology, do you, Detective?"

He uncrossed his legs, sat back in the chair again, looking like a very focused Papa Bear sitting in Baby Bear's chair. "It doesn't take astrology to know whoever's calling you is probably someone you've already had some kind of contact with and that he's hiding things. He's obviously hiding his identity, and he's not even telling you the details of his grievance against you."

Kelly liked the way Stevens said this. He wasn't dismissive or condescending; he was just stating how he assessed what she'd told him.

"Is there anybody in your personal life who might have a reason to threaten you?" he asked.

She responded immediately. "No. Nobody."

"What about your ex-husband?"

"Jack?" The tone of her voice reflected her skepticism. "It wasn't Jack. I'd have recognized his voice."

"You said the caller was whispering."

Kelly was silent.

"Was it you who decided on the divorce?" he asked her.

"Yes, it was."

"Then you were responsible for a woman walking out on him," he observed.

"That's ridiculous. Jack and I get along well. We saw each other just a few months ago at our daughter's high school graduation. Whoever's calling me, it's not Jack."

Stevens was quiet; then he asked, "What about the fireplace? You think the caller was responsible?"

Kelly hesitated; it was another question she'd thought about in the early hours of the morning. "The fire department said it was just debris that the wind carried."

"I read their report."

The way Stevens said this, Kelly couldn't tell if he agreed with what the fire captain had told her or not. His opaque brown eyes and sallow face gave her no clue of what he thought, either.

"We'll put a trace on your phone," he said after a long silence. He ran his fingers through his close-cropped brown hair, a nervous habit, then took the police report he'd brought with him out of his pocket and unfolded it on his lap. "You've already given us the number. 212-555-323—"

Kelly cut him off. "Oh my God! That's my office number! That's what he called the first time. But the second time he called my private number! Nobody has that number except my family and friends. How did he know my private number?"

Stevens saw Kelly's alarm; it seemed she was only now realizing that the caller had already penetrated her life—or that he'd been in her life all along. Before he could say anything, there was a knock on her office door, and he turned around to see the petite black-haired woman who had let him in standing in the doorway.

"Sorry to interrupt," she said. "But someone's here to see you, Kelly. I told him you were busy, but—"

"That's okay, Sarah. Who is it?"

"Chris Palmer."

Stevens saw that this news made Kelly even more unhappy. Rising from her chair, she excused herself and told him she would be back in a minute. As he watched her follow the other woman out of the office, he thought Kelly seemed to disappear behind a facade under which he could sense her fear.

Kelly walked into Sarah's office and found Chris waiting for her, holding a manila envelope. He was wearing the leather jacket he'd worn the night before and a black sweater and jeans. He glanced into the hallway, and then he turned to her and smiled. "Looks like you made a fire after I left last night. You should've let me stay."

Kelly felt the muscles in her jaw tighten; she didn't know what to say to him, what to think of him, so she said nothing.

He smiled again, this time with contrition. "I know I shouldn't be joking about it. What happened, Kelly?"

His dark eyes seemed sympathetic, but all she could think

about was the tattoo of the skull on his arm and what he'd said to her before he left about making a fire in the fireplace. And he'd just talked about it again.

"I'm in the middle of something important," she said, "so if you just came by to chat—"

"I printed some of the photographs for you and the contact sheets. They came out very well." He opened the envelope and started taking out the photographs. "See what you think."

"Thanks. But I don't have time now." She was doing her best to sound in control of herself.

Chris looked at her; then he tossed the envelope with the photos half out of it onto Sarah's desk. "See you around some-time," he said, hostilely sarcastic.

Kelly's eyes remained on him as he walked into the hall and turned toward the front door. The carpenters were still working to replace the door, so it didn't surprise her not to hear the door slam behind him as he left, but she knew he would have slammed it if he could have.

Without looking at Sarah, she walked back into her office, re-lieved that Chris was gone and that Detective Stevens was there.

"Who was that?" he asked.

"Chris Palmer. A photographer for the magazine I write a column for."

Instead of going back to sit in her chair, this time she sat in the other chair she used for clients, on the same side of the desk as Stevens.

"He was here last night?"

Kelly nodded. "Yes."

"Do you know him well?"

"I just met him yesterday afternoon. He took my pictures for the magazine, and I invited him to dinner." She felt foolish telling Stevens this, but there was no point in not telling him.

"He went out of his way to bring you the photographs," Stevens observed. "It would've been easier to send them on the computer. Obviously, he wanted to see you."

Kelly met his eyes but said nothing.

"Maybe he wanted to see what was going on here this morning, after the chimney made the smoke back up."

He saw in Kelly's face that what he'd said troubled her. "What is it, Dr. York?"

"I'm not sure if I'm just imagining that it's important, but—"

"But what?"

"After dinner, Chris suggested making a fire. I told him I was too tired and that he had to leave. But then, when I was alone, I did what he said. I made the fire in the fireplace."

Kelly was looking at him as if she wanted to say something else, but she didn't. She glanced at the floor, as if what she was thinking embarrassed her. Stevens did nothing to fill the void in their conversation. Finally, she looked up at him again.

"He has a tattoo of a skull on his arm. He said he used to be a Goth, and it didn't mean anything. But it scared me. That's why I asked him to go."

"You think he blocked the chimney and that's why he suggested that the two of you make a fire?"

"I don't know," Kelly said, anguished by the thought that she had been ruminating on since the firemen had arrived the night before. "Why would he have wanted to be here with me when the house filled up with smoke?"

"Maybe he wanted to see how upset you'd get. Or maybe he wanted to play the hero and have you become dependent on him."

Kelly met the detective's eyes with hers. He was right; those were reasons Chris might have wanted to be there with her when a fire was lit in the fireplace.

"Do you know any reason he'd want to hurt you?" Stevens asked.

Kelly shook her head. "I told you, we just met yesterday."

"But that doesn't mean his girlfriend or wife didn't come to see you before she walked out on him. When you check your files, see if any of the women who came about relationship problems described their boyfriend or husband in a way that make you think it could've been Chris Palmer."

Kelly felt her jaw tense again. "I will." It was devastating to think that maybe she was right about Chris; she would have preferred Stevens to have told her that her fears about Chris were groundless, that she had no reason to be suspicious of him at all. She'd rather be a fool who'd ruined a potential relationship with a man she'd been attracted to because she'd imagined things about him that were untrue than to find out she might have been attracted to a man who wanted to hurt her.

"Are you all right, Dr. York?" the detective asked her.

Kelly was slow to answer him. "Yes," she said finally. "It's just a lot to absorb."

Stevens looked at her. He didn't get up right up away. Regardless of what she'd just said, he knew that Kelly wasn't all right. He wanted her to know, by his presence, that he would do his best to keep her safe. That was what he wanted to do—keep her safe. It was why, when he'd heard that she had called the station to report the phone call, he had wanted the case. For reasons he wasn't quite ready to tell her, he wanted to help her.

Kelly didn't get up right away, either. Sitting with this giant of a man in her small office, she felt there was a possibility that he could actually protect her. His gravity gave her confidence in him. That was what she needed right now, because each day she lost more confidence in herself.

※

It started raining a few minutes before Stevens went up to the roof of the brownstone, and now it was raining hard. He hadn't thought of asking Kelly for an umbrella, so it didn't take him long to get drenched as he walked across to the spot near the eastern border of the roof where the chimney protruded from the floors below. The bricks from which the chimney was made had once been red; now they were a dull brown from decades of exposure to smoke and to New York City's filthy air. He crouched next to the chimney and studied the silver-coated tar paper lining the roof, but it didn't tell him anything about who had been up there before. It didn't even show the impression of the boots worn by the fireman who had inspected the chimney the night before. If the weather had been hot and humid as it had been this summer and earlier in the fall, it might have softened the silvered tar paper enough to hold footprints, but now the surface was hard, and it told him nothing.

He stood up and looked at the brick wall around the roof. It was about three feet high, the chimney next to it about six feet high. Anybody could have climbed up on the wall and stuck whatever he wanted to in the chimney to clog it up. Anybody. That included Kelly's ex-husband, Jack York, and the photographer Chris Palmer.

Twenty-Three

THE MEDICAL EXAMINER FROM the West Orange Police Department finished his examination of the body on the bed and turned to the police detective in charge of the investigation. "From the temperature and lividity of the body, I'd say she's been dead six or seven hours, which means she was raped and killed sometime around three this morning."

The detective, Vincent Nichols, didn't say anything. He wasn't surprised by what the ME had just told him; from the moment he saw the victim's thigh, he knew that she had been raped before she was strangled and that it had happened between two and four a.m. That was when the other victim—the victim he'd read about in the report from the New Kent PD—had been raped and strangled. The only difference was this victim had a contusion on her jaw. She must have fought back.

The ME saw Nichols staring at the cuts that formed some kind of design on the upper part of the woman's leg. "What do you think that is?"

"It's an astrology sign," Nichols told him. "I don't know which one. I'm not up on those things. But it looks like an old-fashioned scale. The kind they used to weigh things on, using weights."

The ME bent closer to scrutinize the cuts. "You're right. It is a scale. What makes you think it's an astrological sign?"

Nichols glanced at the photograph of the woman on the

night table. In life, she'd been a stunningly pretty blonde. He said to the ME: "This woman, Sheryl Doyle, she's not the first. There was one in New Kent. We're looking for a serial killer. The astrology sign is part of his MO. He rapes women, strangles them, and carves their sign into their thigh."

"Why do you suppose he does that? The astrological sign, I mean."

Nichols thought about it. "Maybe to brand them with their sign. And to show that he knew what their sign was."

"How would he know?"

Nichols looked at the ME somberly. "That's what we have to find out."

Twenty-Four

KELLY KNEW SHE HAD to tell Emma and Sarah about the phone calls. After Detective Stevens left, she decided that she would do it over coffee in the kitchen. The painters and the other workmen were occupied in other parts of the house, so for the time being, at least, the kitchen would afford them privacy. Emma had made coffee early that morning, but Kelly put up a new pot before asking Emma and Sarah to join her. Making the coffee gave her something to do as she anxiously deliberated what she was going to say to them. As they walked into the kitchen, she could see on their faces that the chaotic state of the brownstone was taking a toll on both of them. She could also see that they were apprehensive about why she'd asked them to come into the kitchen with her. She felt that she'd done it awkwardly, with a kind of self-conscious formality that communicated to them that she had an announcement to make. Now that they were there, she wanted to set them at ease, but she didn't know how; she was too uneasy herself.

The best she could do was to gather them around the table with her and serve them the fresh coffee. Just pretend it's an ordinary morning, she told herself. But she couldn't pretend. On ordinary mornings, they drank the coffee Emma prepared, and Kelly didn't serve them. On ordinary mornings, the kitchen walls didn't have dark streaks where smoke residue had been washed away. On ordinary mornings, the house wasn't filled with men trying to put it back together. And on ordinary mornings, a police detective didn't come to see her and have a closed-door conversation with her in her office.

Sitting down at the table with them, she took a sip of the coffee and told them about the phone calls. She explained that she hadn't mentioned about the first call because she'd hoped she wouldn't get another, and if she didn't, there would have been no point in worrying them. But after the second call, she felt he'd be calling again, and that he had meant it when he'd threatened her. She also told them he'd said it was because of her that a woman had left him. She didn't tell them her suspicions about Chris Palmer; she'd had to tell Detective Stevens, but she didn't want to tell Emma and Sarah unless she was sure that Chris was the caller. Emma and Sarah looked at her as she told them Detective Stevens was putting a monitor on her phones and that he'd asked her to go through her records to see if one of her clients in the last year fit the circumstances that the caller had described.

"You don't have to stay here with me," she said, her hands clasped around her hot coffee cup, as if it could make her feel warm and protected, as if anything could. "Emma, why don't you go to Donald's? I'm sure he—"

Emma interrupted her. "Of course we're staying! The firemen said the smoke was just an accident. It wasn't done on purpose or anything!"

"I'm not sure Detective Stevens believes that," Kelly said.

"Well, I believe it!" Emma responded. "And I believe the man who called you is full of hot air!"

Sarah looked at Kelly. "I agree with Emma. I'm not afraid of some coward who calls in the middle of the night. He's just a creep with a telephone. He's not going to *do* anything."

Kelly was grateful for Emma's and Sarah's support, but she wasn't sure they were right.

Sarah saw the doubt in Kelly's face. "Once the house is put back together and everything's running normally again, we'll all feel better. You're strong, Kelly. You're going to be okay. We're all going to be okay."

Kelly felt herself become emotional. She'd prepared herself for Emma and Sarah to leave the house after they'd learned the situation; she hadn't prepared herself for them to stay. She looked at both of them and said, "Thanks," almost unable to get the word out because she didn't want to cry in front of them.

Twenty-Five

GIORDANO SAT AT HIS desk reading the copy of the August issue of *You and Your Sign* that Kim and Hernandez had found in Jennifer McGraw's house. He'd glanced at astrology columns in magazines at his dentist's office and even occasionally perused his horoscope—he was a Taurus—but he'd never known that whole magazines were devoted to the subject, and if he'd known, he wouldn't have cared. He considered reading about astrology to be a frill, and he didn't have time for frills. The only thing he believed in reading was the newspaper, which almost invariably aggravated him, because almost invariably it told him that things were as bad as he'd imagined.

Regardless of his prior attitude about astrology columns, the articles he was reading in *You and Your Sign* fascinated him. They told him something about how the victim, Jennifer McGraw, had thought about herself and about life. They also told him something about how the man who had raped and killed her thought about life. Astrology connected them: Jennifer had been a Sagittarius, the murderer had gouged her sign into her thigh, and Jennifer had an astrology magazine in her possession at the time of her death. Not just *an* astrology magazine; *this* astrology magazine.

Giordano had almost completed his reading. He'd read every word of every article, but he'd paid special attention to the articles Jennifer had marked with dog-eared pages and under-lined sentences. Not surprisingly, she had folded down the corner of the page on which August's predictions for Sagittarius ap-peared. The forecast was generally positive, emphasizing August as a good time for travel to distant places and socializing, with only a vague warning about the need to pay particular attention when negotiating contracts. There was nothing prophesying that in a little more than two months, Jennifer McGraw would be raped and murdered.

Jennifer had also marked an article on decorating your home according to your sign and another article about love relation-ships. In the decorating article, Jennifer had underlined the ad-vice for Sagittarius: *Put a round or oval table in your dining room to encourage wonderful conversations.* Jennifer had never gotten around to fulfilling that suggestion; her dining table, Giordano remembered, had been small and rectangular and stacked with several days' worth of unopened mail. In the article on love re-lationships, Jennifer had underlined the paragraph that had told her the most compatible signs for Sagittarians are Leo, Aries, Aquarius, and Libra. She had also marked a paragraph advis-ing her to find out what sign a potential mate's Venus is in: for Sagittarian women, if his Venus is in Sagittarius, he might be a good match, regardless of his sun sign. Jennifer had underlined that information twice.

Giordano finished the article, the last in the magazine, and turned the page to find several pages of classified ads. Given her interest in finding a love relationship, it didn't surprise him to see that Jennifer had underlined an ad, too. As he began reading it, he heard the sound of Hernandez's rubber-soled shoes plodding toward him on the linoleum floor.

"What do you want?" he asked, continuing to read.

Hernandez was holding a computer printout. "A victim was raped and killed early this morning in West Orange with the same MO. Except this time he cut the sign for Libra into her thigh. They've agreed not to release details to the media."

Giordano's eyes remained on the classified ad in *You and Your Sign*. "And here's how he's choosing his victims," he said to Hernandez. "'Single? Wondering why you're not attracting anyone and what you can do to change it? See the Intuitive Astrologer, Antiochus. Saturday, August fifteenth, Le Grand Hotel, New Kent, New Jersey. Ten a.m. to six p.m. Three hundred dollars for your chart and the answers to your life's most important questions. Appointments on first-come, first-served basis.'"

"So they went to this guy *Antiochus* for readings and they ended up dead."

Giordano didn't take the time to answer Hernandez. He rolled his chair up to his computer and, with two fingers, typed the name *Antiochus* into his search engine and clicked "Search." A moment later, a page of entries on Antiochus filled the screen. Giordano clicked on the first. When it came up, he read aloud: "'Antiochus was the most influential astrologer in Greece in the second century BC.'" Finally looking at Hernandez, he commented, "Not too shabby, naming yourself after the most famous astrologer in ancient Greece." He got up out of his swivel chair. "Let's check out the Le Grand Hotel."

As Giordano headed out of the office, Hernandez, following him, took out his cell phone. "I'll call West Orange. Tell them to look for an ad like that in the victim's place up there."

"Ten to one they'll find it," Giordano said. "Unless she threw it out. I'm telling you: this is who he is and how he finds them."

Twenty-Six

THE TWO-ROOM SUITE ON the eighth floor of the Pierpont Hotel in Tarrytown, New York, was divided into a modest living room and an even more modest bedroom. The living room drapes were closed and the room was dark except for the pinpoint light of a small architectural lamp. He'd brought the lamp with him and set it up on the desk prior to the arrival of his clients. He needed the lamp for his work—not the work his clients thought he was there to do, but his real work, his vocation.

If the client who came up from the lobby to see him was a man, he didn't use the lamp at all; it had no purpose, because he wasn't looking for men. With men, the session was direct and quick, over in half an hour. But when a woman came up from the lobby to consult with him, his procedure was very different. A woman was with him now, which was why he had drawn the drapes and turned on the lamp, so that the pinpoint of light would reflect in the shiny metallic circle that he swung slowly, back and forth, in front of her half-closed eyes on the string from which it was suspended. She was thirty-two and pretty in an exotic way, with medium-length brown hair, skin that looked suntanned, and long, dark eyelashes.

"Very good, Cassie," he said to her. "You are falling asleep so easily, so restfully . . ."

Her eyes closed completely now.

"Are you in that special safe place now?" he asked her.

Her eyes still closed, she answered, "Yes, I am."

Gradually, he let the circle stop moving. "It is the place where you will create the destiny of your dreams. The place where you will fulfill all the potential your planets have given you . . ."

He was pleased to see that she smiled; she was cooperating. "You will stay exactly as you are with your eyes closed until I tell you to open them," he continued as he placed the shiny metallic circle on his lap. "Until then, nothing will disturb you. No sound, no thought, not anything. Do you understand that?"

"Yes." She was still smiling.

"Then repeat my instruction."

"I will stay exactly as I am with my eyes closed until you tell me to open them. Until then, nothing will disturb me. No sound, no thought, not anything."

"Good." He turned the lamp he'd brought with him away from her face but left it on. "As a Cancer, home is very important to you. Do you have your own home?"

"Yes, I do."

"Is it a house or an apartment?"

"A house."

"Do you live alone or with someone?"

"I live alone."

"Are you dating anyone?"

"No. That's why I've come to see you."

"I know." He made his voice sound especially soft and sympathetic as he said: "But before we can expand and look at your relationship path, it's vital that your home—your home base, the place where you draw energy and sustenance—feels safe to you. Does your home feel safe?"

"Yes, it does," she said immediately.

"What makes it feel safe?"

"It's warm and comfortable. I like going home to it every night."

"Good." That wasn't what he wanted to know. He tried a different approach. "Describe what you do to make your house feel safe after you walk in at the end of the day and you close the door."

"I lock the top lock and I make sure that the bottom lock is locked, too."

"Good. Do you do anything else to make it feel safe before you go about your evening?"

"I close the chain."

"Good. Anything else?"

"I turn on the lights."

"Wonderful."

"And I make myself a drink. I need a drink at the end of the day."

"Do you feed the dog?"

"I don't have a dog."

"I see." He felt encouraged. Two locks and a chain. And she drank.

Of course he wouldn't have cared if she also had a dog; he had ways of dealing with dogs. "What is the man of your dreams like?" he asked her. "Describe him for me."

"He's older than me. And successful in whatever he does . . ."

Seeing that her eyes were still closed, he bent forward, reached into her shoulder bag on the floor, found her keys with his fingers, and gripped them so that he could remove them from her bag without jingling them. In his other hand, he held a softened piece of wax.

"He likes music and he has a good sense of humor," she

continued. "He has to be fit . . ."

There were two car keys and two house keys on her keychain. He pressed one of the house keys into the wax and made an impression of it.

"I like to go hiking, and I'd like him to like hiking, too . . ."

As she talked, he took the second key and pressed it into another piece of wax.

"The thing I want most is for him to love me for who I am, not for what I look like or anything."

"Good, Cassie." As he bent down, he said, "Now describe how you would like him to see you."

"I would like him to see me as a loving woman with a lot to give."

He slipped the keys noiselessly back into her purse and sat up, facing her. Her eyes were still closed and she was smiling again.

"The right man will see you that way, Cassie. He'll know you have a lot to give."

He was smiling now, too. Because he was the right man. And soon he would be ready to take everything that she had to give.

Twenty-Seven

AFTER HIS FRUITLESS EXAMINATION of Kelly's roof, Stevens drove back to the precinct house. His clothes were drenched, but instead of changing into the spare jacket and pants he kept in his locker, he went to his desk and put a trace on Kelly's phone lines. Without taking the time to remove his wet jacket, he sat down at his computer and started looking into Chris Palmer. He found that Christopher Palmer had been arrested for assault and battery twice in the last three years, but that Christopher Palmer was twenty-one and at the moment was serving six months in Ossining. The Chris Palmer who had photographed Kelly had no record. But he did have a listed phone number. Stevens called it and got Palmer's answering machine. He didn't bother leaving a message.

Instead, he looked up the phone number of *Luminary World* magazine and called it from his personal cell phone. He asked for the editor and was instructed to hold. He'd decided that, for now, at least, he wasn't going to tell the editor he was making a police inquiry. For five minutes he listened to a canned-music version of old Sinatra songs. When Wendy Storr finally answered, he introduced himself, said he'd seen Chris Palmer's work in her magazine, and was wondering if she would recommend him for an assignment. She answered that she'd recommend him wholeheartedly. He said the assignment was a women's fashion shoot, so he wanted to make sure that she'd never had any complaints about Chris Palmer from women he'd photographed. She told him she hadn't had any complaints about Chris Palmer from anybody, women or men; it was obvious from her tone of voice that his question had surprised and perhaps even offended her. Stevens thanked her and hung up.

He was disappointed he hadn't learned anything about Palmer that added support to Kelly's suspicion of him. But on the other hand, what Wendy Storr had told him didn't mean Palmer hadn't made the early-morning phone calls to Kelly; nor did it mean that he hadn't clogged her chimney to fill her house with smoke.

Looking out the window at the rain pouring from the gray sky, Stevens wondered if Kelly had started searching through her past year's files for the names of the women who'd consulted with her about ending a relationship. He wondered if one of those women had ended a relationship with Chris Palmer.

✳

Giordano and Hernandez entered Le Grand Hotel in New Kent through its brass-framed revolving door. Giordano was the first to push his way through the door and emerge into the lobby. Like the door, the small but high-ceilinged lobby was a relic of the hotel's construction in the 1940s. Maybe at one time it had been a first-class hotel, but the lobby, though clean, needed new furnishings, and Giordano figured that nowadays the hotel appealed to businessmen who wanted to stay someplace economical and well located. Not just businessmen, though; according to the ad in *You and Your Sign*, this was where Antiochus had seen his clients on August 15.

Giordano walked up to the check-in desk, where a balding man in a black jacket with *Le Grand Hotel* embroidered on the outside breast pocket was doing paperwork. He was concentrating so intently on what he was writing that he didn't look up at Giordano or at Hernandez, who arrived as Giordano took out his badge and stuck it under the man's face.

The clerk looked up, startled. "I'm sorry, Officer. I didn't see you come in."

"*Detective*," Giordano corrected him. "*Detective*, not *officer*. I'm Detective Giordano. This is Detective Hernandez." Giordano removed a photocopy of the ad from *You and Your Sign* from his pocket and put it on the marble counter in front of the clerk. "We're hoping you can give us information about this man." With his index finger, he pointed to the name *Antiochus*. "We're hoping you remember him."

The clerk bent over the ad and read it with the same intensity he'd exhibited doing his paperwork. Then he looked at Giordano and Hernandez with watery blue eyes. "I do remember him. He just signed in with that one name. Antiochus." He reached for the maroon faux leather–bound sign-in book and thumbed backward through the pages until he found August 15. He turned the book around so that Giordano and Hernandez could see it. "There," he said, indicating the first entry on the morning of August 15. "See. He registered at seven fifteen a.m. I've had a lot of John Smiths before but never an Antiochus. That's why I remembered him."

Giordano and Hernandez peered at Antiochus's registration. He hadn't written his name in script; he'd written it in perfect block letters.

"Because of his name, I thought he was a foreigner," the clerk continued. "But when he talked, he was just a regular American."

"Did he give you a credit card?" Giordano asked.

The clerk thought a moment before answering. "I think he gave me cash, which is why it sticks in my mind." He went to his computer, clicked away at the keyboard, and then read the information that came up on the screen. "Yeah, he paid one hundred and forty dollars in cash for the room and a deposit of two hundred and fifty dollars in case of damage. That's what we ask for when people don't use a credit card. As I remember it, he had the cash in his attaché case, and he just took it out and plunked it on the counter." He left the computer and returned to Giordano and Hernandez. "He must have had ten or twelve people come to see him that day. Mostly women." He gestured with his chin to the sofa and chairs in the lobby's sitting area. "They sat there till they could go up for their appointment with Antiochus. I could tell they really wanted to see him, but I don't remember any of them telling me he was an 'intuitive astrologer.' They went to him so he could do their horoscopes?"

"Apparently," Giordano responded. "You remember what he looked like?"

The clerk was quiet for a while. He gazed down at the desktop, as if going back in his mind to the morning that Antiochus had appeared at the desk and signed the registration book. "Average build," he said, looking at the two detectives. "Dark hair. I think he was about thirty-five." He closed his eyes, as if trying to retrieve more details; then he opened his eyes and shrugged. "That's about it."

"What about distinguishing marks?" Hernandez asked. "A scar? A mole? A tattoo?"

The clerk thought about it and shook his head. "Sorry. I just don't remember."

"How about the women? Do you happen to know any of them?"

The clerk shook his head again. "Sorry again."

"Thanks," Hernandez said.

Giordano was already heading to the revolving door. Hernandez hurried after him. Sometimes he wished that Giordano would be more polite, but it was a battle he'd given up long ago. It was just Giordano's nature to be rude. Hell, Giordano was even rude to him, and he was Giordano's partner.

Out on the street, he said to Giordano, "At least we got a physical description."

Hernandez wasn't sure, but he thought Giordano nodded in agreement. He wasn't sure because Giordano was already on his way to their car. All part of Giordano's nature. When they were on a case, he wasn't just single minded; he was insatiable. Any information they got that would help them follow a lead just made him want more—and he wanted it *now*.

✳

Vincent Nichols had searched most of Sheryl Doyle's house in West Orange and was now starting to look through the reading matter in her night table. He'd already gone through every magazine and book he'd found in her kitchen, her living room, her den, and her finished basement. It was only because he was thorough that he'd found this cache at all. The top of her cabinet-style night table held only a lamp, a clock, and the photograph of Sheryl Doyle that he'd first seen as he'd stood over her body, listening to the medical examiner's report; her magazines and books were haphazardly piled together on two shelves behind the night table's closed door.

For a moment he glanced up at the wall over the night table and saw another photograph of Sheryl Doyle, this one taken years ago, when she'd still been acting. That was one of the things Nichols had learned about her, that she'd been an actress. More recently she'd become a caterer, and not as successful a caterer as she had been a young actress, before her career had waned. The condition of her house and her bank account testified to that. Her house had been paid for during her acting days, so it no longer had a mortgage, but her checking account revealed that she had lived month to month, and she didn't have a savings account. Looking at her photographs, Nichols asked himself, as he had many times before about other homicide victims, if she would have lived her life differently if she had known when it would come to an end. Would she have sold her house, perhaps, and traveled? Would she have married instead of remaining single?

Single—or more accurately, the desire not to be single—that was part of the connection between Sheryl Doyle and the man who had raped and killed her. Antiochus, the intuitive astrologer. At least that was the theory, based on the victim in New Kent.

"Single? Wondering why you're not attracting anyone and what you can do to change it? See the Intuitive Astrologer, Antiochus. Saturday, August fifteenth, Le Grand Hotel, New Kent, New Jersey. Ten a.m. to six p.m. Three hundred dollars for your chart and the answers to your life's most important questions. Appointments on first-come, first-served basis."

Frank Giordano of the New Kent PD had sent Nichols the ad, and Nichols had read it to himself so many times that by now he had it memorized. As he'd gone through her house, every time he'd picked up one of Sheryl Doyle's magazines, he'd expected it to be *You and Your Sign*, but it never was. He'd found hundreds of cooking magazines with recipes that she'd bookmarked for her catering business. He'd also found women's magazines with recipes she'd bookmarked. The women's magazines also had astrology columns, but there were no indications that she'd read any of them. Sheryl Doyle also had hundreds of books: cookbooks and novels, but not a single book about astrology.

Although the MO of her killer was the same as the MO of the killer in the New Kent case, after spending four hours searching, Nichols was feeling tired and increasingly pessimistic about finding the ad that would tie the two victims together. If Sheryl Doyle had ever had the August issue or any issue of *You and Your Sign*, she'd disposed of it. Or perhaps, unlike the victim in New Kent, she'd never had the magazine. Perhaps she hadn't even been interested in astrology. Perhaps the man who had raped and strangled her and carved her sign, the scales—which Nichols had learned was Libra—into her upper thigh had chosen her another way.

Nichols pulled a stack of magazines and books out of the cabinet onto the scruffy white rug, where he could see them in the daylight. Five issues of *Food & Wine*, three issues of *Gourmet*. A hardback copy of *The Da Vinci Code*, another hardback, *The Thirteenth Tale*. He took a third book, a hardback with a worn blue cover, out of the pile so he could read the title: *One Hundred-Year Ephemeris, 1950 to 2050 at Midnight*. Under the title, the blue cover was dotted with stars. Suddenly, Nichols's weariness turned into excitement. He didn't know what an ephemeris was, but the fact that the cover of the book depicted the night sky and its title included dates and a time made him think it had something to do with astrology.

Opening it, he saw that he was right: On the back of the cover was a list of the symbols for the astrological signs, the planets, the phases of the moon, solar and lunar eclipses, and words— like conjunction, sextile, trine, opposition—that he'd never heard of before but that were obviously part of astrology. The opposite page was a chart, labeled *Longitude*, full of squares containing numbers and symbols for each day of January 1950. Thumbing through the first few pages, he saw the same kind of chart for

subsequent months. Clearly it was an astrology reference man-
ual, and finding it in the night table next to Sheryl Doyle's bed
definitely established her interest in astrology and the likelihood
that, even though she hadn't had a copy of *You and Your Sign* in
her possession at the time of her death, it was astrology that had
led her to Antiochus or Antiochus to her.

Nichols bagged the book. He'd show it to Giordano in New
Kent and see if it told them something new about their serial
killer. But before he did that, because he was thorough, he'd go
through every page to find out if Sheryl Doyle had written any
notes in the book that might help their investigation. And he'd
also check the ads in other issues of *You and Your Sign*. And while
he was at it, he'd check the personals in the West Orange newspapers for an ad taken out by Antiochus. Maybe that's what had
led Sheryl Doyle to her fate.

Stevens, wearing his spare sports jacket and pants and carrying an umbrella, was in midtown Manhattan working on another
case, the murder of a sixty-year-old dentist in Central Park. He'd
gone to the office of one of the dentist's long-term clients in a
building on West 57th Street and 5th Avenue and pressed her to
reveal to him what he'd already suspected: that the dentist had
been selling illegal drugs to patients. Afraid she was facing jail
time, the woman surrendered everything she knew once Stevens
promised he'd make sure she wasn't prosecuted for buying drugs.

She told him that the dentist had started out selling prescrip-
tion painkillers but had branched out into selling cocaine, which
she had bought from him, and heroin, which she swore she'd
never tried. Recently, the dead man had perfected a crown that
he'd placed in a client's mouth to time-release his or her drug

of choice. The woman Stevens questioned hadn't had the crown put in yet; she'd planned to do so, but the dentist had been killed before she'd had a chance. She didn't know who his supplier had been, or if anyone in the dental office knew about the drug dealing, but at least she'd confirmed the suspicions that had been raised in Stevens's mind by the presence of cocaine and heroin in the dentist's body and the presence of too much money in his bank account.

Leaving the office building, he put up the umbrella and headed toward 8th Avenue, where he'd parked his car. As he walked, he took out his cell phone and called Chris Palmer's number but once again reached only a recorded message. He was just about to cross the street to 6th Avenue when he remembered that the corporate headquarters for Gemma Pharmaceuticals was on 59th and 5th. He looked at his watch: It was three fifteen. Calling information for Gemma Pharmaceuticals, he started walking back toward 5th Avenue. There was another man he wanted to talk to about Kelly York, another tree he wanted to shake.

Fifteen minutes later, Stevens was on the thirtieth floor of the Gemma Pharmaceuticals building, standing in front of the receptionist, a young woman with well-cut hair, a tastefully made-up face, and perfectly polished nails. He introduced himself and told her whom he had come to see. Almost immediately, another immaculately groomed young woman appeared through the double doors behind the reception desk and led him through a long corridor to a closed door at the end of it. She knocked on the rosewood door and waited until a male voice said, "Come in," before she opened the door to let him enter. She didn't come in with him.

Two walls of the massive corner office were windows with views of Manhattan. Even when the sky was colorless and filled with rain as it was now, it was a spectacular sight. Jack York, Kelly's ex-husband, was standing at the windows that faced north and looked out over 5th Avenue as he finished a phone call. The first thing that surprised Stevens was that York was as tall as he was. Being six foot five, Stevens was used to most men being shorter than he, and even though he knew York had been a football player, he'd been a quarterback, and Stevens had expected him to be six feet tall, at most; twenty years ago, when he'd first seen York playing, it wasn't unusual for quarterbacks to be six feet or even a shade under. While some football players had let their muscles turn to flab, York, in his stylish suit, looked fit, even leaner than he had in his football days, and since his full head of black hair had yet to turn gray, he looked only a little older than the last time Stevens had watched him in a game on television.

York hung up the phone and focused on Stevens. "I don't understand why you're here. What does my ex-wife getting threatening calls have to do with me?"

Stevens met York's hard stare. "Don't tell me how to investigate a case, Mr. York, and I won't tell you how to run your company, all right?"

York let out an aggravated sigh. "I'm sorry. What do you want to know?"

"I want to know if you and your ex-wife had what you would consider a difficult divorce."

This time York shook his head. Finally, he said, "Yes, Kelly and I had a difficult divorce. But we've worked out our differences and we have a perfectly friendly relationship."

Stevens kept his gaze on York. "Then I would think you'd care if somebody was threatening her."

York responded with a tone of exasperation. "Of course I do. She's my children's mother."

"So you don't care about her personally anymore."

"I didn't say that."

"You said you have a friendly relationship, but you don't seem to care about her the way you'd care about a friend. You care about her just as your children's mother."

York glanced out the window, as if gathering his thoughts. Then he turned to Stevens. "Look, I was a pro football player before I became CEO here—"

"I know," Stevens told him. "I followed your career."

"Then you probably already knew we had a difficult divorce." He didn't say this belligerently, just matter-of-fact. "You must've read about how I didn't know how to keep it in my pants ..." He looked at Stevens for a moment before he went on. "Kelly and I, we had the kids right away, and I figured she would put up with what I did on the road. But that wasn't her way. She needed more, and I couldn't give it to her." His green eyes were sad now, as if suddenly his memories of that melancholy time had taken him over and become more real to him than his corner office with its impressive view. "Her parents died when she was nine. She was raised by her grandmother. She was a pretty lonely kid. She really loved me, and I broke her heart. But she made a life for herself and the children without me. Of course I care if someone's threatening her."

Stevens scrutinized the man in front of him. He seemed to be a completely different Jack York from the one who had challenged him about why he'd come to question him. This Jack York seemed to care deeply about Kelly, maybe even to still be in love with her. But what did that mean? Jack York was a consummate salesman; that was how he had made the transition from football player to CEO at Gemma Pharmaceuticals. Maybe when challenging the detective hadn't worked, York had decided to sell

Stevens on what York wanted him to think of him: that York felt guilty about how he'd treated Kelly and that he still had deep compassion for her. Or maybe Jack York was still in love with her. And maybe if he was, the flip side of that love was anger that she'd divorced him and a desire to retaliate by threatening her. Or to make her so afraid and vulnerable that he could step back into her life and make her dependent on him again.

"Can you think of anyone who would want to scare her or hurt her?" Stevens asked.

"No. But that doesn't mean there isn't somebody. It just means if there is, I don't know about him. Our worlds have been separate for so long. Except for our children, I don't even know the people she knows anymore."

"Whoever's calling her doesn't just have her office phone number. He has her private phone number, too. So it's someone who knows her well enough to access her private number."

"That was her grandmother's old number. Kelly kept it after her grandmother died. I don't know how many people have had access to it over the years."

Stevens took this in. "Thanks, Mr. York." He buttoned his jacket and prepared to go out again into the rain. "By the way, how did she become interested in astrology?"

Jack York smiled. "That's something else Kelly got from her grandmother. Her grandmother was an amateur astrologer. She taught Kelly."

"She seems to owe her grandmother a lot."

York nodded in agreement. "Her grandmother was a lovely woman. I liked her. She was very disappointed in me." He went inside himself again for a moment; then he added, "I was very disappointed in myself."

Stevens picked up his wet umbrella from the floor where he'd dropped it. "Thanks again. If I have any more questions, I'll be in touch."

"You know where to find me," York said to him. He stepped out from behind his desk and shook Stevens's hand. "I'm sorry I got off on the wrong foot, Detective. I want you to know, I'll do anything I can to help you get this guy. Kelly doesn't deserve to have this happen to her. She's a good woman."

As Stevens left the office and headed toward the elevator, he mentally crossed Jack York off his suspect list. However great a salesman York was for Gemma Pharmaceuticals, Stevens believed that York was exactly who he seemed to be: an ex-husband who regretted that his philandering had hurt his ex-wife.

Stevens knew that if he wanted to, he could've called it quits for the day, but that wasn't his personality. With York crossed off, he had the urge to question Chris Palmer.

Twenty-Eight

SITTING AT THE DESK in her office, Kelly opened the last of the files that she and Sarah had taken from her filing cabinet. The first thing inside the folder was the sheet of lined yellow paper on which the client had written her name—Carol Wallen—birth date, time, and place—November 24, 1980, 9:15 a.m., Brookline, Massachusetts—and on which Kelly had written the issue about which the client was consulting her and her impressions of the client from their meeting. Carol had consulted Kelly about whether she should stay in her job as an investment analyst at a brokerage firm or look for a new job or even a new career. Kelly's impression from the time they spent together was that she was strong, direct, and open. Kelly closed the folder; there was no point in reading any further about Carol Wallen; Carol had not come to see her about leaving a relationship.

Kelly turned and looked out the windows. It was no longer raining, but water was still dripping from the trees and the tires of passing cars made a squishing sound on the wet street. She considered taking another batch of folders from the cabinet, but it was almost five p.m., and she decided she needed a break and a cup of coffee. She got up and went to the door to Sarah's office, expecting to see Sarah, but when she opened it, the office was empty and Sarah's coat was gone from the rack in the corner. On Sarah's desk was a neat stack of the files she was supposed to have reviewed. It was unlike Sarah to leave without saying goodbye, but perhaps she hadn't left yet; perhaps she'd just taken King out for a walk and would soon be back.

Kelly walked into the hallway and was surprised to find that the painters had already finished with it. The walls were once again butter yellow and the molding a shiny white. The hall was brighter looking, in fact, than it had been since she'd had the house painted four years ago. She'd meant to have it repainted for the past year, but it was one of those things that she'd kept postponing for lack of time and lack of commitment to put up with the inconvenience. Now she'd had to do it, and despite the reason, she found she was glad that it had been done. She walked into the living room and turned on the light to see that the painters had completed repainting there, too. The other crews Sarah had called in had also done their jobs. The Persian carpet had been taken out to be cleaned and the slipcovers had been removed from the sofa and chairs for cleaning as well. The hardwood floors, the dining table and chairs, and the tiles on the fireplace had been scrubbed clean of smoke.

Kelly was pleased to see that the house was, indeed, returning to normal and that despite everything that had happened, she was, as Sarah had predicted that morning, beginning to feel better. But it wasn't just the house being put back together quickly that had improved her spirits; it was the feeling she'd gotten as she'd read her clients' files. So far, she'd found only three women who matched the criterion Detective Stevens had given her: those thinking about ending a relationship. Most of the men and women who'd seen her since July had come with career questions, as Carol Wallen had, or questions about their parents or siblings or their health. Many had come to her about romance, but generally it was because they wanted a relationship and didn't

have one, not because they had a relationship that wasn't working. Two women who had consulted with her before had gotten
engaged and wanted her to tell them what the best dates were
for their weddings.

She had seen more than two hundred clients since July, and
looking through their files reminded Kelly how much she enjoyed her work and how much her clients appreciated what she
did. Often they would call her about how helpful she had been,
and when they did, she noted their calls on the sheet of yellow
legal paper in their folders. She'd had the pleasure of seeing many
such notes today as she'd searched her files. People thanked her
for her insight into their patterns of behavior, for her encouraging them to enter new professional fields or her supporting them
in remaining patient, based on what their charts told her about
them and on what she intuitively observed in meeting with them.

She remembered that Sarah had referred to the man who had
called her as a coward and that Emma had said he was full of
hot air, and she wondered if maybe the fireplace's backing up had
been an accident just as the fire investigator had said and if really
the caller was just what Sarah had labeled him: "a creep with a
telephone." Kelly's mind began to spin possibilities. Maybe because she was afraid to leave the house, she'd made his threats
more real than they were, that all he would ever do was call, or
even better, he would never call again. Maybe Detective Stevens
was just being polite that morning in his decision to monitor her
phones. Maybe despite the skull tattoo on Chris Palmer's arm
and his suggestion about starting a fire in the fireplace, Chris
Palmer was just a handsome man who'd been interested in her
until she'd all but thrown him out of her house today. If that was
so, it was something she'd just have to live with.

She couldn't dismiss the danger that she saw in her chart, but it was possible she'd been right when she'd thought that the anger that was posing the danger was really her own anger at herself for being unable to go out into the world as she used to. Maybe everything that had happened was making her look at herself and carry through on her promise to understand why she'd suddenly become so scared of leaving the brownstone; maybe it was leading her to be able to free herself. Leaving the living room, she was starting to feel it was possible that she would get control of her life again.

She walked into the kitchen and saw two painters on ladders, rolling yellow glossy paint onto the ceiling. One was the lanky, blond young man who seemed to be in charge of the paint crew, and the other was a graying man with Eastern European features who was concentrating so hard as he painted that his brow was creased from temple to temple.

"Thanks for working late," she said to the young man. "I appreciate you doing so much so fast."

He looked down at her from the ladder and smiled. "That's why we're called Ace Painting. We're good at what we do."

She took a cup and saucer out of the cabinet. "Do either of you want some coffee?"

"No, thanks," the young man said. "How about you, Alton?"

The other man responded with a heavily accented "No, thank you."

Kelly poured herself a cup of coffee and was about to leave the kitchen when she looked out the glass door and saw Sarah, in her coat, sitting on one of the stone benches in the garden. Sarah's head was in her hands, as if she were feeling sick. Kelly put her coffee on the counter and hurried into the garden. Even before she reached Sarah, she could hear that she was sobbing. Kelly ran to her and gently put her hand on her shoulder.

"What is it, Sarah? Tell me. Please, tell me. Is it your mother?"

For a long time, Sarah didn't look at her; she just shook her head and kept crying. Then she lifted her head from her hands and, still crying, looked up at Kelly. "It's Kevin. He's marrying someone else."

Kelly knew what Kevin meant to Sarah and, hearing this news, her own heart ached with Sarah's. "I'm so sorry. So sorry."

"I never thought this would happen. Sometimes I was scared he would meet someone else, but I never really thought . . . " Sarah was crying so hard again that she couldn't speak.

Kelly knelt beside her. "I know. I know."

Still crying, Sarah took a handkerchief from her coat pocket and started to dry her eyes and her cheeks. "Every time he came into town to sing, we would go out," she said between sobs. "And we would sleep together. I know it's silly now, but I thought it would always be like that. I guess I thought that one day when we're old, we'd finally get married."

Kelly was afraid to ask her what she needed to ask her, but she knew there was no way of avoiding it. She looked up at Sarah. "Are you sorry you asked me to do your charts and talk to you about them?"

With hazel eyes filled with tears, Sarah shook her head. "No." She repeated the word more adamantly. "No." She knew Kelly would blame herself, which was precisely why she hadn't wanted to tell Kelly about Kevin right now, not on top of everything Kelly was dealing with. But she didn't blame Kelly, and she didn't want Kelly to blame herself, either. "I was ambivalent or I wouldn't have asked you. And what you told me only reinforced what I already knew about myself. It would've been terrible for me to marry Kevin and give up a music career myself. I love the violin as much as I love him. I couldn't spend my life going from opera company to opera company so he could keep building his career while I would just . . . just be a wife who used to play the violin."

Kelly knew that what Sarah said about herself was true, but she also knew it didn't make Kevin's engagement to another woman any less painful. "I wish it had happened differently, Sarah. I wish it with all my heart. Everything I saw in your chart and Kevin's said it might have turned out just the way you thought it would, with the two of you together. None of this was fated. But that's how it is. It's not the planets that determine our lives; it's the choices each of us makes. And no matter how much we know about our planets and the planets of the people we love, we can't make choices for the people we love. We can only make choices for ourselves."

Sarah nodded again. She was still crying, but not as wrenchingly as she had been. Soon she dried her eyes again with her handkerchief. "A year ago, before he left for Germany, he was so angry when I told him I wouldn't marry him. Even though I told him I loved him, it hurt him deeply. I didn't realize he had so much anger in him."

Kelly suddenly felt cold. It wasn't just the cold dampness of the garden in the waning hours of daylight after the rain; it was the realization that Kevin was a man who could possibly blame her for making a woman leave him. She hadn't made Sarah leave him, but he could certainly think that she had; he could blame Sarah's decision on her because she hadn't encouraged Sarah to accept his proposal.

"What are you thinking, Kelly?" Sarah asked her.

Kelly stood up. She didn't want Sarah to see her eyes, because she didn't want her to see that she was lying. "Nothing. I was just feeling sad." In the gray-blue twilight, she looked at the rain that clung to the ivy on the garden walls and to the panels of glass on the greenhouse. "It's late," she said to Sarah. "Please go home and take care of yourself. I had no idea the strain you were under today. I wish you'd told me."

Sarah rose from the bench. "I didn't want to burden you. Not accepting Kevin's proposal was my choice. You never told me what to do."

Kelly took Sarah's hand and clasped it. She wished she could be sure that Kevin understood that as well as Sarah did. "Thank you."

As they headed back toward the kitchen, the optimism that Kelly had felt minutes before was gone. The realization that Kevin might hate her made the threatening calls all too real again. She reminded herself that that didn't negate the possibility that all they were were calls—that they would never amount to more than that. And it didn't negate the possibility that she would never receive another one. Maybe Kevin's engagement to another woman would gradually lessen his anger at her. Maybe today he was already feeling less angry.

Kelly opened the door for Sarah and let her go into the kitchen first. The two painters were still painting the ceiling. Kelly entered behind Sarah. She squeezed her hand again. "Please rest tonight and take care of yourself. I don't want you coming in tomorrow."

Sarah looked into Kelly's eyes, which were filled with concern. "I want to come in. I want to keep busy, and we don't have a rehearsal till tomorrow night."

"See how you feel," Kelly told her. "You might want to just stay home and practice."

Sarah nodded. "Okay, I'll see how I feel."

Twenty-Nine

HE SAT AT THE worktable, watching the computer screen and drinking a long, slow slug of beer. On the screen, he saw Kelly and Sarah walking through the kitchen toward the doorway to the hall. They looked like they were upset. He also saw the legs of the two painters standing on the ladders, but he couldn't see their faces. He didn't care; the only face he really wanted to see was Kelly York's. It made him feel warm and tingly that she looked so upset. He'd hated her for so long. It was a pleasure to see her so upset. And he knew that however upset she was, it was only the beginning.

Thirty

Kelly is nine years old. She is sitting on the ottoman next to her grand-mother, who is in her wheelchair. The living room walls are light blue and the bulky, brown velvet-upholstered sofa and chairs are the same ones her grandmother had when Kelly's mother was a child. Grandma Irene is showing Kelly a chart with a circle divided into sections and with odd-looking symbols and writing. The chart is on old paper. The reason Kelly knows the paper is old is because it's discolored, the way the pages are in some of her grandmother's old books.

"Do you know who did this chart for me?" her grandmother asks.

Kelly looks at her grandmother and shakes her head, no.

"Evangeline Adams, dear. She was the most famous astrologer in all of America, and when I was very young I was lucky enough to have her do my chart!"

"That's wonderful, Grandma!" Kelly says, impressed.

"When I was your age," her grandmother tells her, "being an as-trologer wasn't a legal profession. Even Evangeline Adams was ar-rested for fortune-telling. When she came before the judge, he told her he was going to give her a test. He wrote down the birth date and time and place of a real person, and he asked her to tell him about what that person's life was like now.

"Evangeline Adams took the information, looked in her ephemeris, and said to the judge, 'I can't tell you what his life is like now because the person is dead.'" Her grandmother pauses dramatically. She sees

that she has Kelly's expectant attention and then continues. "The judge was stunned. The birth date and time belonged to his son, who had died many years before!" Grandma sits up in her wheelchair and announces, "Not only did the judge free Evangeline Adams to practice astrology, but he told her she had 'raised astrology to the dignity of an exact science.'"

Kelly is more than entertained by what her grandmother has just told her about Evangeline Adams; it speaks to her in a way that makes her feel better than she has in months; it gives her the first hope she has felt since she learned that her parents had died when a train had gotten derailed and crashed between New York and New Haven, where they had been professors at Yale. She reaches for her grandmother's ephemeris on the coffee table. She doesn't know exactly what an ephemeris is, but she knows her grandmother is always looking up dates and times in it in order to find out something about astrology.

"Will you show me how to use your ephemeris, Grandma?" Kelly asks her.

"Of course I will, dear." Her grandmother takes the ephemeris and places it onto her lap. "That way you'll be able to help guide yourself and other people, too."

Kelly smiles. "I'd like that. That way, I would always know what to do, and I'll never make a mistake."

She opened her eyes with a start, at first not realizing that she'd been dreaming. The word *mistake* had woken her up. It reminded her of something she had forgotten when she'd spoken to Detective Stevens and that she realized could be important. She felt Meow against her leg, and saw that she was still asleep. She glanced down at King, asleep in his bed on the floor, and then she glanced at the clock on her night table. It was just after two a.m. Her eyes went to the telephone; it was silent. She turned to the window and saw the top of the moon above the treetops. It was a quiet, peaceful night, and yet the word *mistake* had awakened her from her sleep as if it had been a gunshot. She felt anything but peaceful.

She got out of bed, put on her slippers and bathrobe, and headed for her daughter's room. After Sarah had left, the last vestiges of her positive frame of mind had collapsed. She and Emma had shared a quick dinner, and after that she'd spent the night looking through another three months of files. She'd discovered only one other woman who had consulted her about leaving a relationship. So up until now the search had revealed four clients whose names she would give to Detective Stevens because their husbands or boyfriends might have made the calls. But because of what Sarah had told her, she would also give him Kevin's name. And because of what her dream had prompted her to remember, she had another name to give Stevens, too.

And there was Chris Palmer. One of her clients who had consulted her about relationship problems had had a boyfriend who had been a Pisces. Chris Palmer had said he was a Pisces. Maybe the woman's boyfriend had been Chris Palmer and she'd left him after her appointment with Kelly, and Chris Palmer blamed her for his girlfriend's breaking up with him. Maybe she was right to have been afraid of him.

It made her sad, all of it; it wasn't her nature to think about people this way, to probe their lives and their own sadness, looking for reasons they might be filled with hatred. She preferred always to see the potential for light.

She walked into Julie's room, opened the closet, and looked up at the shelf over the clothes rack, wondering if she'd find what she was looking for. She wasn't the type of mother who searched through her daughter's things, and this was the first time she'd been in Julie's closet since Julie had left for school. But she knew, because Julie had not hidden it from her, that Julie kept a shoe box full of letters on the top shelf. The question was, was it still there, or had she taken it with her to college?

At first, Kelly thought the box wasn't there. Then she found it between two piles of sweaters. She took the box down from the shelf and brought it over to Julie's bed. She sat down and removed the lid. She knew what she was looking for because Julie had shown her that particular letter. As she started looking through the letters her daughter had saved, in her head she kept hearing the word *mistake*.

She recognized the handwriting. She'd seen it on Valentine's Day cards, Christmas cards, and birthday cards that Julie had put on the mantel while she was in high school. The letter was dated June 15 of that year. Her eyes focused on the words that he had written in his strong, bold printing: *You're making a big mistake breaking up with me.* Below it, he had blamed Kelly.

Thirty-One

STEVENS HAD CALLED Chris Palmer's number a few times during the day but had never reached him. He didn't know if Palmer just happened to be out or if he was deliberately not answering the phone because, despite Stevens's calling Wendy Storr under the pretext of a potential assignment for Palmer, Storr had told Palmer that a man had called to question her about him. Now Stevens sat in his car at the curb outside Palmer's loft on Prince Street.

Each floor of the four-story building was a loft, and since Stevens had found Palmer listed in the directory as #4, he figured that Palmer's loft was on the top floor. Stevens had first stopped by there at nine o'clock, and the fourth-floor windows had been dark; it was one fifteen a.m. now and they were still dark. He was just about to start his car and go home when he saw Palmer walking arm in arm with an attractive young woman with a mass of black hair and a dress just long enough to keep her from being arrested for indecent exposure. Their wobbly gait and raucous laughter told him they were drunk.

He got out of his car and approached Palmer and the young woman just as Palmer was unlocking the door to his building. He stuck his badge under Palmer's nose and identified himself. "Detective Stevens. I'd like to talk to you."

Palmer looked up at Stevens with alcohol-glazed eyes that

seemed to sober up in the moment it took for him to register the detective's presence. "I think you're making a mistake, Detective. I haven't witnessed a crime or accident or anything."

Stevens stared down at him; he was half a head taller than Palmer and weighed eighty or a hundred pounds more than him. "I'm not making a mistake, Mr. Palmer," he said evenly.

Palmer turned to the young woman, said he'd be right back, and led Stevens out of the doorway so that she wouldn't hear their conversation. "What's this about?" he asked.

"Kelly York."

Palmer's forehead furrowed with confusion. "What about her? Did something happen to her?"

"No. Do you wish something did?"

Palmer laughed dismissively. "Of course not. I just don't understand why you're asking me about her."

"I'm asking you about her because you seemed angry when you left her house this morning."

Palmer's dark brown eyes glanced at the sidewalk for a moment as if he were going back to that morning in his mind; then he looked up at the detective again. "This has to do with what happened to her house because of that smoke, doesn't it?"

"I don't have to tell you what it has to do with," Stevens said. "Why were you so angry at her?"

Palmer shrugged. "I was interested in her, and she gave me the cold shoulder."

Stevens looked at the young woman waiting apprehensively in the doorway. "You seem to have gotten over it pretty fast."

"I didn't realize it was a crime to go out on a date," Palmer said.

Despite Palmer's effort at casual sarcasm, Stevens noticed the tension in his hands and shoulders; he was nervous. Stevens wondered if it was just because he was being questioned by a police detective or because Palmer had been threatening Kelly York.

"How do you know I was angry at Kelly when I left her house today?" Palmer asked almost belligerently. "Did she tell you that?"

Stevens was about to respond that it was none of Palmer's business how he knew when he felt his cell phone vibrating in his jacket pocket. Taking the phone from his pocket, he said, "Excuse me," and walked away from Palmer, keeping his eyes on him as he brought the phone to his ear.

"Stevens here."

On the other end of the phone Stevens heard what he didn't want to hear.

"It's Griffin, Detective Stevens. I'm monitoring Kelly York's phone. The caller is on the phone with her right now."

Stevens turned away from Palmer. "Where's he calling from?"

"Chelsea Piers."

"Shit," Stevens said. "Patch it through." He was already running to his car.

"Hey, can I go now?" Palmer called after him.

"Yeah, you can," Stevens shouted back over his shoulder. He brought the phone to his ear again so he could listen to the call.

✳

Kelly shuddered as she stood at her desk in her third-floor study, speaking to the voice on the other end of the phone. "Please, stop calling me," she begged.

"Why should I? You didn't care what happened to me," the voice whispered back.

"Was it you who blocked up my chimney? Did you make my house fill up with smoke?"

"Oh, your house filled up with smoke. What a shame," he

whispered. "But it didn't kill you, did it?"

She was still holding the letter she'd found in the shoe box from Julie's closet. As she listened on the phone, her eyes drifted to the first few words of the letter:

Dear Julie,

You're making a big mistake breaking up with me. I thought your mother would know that, being an astrologer.

Then she looked at the signature. *Billy*.

*

As Stevens sped uptown on 10th Avenue toward Chelsea Piers, he was listening to Kelly's conversation with the caller, which he'd had patched into his radio phone. The volume was up all the way and he could hear bits of it despite his siren.

"Billy, is that you?" Kelly was asking.

Stevens wondered who Billy was; Kelly had never mentioned him. He was already doing eighty and making good time because there were so few cars on the road at that time of night, but he pushed down the gas pedal and went up to ninety. He wanted to get to the location where the caller was making the call while the call was still in progress.

He could hear that the caller was saying something, but he had trouble hearing him because of the siren, so he turned it off and just used the flashing red light to warn the two other cars on 10th Avenue that he was about to overtake them.

"It doesn't matter who I am," the caller was whispering. "What matters is what I'm going to do to you."

"Whatever I did, I'm sorry," Kelly said.

Stevens could tell she was terrified from the way her voice

was shaking.

"Sorry doesn't cut it, Kelly. Nothing cuts it anymore. Not for you."

Stevens heard the caller click off the line. "Shit," he said to himself. He was only at 10th Avenue and 15th Street; Chelsea Piers was seven blocks away.

The cop who'd been monitoring the call came in over the radio: "Sorry he cut off before you got there."

"Yeah," Stevens said. "Me, too."

"He used a prepaid cell phone. It's probably in the Hudson by now."

"Shit," Stevens said for the third time that night.

Thirty-Two

KELLY WAS IN THE living room sitting on the sofa with King curled up next to her when she heard a knock on the door. Detective Stevens had called to tell her he knew she'd received another phone call and that he was on his way. After that, she'd gotten dressed and had come downstairs to wait for him.

As she got up from the sofa and hurried into the hallway, King came with her, running between her legs as he always did. She had to gently push him out of the way so she could get to the door. She felt relieved when she looked through the peephole and saw Stevens. She unlocked both locks and opened the door for him. The moment he walked into the house and she'd closed the door so King wouldn't get out, she turned to him and asked, "Do you know who he is?"

Stevens shook his head. "No. He used a phone he bought at a convenience store. A throwaway."

She felt herself plunge again into despondency. "Then you're never going to know who he is until it's too late! Until he does something to me!"

All of a sudden she was crying. She hadn't wanted to cry in front of Stevens, but she couldn't stop herself.

He looked at her steadily. "That's not true. I'll find him."

She tried to dry her eyes, but she kept crying. "I shouldn't act like this—"

"That's okay," Stevens said.

Despite his reassuring words, Kelly got her crying under control and dried her eyes again. Then she asked him if he'd like a cup of tea and led him toward the kitchen.

"Have you started looking through your files?" he asked as he followed her and King.

"So far I've found four women who consulted with me about possibly leaving their relationships," she said, turning on the kitchen light. "I wrote down their names, phone numbers, and addresses. Two of them gave me their boyfriends' names, and two just gave me their birth date and time." She handed him the information she'd taken from her files. "Any of these women could've broken off their relationship, and the men might have blamed me."

Kelly watched as Stevens looked at the sheet of paper she gave him. She wished she could leave him with just that, but she knew she couldn't. After a moment, she said: "I've been thinking, Detective. There are two other men it might be . . ."

She stopped speaking, and he could see how painful this was for her. "Just tell me, Dr. York."

Kelly took a deep breath before she continued. "One of them was a boy my daughter, Julie, dated in high school. Billy Whitmore. She broke up with him the middle of her senior year. I remember her showing me this." She took the letter she'd found from the pocket of her pants and gave it to Stevens. "I never told her to break up with him, but he blamed me. He said I was an astrologer and I should've known it was a mistake. But he's only eighteen. Do you really think it could be him?"

Stevens was already reading the letter. So that was who Billy was; he'd heard Kelly ask the man on the phone if he was Billy.

"Age has nothing to do with it," he said. He finished reading the letter and put it in his pocket along with the other piece of paper she had given him. "You said two men. Who's the other one?"

"Kevin Stockman."

"Who's Kevin Stockman?" he asked.

She still felt hesitant. "I don't know . . . I could be wrong . . ."

"If you're wrong, it doesn't matter," Stevens told her. "If you're right, it could matter a lot."

"Kevin is my assistant Sarah's old boyfriend. I've always liked him."

"Like age, that has nothing to do with it. Tell me why you think it might be him."

"Because of what happened in their relationship," Kelly explained. "Kevin is an opera singer. He and Sarah met at Juilliard, and they dated while he lived in New York. Then he started getting jobs in Europe, and he proposed to her. He wanted her to travel with him, but it would've meant giving up her career as a violinist. Today she told me how angry he was when she wouldn't marry him. He knew she'd consulted with me. I never said she should turn him down, just that whatever decision she made, she would have to find a way to fulfill her own need for creativity. But he might not know that . . ."

Her blue eyes looked at Stevens with urgency for him to understand how unfair this was, that someone would hate her for something that she'd never even said. "What we talked about this morning is true, Detective Stevens. It doesn't matter what I really said. It only matters what whoever is calling me thinks I said."

Stevens's eyes met hers; he wished there were something he could say to comfort her, but nothing came to mind. "Where is Kevin Stockman now?" he asked.

"He's in New York, singing at the Met. He told Sarah he's

found another woman, and they're going to get married, but . . . "

Kelly stopped. She knew that if she continued, she would start crying all over again. She looked away from Stevens and took control of the emotions that were threatening to unmoor her and take her over.

"Why don't you go stay with friends for a while or go to a hotel?" he suggested.

That was it, the trick question, a question that would not be a trick for anyone but her to answer. She didn't answer him.

"What is it?" Stevens asked.

She looked at him and unleashed her frustration and bewilderment. "Everything," she said. "Everything! My whole life! I can't stay with anyone or go to a hotel because I can't leave my house. I have agoraphobia. I'm afraid to leave. And now I'm afraid to stay. I don't know what I'm doing anymore!"

If he saw urgency in her eyes before, now he saw desperation.

"I always believed that I knew a lot. I knew psychology and astrology, and between them I could make good decisions and help other people make good decisions and that everything would be better because of what I knew. I married my ex-husband knowing from his chart that he had a predilection for other women, but I thought I could bring out the best side of him instead. When that didn't work, I comforted myself by telling myself I saw the potential for it from the start, and if I thought I could overcome it, that was my choice. But this! This—someone threatening my life—I didn't see it!"

She looked at him and for a time said nothing.

"I told you that Mars is squaring my Pluto at the same time as Pluto is conjuncting my Mars," she said after a while. "And that means danger. But what kind of danger? I'm not going to get run over by a car because I can't leave my house! I never thought somebody would want to come here and kill me! It makes me feel as though I don't know anything anymore, that astrology is worthless . . . or that I'm worthless as an astrologer and as a psychologist."

"I'm sorry you feel that way," he said, "because it's not true."

"How do you know?"

"Because your column helped my wife, Diane."

"How?"

"Two years ago, we were trying to have a baby, and she was about to give up. She'd had two miscarriages, and she felt so bad about herself, she started pulling away from me. I don't know what you wrote, but it was something about obstacles for Aries being more temporary than they seemed and having the faith to stay committed to what you want. She opened up to me, told me how guilty she felt for miscarrying, and I told her I love her no matter what. Two months later she got pregnant."

He took out his wallet and removed a photograph that he held out to Kelly. "That's Anthony," he said. "He was fourteen months old last week."

Kelly took the photo of the small boy with a lot of brown hair, an open smile, full cheeks, and shining brown eyes not unlike his father's. She was still crying, but not for herself anymore; it made her cry to see such a beautiful child.

"My marriage means everything to me," Stevens told her. "I don't know what would've happened if Diane hadn't read your column."

Kelly looked up at him. "I thought you didn't believe in astrology."

"I don't know if I believe in it. But I believe you do help people. And I'm going to get this guy. Whoever he is. You got my word on it."

Kelly could tell these weren't just words to Stevens; he meant them with the full force of his being. "Thank you, Detective Stevens," she said. "And thank you for showing me your lovely son." As she handed the photograph back to him, she was no longer crying.

"I feel like you've given me the most important things in my life," Stevens said to her. "My wife and my son. That's why when I saw the report, I wanted to work this case. I want to do something for you. Why don't you put up that tea now, and I'll go over the information you wrote down about those clients to see if I've got any questions."

He watched Kelly go to the stove for the teakettle and take the kettle to the sink to fill with water. He could tell she was feeling a little better. He hoped that one of the men she'd told him about tonight would turn out to be the caller.

Thirty-Three

HE'D MADE GOOD TIME driving to Tarrytown. And he'd made good time getting to the house, a rambling suburban ranch with mock weathered shingles and a shingled roof. He'd had no trouble getting in, of course; all he'd had to do was use the keys he'd made to open the locks and then cut the chain with a wire cutter. If she'd had an alarm, he could've taken care of that, too; he would've gotten her to tell the code to him the same way he'd gotten her to tell him everything else. Or she might have even written it down and kept it in her purse; he'd seen that before. And if she'd had a dog, he would've taken care of the dog as well. He had his ways.

But it had been easy. All of it. And Cassie herself was the easiest of all of them. When she felt his knees pressing against her body and looked up and saw his ski-masked face, she cried out, but just a little, and then she gave up. And then she gave in. And now she was no more.

Gripping the instrument in his surgical-gloved hand, he inserted the point into her thigh and began to carve what looked like the Roman numeral II, the symbol for Gemini.

He was still hard. It always excited him to see how well his plans worked. He hoped that this time when the police found what he'd done, they'd tell the newspapers and television about how he'd marked her body with her zodiac sign. It was disappointing that until now they'd only said that the women he'd so carefully chosen had been raped and strangled. Leaving out his astrological expertise somehow made his accomplishments less personal, but it didn't render them less satisfying.

Thirty-Four

KELLY FELT THE HOT spray of the shower run over her body. It made her feel almost as if she were starting all over again with the new day. She found herself thinking about what Detective Stevens had told her the night before about how much her column had meant to his wife and to him. It felt good to know she'd helped them, that what she'd written, based on the disposition of the planets, about Diane's problem being temporary and the necessity of staying committed to what she wanted, had not only proven true but had been what Diane had needed to hear.

She turned off the water, got out of the shower, and started to dry herself with her white terry-cloth towel. Besides thinking about his wife, she'd also been thinking about the women whose names she'd given the detective because they'd consulted with her about troubled relationships. As she'd reviewed their files and read her notes about them, she'd begun to picture some of them in her mind. She hadn't had enough time to go over their charts or the charts of their husbands or boyfriends, and now she wondered what their charts would tell her. She decided that she would look at them and see. In the meantime, Detective Stevens was going to find out what he could learn about the men, so no time was being wasted.

She hung the towel on the rack. As she reached for her bathrobe, she was surprised to see King padding into the bathroom carrying a bone in his mouth. She generally didn't give him bones, and neither did Emma or Sarah.

"Where did you get that?" she asked him. "Did someone throw it into the garden?"

King looked up at her with his light blue eyes and gave her a soft howl, as if to say he hoped she would stop asking questions and just let him keep it. She pried the bone out of his mouth and looked it over. It was a leather bone, the kind sold in pet stores. It was in very good shape; in fact, it looked new. She bent down and smiled as she gave it back to King. "Looks like you got yourself a bone," she told him.

✳

Sarah was downstairs straightening her office. She'd been ready to take Kelly's advice and stay home, but when she'd woken up that morning, she realized that she wanted to go to work. The night before she had practiced her part in Janáček's String Quartet no. 1 for three hours, and playing the magnificent music had made her realize that, despite missing Kevin, she was still able to enjoy music and hopeful about the opportunities that the upcoming concert would create for her quartet. Part of what made her feel this sense of hope was the support Kelly gave her to pursue her career as a violinist, and it made her want to come to the brownstone to support Kelly.

All the workmen had left the house except the two painters who ran Ace Painting, Ed Murrin, who'd come today for the first time, and Peter, who'd painted and run the crew in Ed's absence. Emerging from her office, Sarah saw Ed on the stairway, using a small paintbrush on the molding. She could see from the awkward way that he held his neck and head as he painted that he had arthritis. The last time Ed had painted her house was four years ago, when Joe Heath, Peter's father, was still working as Ed's partner. Sarah didn't remember Ed seeming old then, although he was in his 60s. There were times Sarah felt her father shouldn't have retired from his contracting business, but seeing Ed in pain made her feel that maybe her father had been right to stop while he was still feeling well. And, of course, the fact that he had retired meant that he now had the time to devote to taking care of her mother.

Ed hadn't made it to the house the day before because the job he'd been on had taken all day, but Sarah had been impressed to see that he was already there and busy painting in the morning when she'd arrived. It was clear from the meticulous way he painted that he was a master in his trade, and the look of pride Sarah saw on his face as he stood back to inspect his work told her that if he was still painting because he needed the income, he also still found satisfaction in it.

"How's it going?" she asked him, walking to the foot of the stairs.

He turned and straightened up his stooped frame as best he could. "Fine. Just fine."

"Would you like some water?"

He shook his head. "Just want you to know, tell your father thanks for the recommendation. We appreciate the work."

Sarah smiled. "Well, I appreciate your work."

"How's your mother?" Ed asked her.

"She's doing all right. I think she'll be okay."

Ed smiled. "I'm glad."

Peter, on a ladder at the end of the hallway, painting the ceiling, spoke to Sarah as he wiped a blob of white paint off the front of his uncombed mane of blond hair. "We'll be out of here as soon as we finish these touch-ups. Unless you see anything else ..."

Sarah stepped away from the staircase and surveyed the neatly painted hall. "Looks good," she said. "When you're done, come to my office and I'll write you a check."

Walking back to her office, she was certain she'd made the right decision to come to work that day. It gave her a sense of accomplishment to see how much had been done to restore the house in a mere twenty-four hours and that she was the one who had set the renewal process in motion; it made her feel that she would get over Kevin and that she was already starting a new and positive chapter in her life.

*

It had taken Kelly longer to dress than usual. She'd found herself thinking about her grandmother and memories she had of growing up in her grandmother's care. Kelly had been the only child in her class at Rudolf Steiner who had been raised by a woman in her seventies and eighties, yet her grandma Irene had been as creative, interesting, and open-minded as any of the other children's far younger parents. And she had been the only one who had taught the child she was raising about astrology; more important, through astrology, and through her own optimistic spirit, she had taught Kelly that life was a cycle and that death, which had claimed Kelly's parents—her grandmother's daughter and son-in-law—in a train accident, was part of that cycle. Her grandmother had explained that just as the cycle of each day included dawn and night and everything in between, so the cycle of each life included birth and death and everything in between.

Kelly had been grieving over the loss of her parents; for days she had stayed in bed, coming out for meals only at her grandmother's and Emma's insistence. Gradually, she had begun spending time with her grandmother, whom she had always deeply loved, in the living room or the downstairs library, which was now Kelly's office, or in her grandmother's garden. All the while, her grandmother had talked to her. Slowly her words had begun to take root in Kelly's consciousness, and Kelly had begun to believe that life wasn't necessarily all bleak because something terrible had happened, to believe that one day she could find her spirit reborn, perhaps even find her grandmother's optimism in herself.

She knew how very much her grandmother had loved her mother and father, and yet her grandmother was able to mourn them and, at the same time, to love life enough to take care of her and to encourage her to find delight in life again. In a very real way, Kelly felt that her grandmother had saved her life, and later she had made it possible for Kelly to survive her divorce, go back to school, and raise Jeff and Julie. Despite being in a wheelchair and unable to stand on her own, her grandmother had had the strength to teach Kelly to stand on her own, not just once, but twice.

As she started down the staircase from the third floor, Kelly was thinking about the interconnections between her grandmother's chart and her own. When her grandmother had taught her how to draw a chart, the first two charts Kelly had done by herself were her grandmother's and hers. She had immediately seen how much they had in common and that the charts showed how they complemented each other's strengths and weaknesses. Like Kelly, her grandmother had been a Pisces with Aries rising—which made both of them emotional and intuitive as well as pioneering—but where Kelly had a moon in Capricorn, which made her reflective and focused, with a tendency toward fixed opinions, her grandmother's moon was in Cancer, which made her protective and nurturing. Their charts also showed that they had a deep connection in the fourth house, the house of family, where her grandmother's moon conjuncted Kelly's south node; they were profoundly bonded to each other like a mother and daughter on a soul level from a past life.

Kelly was thinking about her dream about her grandmother from the night before when she stepped down to the next step and felt herself slip on the runner and lose her balance. Disoriented, she slid down the staircase, each step hitting her back as she fell until her body hit the second-floor landing. She took stock of herself, saw that she was still in one piece, so at first she thought that the worst was over, that she was a bit shaken and her back might be bruised a little, but other than that she was okay. Then she tried to stand and fell to the floor again; the pain in her right ankle was excruciating.

She lifted herself on her hands to a sitting position and saw that King was running up the stairs toward her from the first floor. He padded onto the landing and howled softly as he approached her. "It's all right, King," she told him, patting his nose. "I just had a little fall." She looked toward the first floor and called out, "Emma! Emma!" A moment later she heard footsteps in the first-floor hallway and looked down the stairs, expecting to see Emma, but instead she saw a gray-haired man in paint-spattered coveralls climbing the steps as quickly as his stiff legs could carry him. She remembered him from the last time she'd had the house painted.

"I'll be there in a minute," he said, looking up the stairs toward her. "Hold tight."

"Thanks," Kelly said. "I'm sorry to be such a bother."

"That's okay. What happened?" he asked as he reached the landing.

"I must've tripped on the carpet."

He extended his hand toward her to help her up. She took hold of his hand and was surprised to find that he had the strength to pull her to her feet.

"Now take hold of my arm," he instructed, "and lean on me. We'll get you someplace where you can sit down."

Kelly held on to his arm. So far she was putting all her weight on her left foot; now she tried to put some weight on her right foot, but the pain was too great.

"Be careful," he told her. "It might be broken. You've got to have someone look at it."

She nodded and did as she was told, leaning on him as he slowly led her into Jeff's room. She sat down on the bed and looked up as Sarah came in.

Sarah's eyes went to Kelly's right foot, which she saw Kelly was barely letting touch the floor. "What is it, Kelly?" Sarah asked worriedly.

"I was clumsy and I fell. That's all." Kelly tried to keep the pain out of her voice. "I didn't know you were coming in today. I thought you were staying home to take care of yourself."

"I didn't need to stay home," Sarah told her. "Is it your leg or your ankle?"

Kelly felt like a fool; she wished she'd paid more attention as she'd gone down the stairs so she wouldn't have tripped. "I think it's my ankle," she said.

"I was just telling her she has to go to a doctor," Ed told Sarah; then he turned to Kelly. "I'll drive you to the emergency room if you like."

Sarah glanced at Kelly and saw that she was looking down at her ankle; to Ed it might look as if the pain had drawn her attention to it, but Sarah knew Kelly was looking down to avoid his eyes, so he wouldn't see how tense his suggestion of going to the hospital had made her. Going to the hospital would mean leaving the house, and Kelly couldn't do that.

Sarah answered before Kelly could come up with a reason not to go. "I appreciate it, Ed," Sarah said. "But I know you have to leave for your next job. I'll stay with Kelly and make sure she sees someone."

Kelly was looking at Ed now. "Thank you again for helping me, and for your offer. It's very kind of you."

"My pleasure, Dr. York. You just get that ankle healed soon." He was already out the door.

Kelly listened to his footsteps in the hallway heading toward the staircase and then descending the steps. When she could no longer hear them, she said to Sarah: "You really don't have to be here. You should be home."

"It would be depressing to stay home," Sarah said. "I could practice for a few hours, but I'll be doing that later anyway. The rest of the time, what am I going to do? Sit around thinking about Kevin? What's the point of that?" She looked at Kelly with an expression that told her she meant what she was saying. "I'll get over it. I have the concert coming up. And I have at least another fifty years to live. I'm not going to be one of those women who spends her life pining over a man. Now, what are we going to do about your ankle?"

Kelly moved to the edge of the bed and let some of her weight fall onto her right foot. The pain was just as sharp and intolerable as it had been when she'd tried standing up on the landing. She looked up at Sarah. "If you don't mind, please call Michelle. Ask her if it's possible for her to come by today to examine it."

Sarah met Kelly's eyes. She sensed that Kelly was avoiding making the call herself because she hadn't yet told Michelle about her agoraphobia, and she wanted to leave it up to Sarah to make up a reason why she needed Michelle to come to the house instead of her going to Michelle's office.

"Of course I'll call her," Sarah said. "In the meantime, I'll get you some ice."

"Thanks. I feel like an idiot for being so clumsy."

"You're not an idiot. You're just human."

She looked at Kelly a moment longer to make sure that she was okay; then she left the room.

Kelly removed her shoes, pulled her legs up on the bed, and leaned back against the pillows. Taking off her right shoe hurt her ankle, and so did the pressure of her right foot coming up onto the bed. The pain made her feel incredibly vulnerable. She had already been feeling emotionally vulnerable; now she was physically unable to walk, which made her feel even more vulnerable. She hated it. She looked around Jeff's room, her eyes focusing on a photograph of him in his high school football uniform, standing with her and Julie on the football field. She loved seeing the three of them enjoying each other's company; it made her think about how they would all be together again on Thanksgiving and how far away Thanksgiving suddenly seemed. She picked up the telephone on Jeff's night table, put it on her lap, and punched in his cell phone number. It was already ringing when she noticed that it was only ten fifteen a.m., which meant that it was seven fifteen in Los Angeles. She was thinking about hanging up when her son answered.

"Oh, Jeff," she said apologetically, "I hope I didn't wake you."

"I'm already up and dressed, Mom. I've got an eight-thirty class. Biology. The teacher's terrific."

She was glad to hear that his voice sounded strong and happy.

"How come you're calling during the week?" he asked her.

"You usually only call on weekends."

Kelly was still gazing at the photograph of Jeff in his football uniform with herself and Julie. "No particular reason," she said. "I missed you, so I thought I'd give you a call."

He laughed. "Between clients, of course. I know how busy you are. When's your last appointment today, six o'clock?"

"Six o'clock, that's right," Kelly responded. She was lying again, but she didn't want to tell him the truth, not about her agoraphobia or the man who had been stalking her on the telephone or even about her ankle. She didn't want him to worry about her. "How are you, honey?" she asked him.

"Working hard, just like you," he said. "No matter what you hear, it's not all parties at this place. I haven't put on a toga in days."

She broke into a smile; her son always managed to make her smile. He was referring to the toga fraternity parties in *Animal House,* of course; they'd rented the DVD and watched it with Julie before he'd gone off to college. "I hope you're going to some parties, at least," she said.

"I am, but only if they're drunken orgies. What about you?"

Kelly did her best to keep up her end of the joking. "Oh, I'm going to my fair share."

"How many drunken orgies have you been to this week?"

"Five or six," she said. "I've lost count."

All at once, even before she finished talking, the vulnerability and helplessness she'd been feeling returned. She hoped it hadn't come through in her voice, but her son's next words told her that it had.

"How are you really, Mom?" he asked. "You don't sound too good."

She forced the smile back on her face, determined that it

would make her sound as well as she was going to tell him she was. "I'm fine, Jeff. Absolutely fine. I called to say hello, that's all."

"If anything was wrong, you'd tell me, wouldn't you?"

He sounded very earnest now, as he had when he was a child and had wanted to talk to her about something serious, like whether or not there was a God and, if there was, was there a heaven and a hell.

"Of course I'd tell you," she said, just as seriously as when she'd told him that she did believe in God and that she didn't believe in heaven or hell except those that people created for themselves here on earth through their good or bad actions.

"I'd want you to tell me. I'm not a kid anymore. You can rely on me."

"I know I can, Jeff." She was feeling more and more emotional. She wondered how much longer she could keep it together if they continued their conversation. "You better leave for breakfast so you can be on time for class. "I don't want you to be late."

He laughed. "You're right. It's not like the days when you could write a note to the teacher for me, is it?"

"I'm very proud of you, Jeff," she said, not caring if it seemed to come out of nowhere; it was how she felt, and she needed to tell him.

"I'm proud of you, too, Mom," he told her; then he added: "I'll call you later."

"You don't have to—"

"I know I don't have to. I want to."

Then he was gone, and suddenly she could feel the three thousand miles between them, the same three thousand miles that separated her from Julie. Suddenly she missed them so deeply that the pain she felt throbbing in her ankle seemed to have risen to her heart. She hung up the phone and looked around his room again, wishing desperately that Thanksgiving were tomorrow instead of a month away.

Thirty-Five

AFTER TAKING MICHELLE UP to Jeff's room to see Kelly, Sarah came downstairs again. She was about to go into her office to start going through the next three months of files to search for women who'd come to see Kelly with relationship problems, but she realized it was lunchtime and that she was hungry. She walked into the kitchen and saw Emma at the counter, making a salad.

"How's Kelly's ankle?" Emma asked, continuing her preparations.

"I don't know. We'll have to wait to see what Michelle says." Sarah took a cup and saucer out of the cabinet and poured herself a fresh cup of coffee. "What are you making for lunch?"

"Chicken and a salad," Emma said. She turned to Sarah, her face showing the worry that had been with her all morning. "Kelly's always telling me Mars or one of those other planets is conjuncting another planet or squaring it or whatever and what I'm supposed to watch out for. Before all this, I only half believed it. But now . . ." She didn't finish her thought right away. When she spoke again, there were tears in her sweet gray eyes. "I'm scared for her, Sarah. She seems so strong, but underneath she's always been delicate, ever since she was a child. I'm worried about what's going to happen to her . . ."

Sarah put her coffee down, came over to Emma, and put her

arms around her. As she hugged her, Emma was crying. "You don't have to worry about Kelly," she told her. "Kelly's a survivor."

Emma, still crying, looked at her with wet eyes. "But what if it's the planets? What if whatever is happening with them means this is just the beginning of her bad luck?"

"You can't think that way, Emma," Sarah said sternly. "Remember what Kelly says in her column. The planets can present you with a challenge, but they don't determine your fate."

"What determines your fate?" Emma asked, her voice quavering.

"Your choices," Sarah said. "And Kelly makes good choices. She's not going to let this challenge overcome her. She's going to meet it. You'll see."

Emma nodded, crying less now. She was starting to feel better.

Sarah was relieved to see this. She didn't want Emma to worry. But despite her positive words to Emma, Sarah, too, was worried. She knew the pressure Kelly had already been under before falling down the stairs, and she worried that the accident would further undermine her belief in herself.

✳

Kelly sat on the edge of the bed as Michelle held her right foot and inspected her ankle, which was puffed up well beyond its normal size.

"It's very swollen," Michelle said. "But it's not crooked. That's a good sign. No bones sticking out. Did you hear a cracking noise when you fell or just a pop?"

Kelly thought about it for a moment. "I didn't hear anything. I was too busy falling."

"See if you can move the joint," Michelle said, the ankle still in her hand. "Take it easy, but just try."

Kelly tried to move her ankle joint. She felt a knifelike pain that made her wince, but her ankle joint moved and allowed her to turn her foot slightly to the right.

"Good," Michelle said. She gently released Kelly's ankle. "Now lower your foot to the floor."

Kelly slowly brought her right foot to the floor alongside her left foot.

"Let me help you up. I want to see if you can put any weight on it at all."

"It really hurt when I tried to stand on it before," Kelly said.

"I understand that," Michelle said, all doctor now. "But I want you to try again."

Taking Michelle's hand, Kelly rose from the bed with all her weight on her left foot. Once she was standing, she lowered her right foot onto the carpeted floor and slowly redistributed some of her weight onto that foot. "I can, a little."

"I'd say it's a bad sprain," Michelle said, "but it's probably not broken. The only way to be sure is if you come in for an X-ray."

Kelly looked into her best friend's eyes. She'd told Michelle so many secrets in the years they'd known each other, but this was different; this was the first time she had a secret that made her feel humiliated. "I can't," she said after a while. "I can't leave my house. I suppose you must've suspected by now. I just can't."

"How long have you been afraid to leave?" Michelle asked. Neither her face nor voice showed any sign of judgment.

Kelly had thought about this often, and she gave Michelle the most accurate answer that she'd come up with for herself. "I'm not sure exactly. Around the time Julie left for school. I don't know if it was the same day or the day after or the day after that. But ever since the morning it first happened, every time I try to leave, I get panicky. I start sweating. My heart beats fast. I breathe so hard I feel like I'm going to die. I know it doesn't make any sense, but I just get so frightened. This is the only place I feel safe. Or at least I did . . ."

Michelle's dark eyes became somber. "Has that man called you again?"

"Yes," Kelly said, "but the police are investigating it. The detective said that he's going to find him. They're monitoring my phones and they're beginning to look at suspects—"

"You've got to learn to go out of your house again, Kelly. You've got to find the key." As she said this, Michelle's voice was no longer even and professional; it was insistent.

Kelly laughed grimly. "That's what I keep saying to myself. The 'key.' KEY. My initials. Kelly Elizabeth York. People come to me to give them the key to their lives, and I can't help myself."

"But you have to," Michelle told her. "You can't just be trapped in here, afraid in your own home and afraid to go out."

"I don't want to be afraid, Michelle," Kelly said. "I really don't."

"Then it's up to you. Either you have to get help, or you have to help yourself." Michelle was looking at her urgently now. "Whatever is making you feel like this, you really do have the key. You just have to find out what it is and use it."

Kelly continued to meet her friend's eyes, but she didn't answer right away. When she did, she said emphatically: "I will."

Michelle smiled. "I know you, Kelly," she said. "If you tell me you will, you will. I just wanted to hear you say it. When we've made a pledge to each other, we've never let each other down."

Kelly smiled, too. "No, we never have. And I'm not going to start now. I'm going to find the key. I will. I'm going to find the key."

Thirty-Six

FBI AGENT MARY ANN Winslow was filling in her junior colleague, Eric Broadbent, on the serial killer case she'd just been handed as they walked toward the elevator in the agency's headquarters on East 57th Street. Winslow walked at her usual fast pace, and Broadbent had to quicken his steps to keep up with her. She talked as quickly as she walked, and he had to make sure he caught every word because he knew she expected that he'd remember everything. Whenever he forgot something she told him, she'd get icy and condescending, and he hated being treated that way. He wished he had a kinder, gentler boss, but the powers that be had assigned him to Winslow, so that's the way it was. At least she was good at her job.

"Four victims raped and strangled," she was saying. "All with the same MO. Two in New Jersey suburbs—New Kent and West Orange. Two in New York, about an hour or so outside the city. Long Beach and Tarrytown. Those two were just found this morning. Long Beach had been dead for five days. Tarrytown was killed last night. There are peculiarities to the MO the cops didn't release to the media."

Broadbent nodded; he'd gotten it all. The thing about Winslow that was most disconcerting to him was how attractive she was: five foot five, with auburn hair, blue eyes, a pretty face, and a great figure. Sometimes it was difficult to listen to her because he found himself just staring at her. He brought himself down to reality again. "Do we know anything about the killer?" he asked.

"The New Kent cops are calling him the *Astrologer*," Winslow said. She reached into her briefcase and handed him the file. "You can read about why in the car. We've got a lead we've got to follow up right now."

"In Tarrytown?" Broadbent asked.

"No, about thirty blocks from here, on the Upper West Side."

They reached the elevator, and Winslow pressed the button. The door opened seconds later, and she stepped inside. Broadbent, carrying the file, followed her in. He wanted to ask her more, but she'd closed herself off and was absorbed in her own thoughts. That was how she got, and he knew better than to annoy her. They rode down to the garage in silence.

Thirty-Seven

KELLY, HER ANKLE WRAPPED in the bandage Michelle had put on it, sat at her desk in her upstairs study, looking over the new files she'd asked Sarah to bring her from her office. So far she'd reviewed six files belonging to female clients, and none of the women had consulted her about leaving a relationship. She opened the seventh file folder and was about to read her notes when one of the phones on her desk rang. It was her private phone. She felt a moment of nervousness but then remembered her son had said he'd call her back, and she picked up the receiver before the end of the second ring.

"Jeffrey," she said brightly. "I almost forgot you were going to call."

"It's not Jeffrey," the voice on the other end whispered into her ear.

Kelly felt her hand holding the receiver starting to sweat. She wanted to hang up, but she knew she couldn't; the longer she kept him on the line, the more possibility there was for Detective Stevens to trace the call. She forced herself to keep holding on to the receiver and listening.

"You've been a bad girl," the voice continued, "but you've been punished, haven't you? It's not going to be so easy for you to get around anymore. Not that getting around outside the house was easy for you before."

Kelly felt her body tense. How could he know? Her mind told her it must have just been a lucky guess.

"What do you mean?" she asked.

"You know what I mean. You're frightened to go out."

She felt her mouth growing dry; she couldn't bring herself to say anything.

"You think you're the only one who knows things, Kelly. You say you know things from the stars. But I just *know* them, like I was right there."

Kelly suddenly looked around her study, half expecting to see him; that he, whoever he was, had mysteriously materialized in the room as he had mysteriously materialized in her life. But she was the only one there.

"You'll never find the key to me," he said. "But I've already found the key to you!"

That was it. The last words she could make herself listen to from him. She slammed down the phone. But even that didn't stop her from feeling scared and enraged and violated. What he'd said wasn't a lucky guess. Somehow he knew these things about her; in fact, he seemed to know everything about her. As if he really were in the room with her.

She looked around the study again, and still she was the only one in the room. She was so scared she was trembling. How did he know? she kept asking herself. How could he possibly know what she had said to Michelle?

Thirty-Eight

STEVENS WAS IN HIS car, talking to the officer who had monitored the call to Kelly.

"Did you get a location?" he asked.

"He made the call near the old World's Fair grounds in Queens. The signal changed transmission towers while he was talking, so he was on the move. He might've been on the Long Island Expressway or the Grand Central Parkway or getting onto the BQE. Before you ask, it was another disposable phone."

"Shit," Stevens said. He hung up as he pulled onto the West Side Highway. Speeding up the entrance ramp, he punched in Kelly's number. It took her a while to answer; he wasn't surprised; she was probably frightened out of her mind. When she finally picked up, he didn't wait for her to speak. He just said: "It's Detective Stevens. I heard the whole thing. I'm on my way."

Thirty-Nine

KELLY WAS LEANING ON the crutches that Sarah had bought for her as she opened the front door for Stevens. She was so shaken that she barely let him step inside before she assailed him with everything she was thinking and feeling.

"You heard what he said! He found 'the key' to me. He used the word *key*—the same word I used when I was in my son's room, talking with my friend Michelle! It's like he can see and hear everything I do and say! But how could that be possible? I feel like I'm going crazy!"

Almost crying, not just from fear but from anger and incomprehension, she looked at Stevens, her intense, dark blue eyes demanding an answer.

Stevens saw the state she was in; he'd seen it hundreds of times before, in people who found themselves confronting circumstances the violence of which was outside their experience and that they didn't understand and had never thought they would encounter. If he wasn't careful, he knew that she could become hysterical. He forced himself to remain centered and focused. When she'd appeared at the door, he'd been surprised to see her on crutches with her ankle in a bandage. He decided to concentrate on that.

"What happened to your ankle?" he asked.

Kelly grimaced. "It was a stupid accident. I tripped on the

carpet and fell down the stairs."

She wasn't raising her voice anymore, Stevens observed; she was calming down. But she was still looking at him, waiting for his answer to her question. After what she'd just told him, he knew he didn't want to try to answer her in the entry hall. For a moment, he didn't say anything; he just gave her a look that said she should pay close attention. Then he whispered, "Do you have a portable radio that plays on batteries?"

Kelly nodded, her eyes staying on his.

He whispered again. "Where?"

She whispered, too. "My daughter Julie's room."

Forty

IN THE SCREEN ON his iPhone he could see Kelly and the police detective walking down the front hallway toward the rear of the brownstone. He'd heard every word Kelly had blurted to the detective. She'd been so scared, she'd almost been screaming at him. He loved seeing her so raw, so unnerved, so close to the edge. She deserved it. And he loved seeing her on her crutches with her ankle wrapped up. He hoped that every moment it pulsated with pain. He loved knowing that he'd hurt her and confused her and made her so afraid that she was almost out of control. He loved knowing that his plan was going so well.

After her outburst at the front door, the cop's voice and hers had grown too quiet and muffled for him to hear. He figured that the cop had tried to comfort her, and now he was probably bringing her to the elevator to take her back upstairs, or they were going into the kitchen. Wherever they were going, for the time being they'd left the range of his miniature cameras and microphones.

He wondered if he shouldn't have commented to Kelly about finding the *key* to her. He wondered if the cop would suspect that he'd bugged her house. If he did, the cop would find the bugs and use them to try to find him. The thought just made him laugh. Let him try!

On the other hand, Kelly hadn't realized that she was *actually* being watched and listened to, and it might not occur to the cop, either. After all, anybody could realize that the initials in Kelly Elizabeth York's name spelled *KEY*, and anybody could tease her with it. Maybe the cop would regard it as just a coincidence. Maybe they would both see it in her stars. She was an astrologer, wasn't she?

He took the iPhone off his lap and put it on the mounting between his seat and the empty passenger seat. He remembered sitting in that seat a long time ago. It was after the trouble started. And the trouble had come because of Kelly York. Kelly Elizabeth York. That was why she didn't just deserve what he'd done to her up until now; she deserved to die.

Forty-One

USING HER CRUTCHES, KELLY slowly and awkwardly descended the steps into the garden behind the brownstone; then she made her way into the greenhouse as Detective Stevens had instructed before he'd gotten into the elevator. She didn't know why he'd asked her to wait there or why he wanted the radio from Julie's room; she knew only that he'd made the requests after she'd told him about her ankle and about the man who was threatening her on the phone repeating to her the exact words she had said to Michelle.

The greenhouse was small, just two rows of shelves holding pots with roses and herbs on either side of the narrow gravel path between them. She leaned on her crutches, looking at the plants, and waited for the detective, thinking about her promise to Michelle to find the key to releasing her from her fear of leaving her house and going into the outside world again. Why did she feel that she couldn't go beyond the rooms that she lived in and the garden behind them? Why had it happened so suddenly? She knew there was a reason for it, and that if she looked hard enough, she would find a clue, and the clue could lead her to escape from the fear that was making her feel so helpless. A key really was the right image. Something in her past had caused this fear; the key was remembering what it was.

She heard Stevens before she turned around and saw him

approaching, carrying Julie's radio. He entered the greenhouse, and, without saying a word, placed the radio on a shelf between two pots, clicked the "On" button, and moved the dial until he found a rock station. He raised the volume, and then he faced her, his brown eyes focused on her intensely, telling her to listen closely. When he finally spoke, he whispered as he had in the entry hall, but now she had to hear him over the din of the loud music.

"He may have found a way to set up surveillance equipment in your house," he said in a hushed voice. "Keep your voice down in case he set it up out here, too."

Kelly felt anxiety taking her over again, but she made herself whisper as he'd counseled. "But how—?"

"If he's set up the equipment," he said, "I'll find out how."

She took this in. The steadiness of his eyes and the confidence in his voice made her feel that he was telling the truth, that he would find out how. "Do you know who he is yet?" she asked.

"No. But I know who it's not. The calls are being made locally. Your daughter's ex-boyfriend Billy Whitmore is in college in Indiana, and he hasn't left since September. Kevin Stockman's in Boston, visiting his fiancée's family. And I was questioning Chris Palmer when you got the call the night before last, so it's not him."

"To tell the truth," she said, "I'm glad it's not any of them."

"And it's not any of the husbands of the women whose names you gave me from your files. Three of the men are still married to or in a relationship with the women, and the fourth died six months ago." He glanced at her bandaged ankle and asked: "Tell me how you fell down the stairs."

Forty-Two

HE WAS STILL DRIVING, which meant he had to split his attention between the traffic and the iPhone on the mounting between the seats. Every now and then he looked at the screen of the iPhone, but for the past fifteen minutes he hadn't seen Kelly or the detective. In fact, he hadn't seen anybody: not on the first floor, the second floor, or the third floor. Before that, he'd seen Kelly, on her crutches, walking through the kitchen into the garden; a few minutes later he'd seen the detective, a portable radio in his large hand, making the same trip. He knew that's where they were now.

He changed lanes as he neared his exit; then he looked again at the iPhone screen. This time he saw the detective entering the kitchen from the garden, crossing through the kitchen, and walking into the first-floor hallway. A honking horn pulled him away from the screen, and he turned the steering wheel to the right, narrowly avoiding drifting to the left again in front of the honking car. The other motorist, a well-dressed man in a maroon Jaguar, gave him the finger. Much as he wanted to reciprocate and do worse—say, ram his car into the Jag—he cursed under his breath and held back on any outward display of his temper. The last thing he needed was an altercation that brought in the police, not when everything was going so beautifully.

The next time he looked at the screen, the detective was

walking toward the staircase that led from the second floor to the third. He disappeared from the camera's view, but his footsteps were audible on the stairs.

He took his eyes off the screen again so he wouldn't miss his exit. He didn't get to look at the iPhone again until the detective was coming out of Kelly's third-floor study. This time, the detective was holding a book. He couldn't tell what it was, but the detective was walking toward the staircase, and he assumed he was bringing the book to Kelly, since she had so much trouble getting around herself.

Yes, his plan was working.

And despite what he'd said to Kelly, they hadn't realized yet that he'd planted the mini-cameras and microphones. Not that it would've mattered if they did. Or even if they found them. He'd made sure they couldn't trace the equipment back to him; he'd made sure they couldn't trace anything back to him. He'd even filed off the ID numbers. That was the thing about being smart. And being someone they wouldn't suspect of being smart. That was the thing about being someone they wouldn't suspect at all.

Forty-Three

STEVENS CAME DOWN THE stairs from the third floor at the same ambling pace as he'd ascended them. He tried to seem distracted, as if he had nothing particular on his mind, but actually he was observing the condition of the runner on the staircase, particularly on the steps where Kelly had fallen. On his way up to Kelly's study, he'd noted the hanging lighting fixtures in the first-, second-, and third-floor halls as possible places for surveillance equipment, but he couldn't inspect them because at the moment he didn't want to tip off the caller that he was aware that the man could be watching him. That's why he affected the distracted expression, why he hadn't gotten down on his hands and knees to examine the steps where Kelly had tripped but only glanced down at them in passing.

Getting the book from Kelly's third-floor study was just an excuse for the journey up and down the stairs, in case the caller was watching him at any point along the way. Any book would have done; Stevens had grabbed this one from her desk. It was a biography of Carl Jung. He handed it to her as he walked into the greenhouse where the rock station was still playing loudly. As he gave her the book, he spoke to her in a hushed voice.

"Does anybody besides you regularly use the stairs to the third floor?"

Kelly shook her head. "Emma usually takes the elevator."

"The runner's loose on two steps. It's not tacked down anymore. It's coming off the steps. It could've just come loose, but I don't think so. I think he made it happen. I think he did it because he wanted you to fall down the stairs."

She stared at him. "I don't understand," she whispered. "How could he have gotten into my house?"

"You had a dozen men here cleaning up the smoke damage. He probably clogged up the chimney to create the damage and give him the opportunity to get inside."

Kelly took in what Stevens said. It made sense, dreadful sense, but she could still see an objection to it. "But how could he know he'd be one of the men I would hire?" she asked. "I could've hired anybody."

Stevens's next question was the one he was about to ask her anyway. "How did you choose the men who did the work?"

"I left it up to Sarah. Her father used to be a contractor. I asked her to call people that used to work for him."

＊

Stevens sat with Sarah on the front steps of the brownstone. It was one spot where he was sure that the caller hadn't set up surveillance cameras or bugs. While Sarah went through the bills on her lap from the various people she'd called in to put the house back in order, he was on his cell phone with Bob Grossman, the 20th Precinct's resident expert on technology. He'd just given him Kelly's address and told him to come there ASAP, and now he was finishing the conversation. "I want you to find the equipment and see if we can use it to trace him." He ended the call before Grossman had a chance to respond.

Returning the cell phone to his jacket pocket, he watched Sarah writing a list for him on a sheet of notepaper. She was a bright, efficient woman, and pretty, but the way she shouldered responsibility told him that she had backbone, too; she wasn't someone who could be pushed around or easily gotten off course. It was clear that she cared deeply about Kelly, and Kelly felt the same about her. Kelly trusted her, and so, Stevens found, did he.

"I got the carpet cleaners, the house cleaners, and the upholstery cleaners from companies my father used to recommend to clients," she told him as she continued writing on the notepaper. "The electrician, the painters, and the carpenters were subcontractors who worked for my father. Here are their names and phone numbers."

She handed him the list and went on talking as he read it. "I don't see how it could be any of the men I know, Detective. Some of them worked on Kelly's house before, some I think even when her grandmother was alive. There were a couple of new men on some of the crews, of course, but . . . Do you really think it's one of them?"

When he looked up from the list, he saw that her hazel eyes were challenging him for a response. "Whoever it is," he said, "we're going to stop him before he hurts her any more than he already has." He stood up. "Thanks for the list."

Sarah stood, too. She was confused and upset by Stevens's theory. She hadn't questioned the firemen's assessment that refuse carried by the wind had blocked up the chimney; nor had she questioned that Kelly's fall down the stairs was accidental. Her stomach churned to think that both might have been deliberate, that the man who had been calling Kelly had already been to the house, that he might have even been inside it and installed hidden cameras and microphones to spy on Kelly. Most of all, it hurt Sarah to think that she might have made the phone call that brought him into the house. She didn't want to believe it.

She looked at Stevens. "The man who's calling Kelly is blaming her for making his wife or girlfriend leave him. None of the men I knew on the crews had wives or girlfriends who came to Kelly to have their charts done. I would know because they would've called me to set up the appointment."

"Not necessarily. A woman could've called on her own and used her own name. A name you might not have recognized. Like you said, there were some new men on the crews. Men who'd never worked here before."

Sarah's face fell; he was right, of course.

Stevens was just about to head back into the house when he noticed a black sedan pulling up to the curb. It looked like an unmarked police car except for the license plate, which told him the car belonged to the FBI. In the front seat were a woman, who was driving, and a man, who sat in the passenger seat. The woman parked the car; thirty seconds later the two of them got out and started walking toward the brownstone. The woman, carrying an attaché case and wearing a black suit and an air of officiousness that made her good looks beside the point, walked two feet in front of the man, whom Stevens judged to be four or five years younger than she and a great deal friendlier.

Now the woman led the man up the steps. Her eyes scrutinized Sarah. "Kelly Elizabeth York?" she asked.

"No, I'm Sarah Stein, her assistant," Sarah said. "Who are you?"

The woman stopped on the fourth step, took out her badge, and showed it to Sarah. "Mary Ann Winslow, FBI." She gestured to the young man behind her. "Agent Broadbent." Then she looked at Stevens. "And you are?"

Stevens didn't bother with his badge. "Detective Michael Stevens. NYPD."

Winslow's face lost what little color it had. "Why are you here? Has something happened to Dr. York?"

"Yes, that's why—"

"Is she dead?"

"No," Stevens said evenly. "That's what I'm here to prevent."

He looked over Winslow's and Broadbent's shoulders and saw that another unmarked car was pulling up nearby. This time he recognized the car and the driver. He watched as the man parked in a red zone and exited the car with his computer bag.

Winslow noticed that Stevens's attention was on the street. She turned around and saw the wiry, brown-haired man with the computer bag approaching the steps and making eye contact with Stevens.

She turned to Stevens again. "Who's he?"

"Lieutenant Grossman. He's here to look for surveillance equipment I think has been installed in Dr. York's house by a man who's been harassing her on the phone."

Winslow turned to Broadbent. "So he's stalking her on the phone."

"You say 'he' like you know who 'he' is," Stevens said. "Do you?"

Instead of answering Stevens's question, Winslow addressed Grossman, who had stopped beside her, on the fourth step. "You can go, Lieutenant. We're taking over."

Stevens felt his blood become hot. He'd disliked the woman before she'd even opened her mouth; now he couldn't stand her. "On what grounds?" he asked. "This is New York. It's an NYPD case. It's my case."

Winslow's blue-gray eyes stared at him. "The killer crossed state lines, Detective. It's an FBI case. It's *my* case." She focused on the sheet of notepaper in his hand. "What's that?"

Stevens didn't answer right away; he didn't want to answer at all, but he knew he had to. Finally, he said: "A list of men who had access to the house to—"

She cut him off again. "You can fill us in on it later." She turned to Grossman. "I said you can go, Lieutenant Grossman."

Grossman glanced up at Stevens to find out if he should stay or go. Stevens nodded reluctantly, and Grossman started down the steps and back to his car.

Winslow didn't bother to show satisfaction that she'd won the territorial battle; the expression on her face said she'd known she would, that it had been a foregone conclusion. He was a cop, and she was FBI, and if there was a pissing contest, of course she'd win.

Once Grossman left, she addressed Stevens again. "We're looking for a serial rapist and killer. He's raped and murdered four women. We have reason to believe he has a connection to Dr. York. Now you tell me he's been calling her on the phone and he may even have already been to her house. Obviously, we don't have a lot of time."

Stevens was surprised to find how unsurprised he was to discover that the man who'd been calling Kelly was a rapist and a murderer. From the moment he'd interviewed Kelly, he'd felt that the man had not just been making idle threats, that he meant to harm her, and that he could. He looked at Sarah and saw that she was frightened. He put his hand briefly on her shoulder in an effort to comfort her, but there was nothing he could do to assuage his own discomfort except vow that he would do whatever he could to help the FBI and protect Kelly.

Winslow turned to Sarah. "Get Dr. York and I'll take her to my office. There's no point talking in the house if it's bugged, and I don't want to have the bugs removed right away."

Sarah swallowed; it took her a while to find her voice. She was horrified by what she had heard and at a loss how to explain to these two FBI agents what she had never explained before to anyone, not even her parents. "I'm sorry," she said finally, "but Dr. York doesn't leave the house. She can't leave the house. She just . . . can't."

Winslow's jaw tightened. "She has agoraphobia?"

Sarah nodded.

Stevens saw Winslow's face fill with annoyance and disapproval. "Behind the brownstone, there's a walled garden with a greenhouse," he said. "I've talked with her out there, but we don't know if he's got that bugged, too. I turned a radio on in there just in case, to throw noise over us talking."

Winslow thought for a few moments before she spoke. "I'm not taking any chances. I'll wait for my specialist to get here. He can find out where the bugs are before I go into the house, and we can see if we can trace this son-of-a-bitch by finding out where the cameras are broadcasting to. That'll give us his location, which is a hell of a lot better than going in, finding the bugs, searching out where he bought them, and hoping he paid with a credit card that has his name on it instead of cash. In the meantime, we'll keep acting like we don't know they're there. I don't want to give him any more advance warning than we have to about what we know and what we don't know."

She paused before continuing. "In answer to the question you asked before, Detective Stevens, we don't know who he is yet. But we know a lot about him."

Stevens looked at her, expecting her to tell him more. But she didn't. Instead, she opened her attaché case, took out a notepad and pen, handed them to Sarah, and said: "I'd like you to write Dr. York a note."

Sarah took the pad and pen and prepared to take Winslow's dictation.

But Winslow wasn't ready yet. "Before we get to the note, I want to make something clear to you, Ms. Stein. I don't want you telling Dr. York anything that I've told you. You're just going to give her the note and leave the rest to me. Do you understand that?"

Sarah nodded glumly.

∗

Although it was sunny, there was a cool breeze, and Kelly was glad she'd put on a sweater before going into the garden again. Sitting on one of the stone benches, waiting for Stevens, she felt a shiver, and she buttoned her sweater. She wondered why Stevens was taking so long to get from Sarah the names of the men who'd repaired and cleaned up the brownstone. She was relieved to know that the caller wasn't Chris Palmer or Kevin or Julie's old boyfriend, Billy, but if Stevens was right, the man hadn't just threatened her on the phone; he'd actually been inside her house and had set up spying equipment and caused her accident. She looked at the crutches propped up beside her against the stone bench and trembled again, knowing how close the man may have been to her without her even realizing it.

She wondered if, when she saw the names of the men who'd worked on the house, she would find that the wife of one of them had consulted her about leaving their marriage. If it was a wife, she'd find the woman's name in her client list, but if it was a girlfriend and not a wife, the only way to find her would be to continue searching through her files for women who had come to see her about a relationship and then for Stevens to follow up with the women until he located the one who had gone with one of the workmen. It could take days; it could take weeks; it might never happen.

She looked up and saw Sarah coming through the door from the kitchen, holding the large appointment book she usually kept on the desk in her office. Sarah's face looked tense and troubled, as if something had happened that had disturbed her so deeply that she couldn't even try to cover her fear. Or perhaps she was trying; perhaps this was just the best she could do. Her expression was solemn as she extended the book toward her and said, "I'm starting to reschedule appointments and I'd like you to look at next week's schedule. See if you'd like me to book a client on Wednesday at six p.m., or if you think that's too much."

Kelly took the book. There was something odd about the way Sarah made the request, and opening the appointment book, she saw that Sarah hadn't wanted her to look at her schedule at all; Sarah had inserted a note between the pages she had marked. The note was in Sarah's handwriting, but the notepaper was printed with a heading Kelly had never seen before, and it stunned her. It was from the Federal Bureau of Investigation.

Kelly's eyes blurred the words on the page, but gradually they came into focus and she was able to read what Sarah had written:

> FBI Agent Mary Ann Winslow is here about the man who has been calling you. She understands you can't leave the house. She's staying outside until she knows where the surveillance equipment is. When she comes in, call her Mary Ann. Treat her like an old friend. This is very important. Pretend that she's come to visit you from Boston.

Kelly stared at the note for a long time. She understood the literal meaning of the words; she understood what she was being told to do, but the fact of an FBI agent's being there to see her about the man Stevens was already trying to find made no sense to her. Why would the FBI be interested? She glanced up at Sarah's frightened eyes and found that she'd forgotten the question Sarah had asked her as a cover for showing her the note. Soon she remembered that Sarah had asked if she would like her to schedule an additional appointment for late next Wednesday. Now she could see that Sarah had asked the question to give her the opportunity to respond affirmatively to the instructions.

"Yes, I can do that," Kelly said.

"I'm glad," Sarah said.

Kelly saw that her eyes looked no less frightened.

Forty-Four

STEVENS SAT IN THE backseat of Winslow's car with Broadbent while Winslow and another FBI agent, Keith Barr, the computer expert Winslow had called in, sat in the front. Stevens hated backseats; his six-foot-five frame made it hard for him to squeeze into the limited space, and he especially hated what squeezing in did to his long legs, but he was relieved that Winslow was including him in the investigation. Barr sat in front of him in the passenger seat, his laptop on his thighs, using a program that would show whether there was any surveillance equipment in the brownstone and, if there was, where it was located.

For several minutes, Stevens filled Winslow in on the calls, the clogged chimney, and Kelly's fall down the stairs, while Barr worked on the keyboard. Then Barr glanced up at the screen and announced, "Okay, I've got something."

Winslow leaned over and looked at the screen with Barr.

Making himself even more uncomfortable, Stevens came forward in the backseat to look over Barr's shoulder. All he saw on the screen were white lines crossing the black space.

He pointed to the white lines. "What are those?"

"They're broadcasting patterns," Barr explained, fixated on the screen. "There are four mini-cams. One on the first floor, near the front door, toward the right if you face the house from the street, like from where we're parked—"

"That's the first-floor hall," Stevens said.

"Another one's on the first floor about twenty feet behind it."

"The kitchen."

"Another on the second floor, on the right, in the middle—"

"Second-floor hall. Probably looks into the son's room."

"The last one's on the third floor," Barr continued, "near the back of the house. I guess that's a hall, too."

"That's the floor with her bedroom and study," Stevens commented.

Winslow ignored him. She was still looking at the screen with Barr. "None in the garden, then, or in the housekeeper's apartment?" she asked.

"No. Just those four."

"Where are they broadcasting to?" Winslow asked.

"I need to open another program," Barr said. His fingers moved quickly on the keyboard, and Stevens saw the white lines disappear.

Winslow turned to him. "Sit back, Detective Stevens. You're making me nervous."

Stevens moved back in the seat, joining Broadbent, who, throughout all of this, had remained a mute observer. He'd wondered why Broadbent hadn't leaned forward with him to look at the screen; he realized now that Broadbent had wanted to avoid having Winslow reprimand him.

Barr was scrutinizing the information on the screen again. "The mini-cams are broadcasting to a wireless modem," he said. "It belongs to . . . " He punched a series of keys, then looked at the screen and concluded his sentence: "Kelly York." He sighed with disgust. "The fucker's using her modem to send whatever the equipment's picking up into the ether."

"Translate," Winslow demanded.

"The Internet cloud," Barr explained. "The Wide Area Network. From there it can go anywhere."

Winslow was clearly annoyed. "Isn't there something you can do to find out where he's picking it up? I want to know who this man is, not just how clever he's being."

"I can use my packet sniffer," Barr said, "and see if I can track the packets to where he's receiving them." His fingers tapped on the keyboard again. "Of course, that depends on him leaving his equipment on. If he stops picking it up on his equipment, I won't be able to trace it."

Winslow was already grabbing her attaché case and getting out of the car. "Oh, he'll leave it on," she said. "He's too curious not to. And we're not going to give him a reason to turn it off, because we're not going to let him know we're aware that he's watching her."

Stevens's eyes followed Winslow as she walked toward the brownstone and up the steps. When she got to the front door, he leaned forward in the seat again so he could see the computer screen. This time Broadbent leaned forward, too.

*

Mary Ann Winslow rang the bell and waited. She noted that the door was new, and she wondered if it had been replaced after the incident with the fireplace. It was an inconsequential question and lasted in her mind no more than an instant before she thought about what had just transpired in the car. She was optimistic about Barr using his computer to find the serial rapist and killer who was targeting Kelly York. They hadn't found surveillance equipment in the homes of the four women he had already raped and murdered, but in a way it made sense that he'd installed it in Kelly's home. Kelly wasn't like his other targets; she held a special fascination for him. That's what had led Winslow here.

Her mind returned to the three men she had just left in the car. She knew that Stevens didn't like her and Broadbent and Barr were intimidated by her, and she didn't care. Indeed, she preferred it that way; she liked to keep cops at a distance and off balance, and she liked agents who worked under her to do what she wanted them to do when she wanted them to do it and at other times to stay out of her way. She didn't view being popular as a requisite of her job; in fact, despite her looks, she'd never cared about being popular, not in high school, not in college, and not at Quantico, where she'd done her FBI training. What she had cared about, at each place, was being at the top of her class, which she had been, and now what she wanted was to be on top of the investigation and leave the others working on it in her dust.

She hadn't met Kelly York yet, but she'd seen her photograph in *Luminary World* magazine next to her astrology column. Winslow had no interest in astrology and had never even heard of the column before Kelly's name had come up in the investigation. She dutifully read it just to see the kinds of things that Kelly wrote about, but it was the photograph that interested her most. It showed Kelly to be a slender blond woman with a warm smile, an attractive woman like the four women the killer had raped and murdered. The photograph also showed Kelly to be a woman who projected ease and confidence; Winslow was annoyed to find out that Kelly was agoraphobic. To Winslow that meant that she was fragile, and to Winslow fragile meant weak.

Despite her distaste for weakness, as Winslow had thought about it, she'd realized there was an advantage to Kelly's being afraid to leave her house: allowing Kelly to stay in the brownstone instead of moving her to a neutral spot that the killer didn't know about would keep the killer watching the broadcast from the mini-cams he'd set up, which increased the odds of Barr's being able to trace him that way. And it didn't really make it any harder to protect Kelly in the brownstone. Winslow could station agents outside of it until they caught the man they were looking for.

Forty-Five

KELLY, LEANING ON HER crutches, opened the front door and found herself facing a strikingly pretty, auburn-haired woman with hard gray-blue eyes that didn't quite go with the broad grin and effusive greeting she gave Kelly on seeing her.

"It's been so long, Kelly!" Winslow bubbled. "It's wonderful to see you!"

Kelly smiled as she opened the door wider to let her inside. "It's great to see you, too, Mary Ann."

Winslow walked into the house, and Kelly kissed her on the cheek before closing the front door.

Winslow's eyes went to Kelly's crutches; she knew there was a mini-cam somewhere on the ceiling overhead and wanted to be sure to put on a good show.

"Why are you on crutches?" she asked Kelly sympathetically.

Kelly shook her head self-deprecatingly. She didn't like acting a role, but she knew how important it was, and she hoped she was convincing. "You know how clumsy I am," she said. "I fell. But it's only a sprain. How was your drive from Boston?"

"Long," Winslow said. "I'd love a cup of coffee."

"Coffee's a great idea," Kelly responded. Balancing herself on her crutches, she led the way down the hallway toward the kitchen.

The hall was narrow, and Winslow walked behind her. When

they were both in the kitchen, as Winslow put her attaché case on a chair, she said, "I brought my photographs so you could see my latest work."

"Wonderful," Kelly said. "I hoped you'd bring them." She made her way to the coffeepot. "I forgot, black or with cream?"

"Black," Winslow told her. "You know I don't like to dilute my caffeine."

Kelly got a cup and saucer from the cabinet and poured Winslow a cup of coffee.

Winslow watched Kelly, assessing the way she was handling herself. She didn't seem quite the delicate leaf in the wind that Winslow had expected when she'd heard that Kelly was agoraphobic. But that still didn't mean she was going to like her.

*

Kelly lowered herself onto one of the benches in the garden and then leaned the crutches against it as Winslow, attaché case in one hand, cup of coffee in the other, sat on the bench opposite her. Now that Kelly wasn't playacting anymore, her anxiety took over. She still didn't know why the FBI was involving itself in investigating the man who was threatening her when Detective Stevens was already on the case. Whatever the reason, Winslow's being there made Kelly feel less rather than more safe.

Alone with Kelly, out of the range of the surveillance equipment, Winslow dropped her pretense of friendship and, after a quick sip of coffee, got down to business.

"We've determined that four mini-cams with mikes were installed in your house," she said with the same matter-of-fact voice she used when she filed a report into her digital recorder. "One in the hall on each floor and one in the kitchen. There are none here in the garden or in your housekeeper's apartment downstairs."

Kelly took in the information. She had the feeling that it was a preamble for what the FBI agent was really leading up to. She sensed that when the second shoe dropped, it was going to drop heavily, and she steeled herself in an effort to prepare for it. Suddenly, from the corner of her eye, she caught sight of someone coming up into the garden from Emma's apartment. She jumped back with a start before she saw that it was Stevens. She was glad he was there.

Stevens remained standing, towering over the two seated women. He knew he'd taken a chance joining Winslow and Kelly unasked, but he'd realized he had nothing to contribute to Barr's effort to track the killer's Internet trail, and he wanted to be present when Winslow acquainted Kelly with the horrendous acts of the man that they were looking for. He gave Winslow a slight nod of his head, but he addressed Kelly.

"With four cameras and microphones, he has your house just about covered," he said. "That's how he knew you were injured and could use the same words you used talking to your friend in your son's room. He could see you and hear you."

Winslow didn't give Stevens a chance to continue or Kelly a chance to respond. "This man is methodical," she said to Kelly. "And not just about the surveillance equipment."

Kelly sat up straight and met the FBI agent's eyes with an unflinching gaze that she hoped would hide her fear. She knew people like Mary Ann Winslow; they liked power, and they despised those who were not as powerful as they were. She sensed that Mary Ann Winslow had no patience for fear, or even for vulnerability. It was bad enough being afraid; Kelly didn't want to be looked down on or pitied.

"How do you know he's methodical?" she asked Winslow.

"How does the FBI know anything about him? And why does the FBI care?"

"Because he's not just threatening you on the phone and spying on you, Dr. York," Winslow said. "He's a sexual predator and a murderer, and he's already killed four victims that we know of."

Kelly kept her eyes meeting Winslow's, but she had to hold on to the bench to steady herself.

Stevens saw Kelly's distress, and also her bravery. "Are you all right?" he asked.

Kelly glanced up at him. "Yes, I am. Just shocked."

"That's understandable," Stevens said. "What this man has done is shocking."

Winslow was getting increasingly irritated by Stevens, but she didn't want to deal with him in front of Kelly. She'd had confrontations before in front of people whose cases she was working on, and she'd discovered that besides increasing the tension, it also decreased people's confidence in her. Under circumstances such as these, she'd found that the best course in dealing with an irritant like Stevens was to act as if he wasn't there and then to resolve the matter later.

"The police discovered that he put ads in a magazine called *You and Your Sign*," Winslow told Kelly, "in August and September. And also in local papers, in New Jersey and New York suburbs."

Kelly felt her throat constricting. "*You and Your Sign* . . . I know the magazine."

"The ads were aimed at singles," Winslow explained. "They said he's an astrologer who can help them find the love of their lives. On the date specified in the ad, he checked into the hotel where he said he'd be available for consultations. He calls himself Antiochus. Antiochus is—"

"An ancient Greek astrologer," Kelly said. "He lived in the

second century BC.”

"He targets women who live by themselves,” Winslow continued. "He gets into their houses. He rapes and strangles them, and then he uses an object with a sharp point to gouge their astrological sign into their thigh. It's not a needle or an ice pick. The police lab in New Kent found traces of bronze in the victim's flesh. Our profiler thinks it might be connected to some kind of astrological instrument—”

"It could be a sharp-pointed rule or an alidade, from an astrolabe,” Kelly said. "Around the time of Antiochus, astrologers in ancient Greece used astrolabes to calculate the positions of the planets. The real Antiochus probably used one to do horoscopes. It would make sense for the killer to use part of an astrolabe to mark his victims with their signs.” She was finding that it helped not simply to listen passively, but to talk, to share what she knew about astrology; it made her feel that she had a reason to be there other than just as a potential victim, that she had value and, perhaps, at least some degree of control.

She noticed that for the first time since they'd met, Winslow was looking at her with interest, perhaps even with grudging respect.

"I'll pass that along,” Winslow said. She removed a pad from her attaché case and wrote a note to herself before picking up her train of thought.

"We don't have any fingerprints, but the clerks at both hotels provided the same description of him. Caucasian, midthirties, average build, dark eyes, dark hair. Rather nondescript. No distinguishing features. Not someone who'd stand out in a crowd. He speaks standard American English.

"Another thing we know about him is he doesn't need money. He didn't take anything of value from the victims' homes. Also, the victims' checkbooks show they wrote checks to Antiochus when they consulted with him, but their bank records show that the checks weren't cashed.

"Our profiler describes him as isolated, never been married or in a long-term relationship. He has delusions of grandeur; he's superficially attractive and so obsessed with dominating and punishing women that he feels compelled to rape them, kill them, and brand them to show his special knowledge of who they are astrologically and to identify them as his."

"Is that what led you to me?" Kelly asked. "Because he calls himself an astrologer and brands his victims with astrological signs?"

"No," Winslow said. Without further comment, she reached into her attaché case again and this time removed a clear plastic bag inside of which was the hardback book whose worn blue cover was illustrated with stars. On the spine was its title: *One Hundred-Year Ephemeris, 1950 to 2050 at Midnight.*

Kelly was stunned. "That's my ephemeris! Where did you find it?"

"It was in the night table of the victim in West Orange, New Jersey. Sheryl Doyle. Did you know her?"

Kelly repeated the name silently to herself and then shook her head. "It doesn't sound familiar, but I'm not good with names. I remember faces."

Winslow was already taking a photograph out of her attaché case. Now she gave it to Kelly. Kelly found herself staring at a beautiful woman in her forties, with long, straight blond hair and sculpted features. "She was lovely. She looks like an actress."

"She was an actress. When she was younger, she had a running part on a soap opera."

Tears in her eyes as she continued staring at the photo, Kelly shook her head again. "Poor woman. I can't bear to think about what happened to her. But I don't remember ever seeing her as a client. " She looked up at Winslow again and gave her back the photograph. "Sheryl Doyle . . . I'm sure I'd remember her face, it was so distinctive. But I'll check my records." She wiped her eyes with her hand. "I can tell you right now, though, when my ephemeris went missing. It was five years ago, when I was on tour for the book I wrote. I did consultations for people in the cities where I stopped to do publicity. I had a paperback ephemeris I used with clients and this one that I always kept with me. It was given to me by my grandmother on my tenth birthday. One morning, I went to look for it, and it was gone. I always thought somebody stole it."

Winslow removed another evidence bag from her attaché case and showed it to Kelly. Inside the bag was a white business card with the name and other information printed in blue. The card read *Kelly Elizabeth York, PhD, Intuitive Astrologer*, and it gave her business phone number.

"It was in the book," Winslow told her.

"I used it as a bookmark," Kelly said. She found that it took all of her energy and concentration to speak.

"Do you remember what city you were in when the ephemeris went missing?" Winslow asked.

Kelly didn't have to think about it; she remembered the morning she'd discovered that her book was gone as vividly as if it had just happened. "I was in Washington, DC, when I noticed it was gone. But I didn't look at it every day. As I said, I used a paperback ephemeris when I did consultations, so it could have been stolen a day or two before that, when I was in Philadelphia or Baltimore."

Winslow found that, despite her initial reservations, she was increasingly impressed with Kelly. "Why don't you look through your records to see if Sheryl Doyle ever had an appointment with you? And if she did, see if it was during your book tour."

Kelly stood up, putting her weight on her left foot and gingerly touching the ground with her right. Then she took the crutches off the bench, got them in place under her arms, and started toward the steps that led to the glass door to the kitchen.

"If you close the door to your waiting room and office," Winslow instructed, "he won't be able to see you in there."

Kelly nodded as she started up the steps toward the door. Stevens got there ahead of her and opened the door for her. "I'll come with you," he said.

Winslow's teeth clenched, and her blood felt as if it had surged to one hundred and fifty degrees. She was enraged; who did Stevens think he was? She was about to shout that he should stay where he was and remind him who had jurisdiction over the case, but she stopped herself when she realized that with the kitchen door open, the microphone inside might pick up her shouting. To the surveillance equipment, she had to appear to be an old friend of Kelly's, not an angry FBI agent telling a cop where he could stuff it.

As she watched Stevens disappear inside with Kelly, she took a deep breath and consoled herself with the thought that she would deal with Stevens later.

Forty-Six

HE'D SEEN HER HOBBLE to the front door on her crutches to let in the woman with red-brown hair, who turned out to be an old friend. It bothered him to see how glad Kelly was that the woman was visiting her. It meant Kelly could still enjoy something about her life. When he watched Kelly, the only thing he wanted to see was how scared and in pain she was. He relished her fear and her pain all the more because he knew it was just a taste of what was going to happen to her.

He'd watched her in the kitchen, making coffee for her friend, and then watched them go through the door at the back of the kitchen into the garden.

He couldn't see them when they were in the garden. But, of course, he knew what the garden looked like, with its stone benches and its high brick walls. Her friend had brought her attaché case so she could show Kelly her photos. He could imagine the two women in the garden, talking, looking at pictures.

He hadn't realized that at some point the cop had gone out there, too, but he must have, because now he saw the cop walking with Kelly through the kitchen toward the front hall. They had come into the kitchen together, through the glass door. He figured the cop must have gone into the garden through the housekeeper's apartment downstairs. He knew about that apartment, too, of course.

He opened a can of beer as he watched Kelly come into the hall on her crutches and make her way toward her office. The cop followed her. She opened the door to her waiting room, but he couldn't see inside. Kelly blocked his view. She let the cop in and then she closed the door behind them. His fingers and hand ached from opening the beer; it always did. But that's just the way it was. The only remedy he'd found for it was more beer. Drinking from the new can, he thought about what was awaiting Kelly and how much he was looking forward to it.

He smiled again about how satisfying it was to have things set up so that he could watch it all. He was happy the cop still hadn't figured out there were cameras and microphones in the house. Even if he found them, it wouldn't matter, of course, since they wouldn't tell him about who had put them there or about what was planned for Kelly.

He finished the beer and watched the empty first-floor hallway of Kelly's brownstone, waiting for her and the cop to come out of her office. It felt good to know that whatever they did, she was doomed. He had doomed her just as she had doomed him. Because of Kelly, he knew what it was to live with the darkness of death every day; now she was learning what it was like to live with it—only the darkness of death that she was living with was her own.

Forty-Seven

BROADBENT WAS NOW SITTING next to Barr in the front seat of the car. He craned his neck so he could see the screen of Barr's laptop as Barr continued searching for the computer that was picking up the transmission from Kelly York's brownstone. Barr had explained to him that the flashes of white radiating outward in a circle on the screen were packets of data from the transmission that were being sent from Kelly's computer into the Internet cloud. By some means that Barr was still working to uncover, that transmission was then being received by the computer that they were looking for.

Barr had been at it for more than an hour, and Broadbent was getting a crick in his neck. He straightened up in the seat and massaged his neck muscles. As he kneaded the sides of his neck with his fingers, his thoughts returned to what they knew about the serial rapist and killer they were looking for: his physical description, his obsession with astrology, the ads he placed to attract potential victims, the skill with which he planned and executed his crimes without leaving DNA or fingerprints behind.

His reflections were interrupted by Barr's voice. "The good news," Barr was saying, "is that the transmission from her house is still going out and being picked up, so I can see that the packets are going somewhere. The bad news is I still don't know where."

Broadbent looked at Barr. He wanted to say something to

Barr to encourage him, but he didn't know what to say, so instead he just watched as Barr tapped a series of keys on the laptop while keeping his eyes on the screen, trying to get his packet sniffer to sniff out the killer.

✳

Coming back into the garden, Kelly found Winslow still seated on the bench, but now she was reading a document from a folder.

"I looked through my list of clients," Kelly said, moving on her crutches toward the other bench. "Sheryl Doyle was never a client. She couldn't have stolen my ephemeris."

Winslow put the document she'd been reading back into the folder. "Actually," she said, "we thought it was possible that she didn't steal it from you."

As Kelly sat down on the bench facing Winslow, she saw the FBI agent glancing up with annoyance at Detective Stevens, who had come into the garden behind Kelly.

Winslow didn't waste a word on him. "We think your ephemeris was taken by the killer, and Sheryl Doyle got it from him," Winslow told Kelly. "Maybe by stealing it like he stole it from you. Sheryl Doyle went to him to help her solve her problems through astrology. She saw him as an authority. People often fetishize authorities, investing them with magical powers. When they fetishize them, they want to own something that belonged to them. We think the killer has fetishized you. He didn't just take your ephemeris and your card, he took something else from you, too."

Winslow leafed through the papers in the folder. When she found the document she was looking for, she removed it from the folder and gave it to Kelly. "This is a copy of the ad he placed in

You and Your Sign and in the suburban papers."

As Kelly read the ad silently to herself, Winslow continued: "He calls himself an *intuitive astrologer*. That's who you are. He's taken part of your identity. Now, by targeting you as a victim, he's showing that he's superior even to you. The phone calls, the 'accident' on the stairs, he's taunting you. Punishing you. He's letting you know he has power over you. And he's spying on you so he can watch the effects of what he's doing."

Kelly finished reading the ad. She didn't need the FBI agent to point out that Antiochus had used the words *intuitive astrologer* to describe himself; the words seemed to vibrate on the page as she read them. That this man who had raped and killed was identifying himself the same way that she described herself constricted her throat and made her feel as if she would suffocate. It took her time to start breathing again and to think and start sorting things out.

Eventually, she looked at Winslow. "You mentioned he's never been in a relationship, but on the phone he said I made his wife or his girlfriend leave him. I've been going through my files with Detective Stevens to find a woman who saw me about troubles with her husband or boyfriend and—"

Winslow stopped her. "That's a cover," she said, "to keep you from figuring out who he is. Start concentrating on the men who came to see you on your book tour, around the time you discovered your ephemeris was missing. Look for a man who was in his late twenties or early thirties at the time. Do you write down descriptions of the people who come to you for appointments?"

"Usually not physical descriptions. But most of the time I write down my impressions. And—"

Winslow cut her off again. "Good. Look for a man in that age group who struck you as isolated, impressed with himself, not only interested in astrology but perhaps someone who considered himself an expert in it. Perhaps someone who was a little too interested in you. A man you had a bad feeling about. As you review your records, see what you can remember, what comes back to you—"

Kelly nodded. "I'll look at their charts, too, to see what they can tell me."

"If that helps you remember, fine."

Stevens had been pacing near the greenhouse, listening to Winslow and Kelly. Now he walked up to Winslow, taking the list that Sarah had written for him out of his pocket. "What about seeing if any of the men who worked here after the smoke damage match the profile? They had access to put in the surveillance equipment."

Winslow took the list from Stevens before he offered it. "We'll check out any man on here that fits the physical description. But, Detective, this killer has already proved he's a master of breaking into houses. If he wanted to get in here, he'd get in without anybody knowing he'd been here till he'd done whatever he'd come to do. That's what makes him so dangerous."

"But Dr. York's been in the house the whole time. And she has a dog. Don't you think—?"

Winslow interrupted him. "We don't know when he installed the equipment. We only know when he made the first call to Dr. York and when what he said to her made it seem like he could see and hear her." She focused on Kelly now. "He may have broken in and installed the mini-cams and microphones before you developed agoraphobia. I assume before that there were times you went out at night."

Kelly nodded. "Of course."

"And times you were away on vacation?"

"Yes."

"And your dog, where does it sleep at night?"

"In my room to begin with," Kelly said, "but usually during the night he goes down to my housekeeper's apartment. There's a door to it on the first floor."

"After your housekeeper lets him in," Winslow continued officiously, "does she leave her door shut or open?"

"Shut, until she wakes up in the morning. If he wants to go out before that, she lets him into the garden."

Winslow looked at Stevens, her lips curled up slightly in a smile of superiority, as if she were about to reveal a winning hand in poker, "I told you, Detective, if this SOB wanted to break into the house, he'd get in without anybody knowing. He's had plenty of opportunity to do whatever he wanted to do before Dr. York's agoraphobia and after." She looked at Kelly again. "Why don't you review your files from your book tour and see if you can find a man who matches the description I gave you?"

As Kelly stood up and put the crutches in place under her arms, Winslow addressed Stevens. "You can go, Detective. I'll call you if I need you."

Kelly saw anger rising in Stevens's face. He was about to protest when Winslow added, "Since Dr. York doesn't leave the house, I'll stay here. And I'll keep two men outside around the clock."

Stevens didn't move; he looked at Winslow; then he looked at Kelly. "Goodbye, Dr. York," he said, as if he had to force the words out.

"Goodbye, Detective Stevens," she responded. This time she let him precede her from the garden toward the kitchen. She kept thinking about Agent Winslow's observation that she didn't really know when the surveillance equipment had been placed in her house. That meant she didn't really know how long she had been observed and listened to. Watching Stevens walk up the steps, open the glass door, and disappear inside, she felt forlorn and alone, even though she knew that the FBI was there to protect her.

Before heading for her office, she looked at Mary Ann Winslow again.

"What is it?" Winslow asked her.

"I don't understand," she said. "Why couldn't Detective Stevens stay?"

"Because it's my case and he's getting in the way," Winslow told her.

The FBI agent's coldness only made Kelly feel worse.

"I intend to catch this killer," Winslow assured her. "And you're going to make it easier for me if you cooperate."

Kelly felt she was being talked to as if she were a child. Still not feeling the reassurance she needed, she headed toward the door. She fully intended to cooperate with Mary Ann Winslow; she only hoped it would be enough.

As Stevens descended the front steps of Kelly's brownstone, he felt an overwhelming sense of remorse. He'd been taken off cases before, but the other times it had been because of departmental politics, not because of the way he'd conducted himself; this time he'd been kicked off because he'd misplayed his hand. He'd known that he was flouting Winslow's authority when he'd joined her and Kelly in the garden and when he'd gone with Kelly into her office instead of remaining alone with Winslow. That had been the kiss of death, hadn't it? Going with Kelly to her office; if he'd stayed in the garden with Winslow, she would have rebuked him for not asking her permission to be there when she'd talked with Kelly, but she might have let him continue to be part of the investigation.

And why had he gone with Kelly to her office? If he was honest with himself, it wasn't because he thought she needed his assistance in looking at her client list for Sheryl Doyle's name; it was because he didn't feel like giving Winslow the opportunity to tell him off. He could kick himself for acting so stupidly. He'd recognized Winslow for the power grabber that she was, but he'd thought he had enough value to the investigation that she'd put up with his transgressions. Obviously, he'd thought wrong.

It wasn't just his ego that was hurt; what hurt him was that he'd wanted to find the man who was targeting Kelly, and now he wouldn't even be able to help. He'd already called his captain to tell him that the FBI had stepped in; now he had to call him to say that he was no longer involved in the investigation.

Walking by the FBI car, he saw Broadbent's and Barr's heads bent down in concentration over Barr's laptop. They didn't notice him as he headed toward his car. It was just as well.

*

Broadbent glanced up briefly as Stevens crossed in front of the car, but seeing the hangdog expression on Stevens's face, he quickly looked down again at the computer screen. He could tell from the way Stevens was staring blankly ahead as he walked that Winslow had sent the detective packing. Broadbent was sorry that she had forced Stevens to go; he sensed that Stevens was a good man and a good detective. But in a way it made it easier. There would be no ambiguities; the FBI could take all the credit for finding the serial rapist and killer that was calling himself Antiochus.

Broadbent saw a new image coming up on the computer screen. A straight line with letters and numbers underneath.

"What's that?" he asked Barr.

Barr kept his eyes on the screen as he responded: "It's a link to a Web site. The packets are going to a Web site."

Broadbent watched as Barr clicked on the link to the Web site.

A second later, Barr shouted, "Fuck!"

Broadbent didn't need to ask Barr why he had cursed. On the screen were two thin, white rectangular boxes, one on top of the other. They were white because they were blank, waiting for whoever was at the computer to fill in the letters and numbers that would give him access to the Web site. Broadbent had seen blank boxes like these countless times before. The first box was labeled "User Name" and the second "Password."

Barr leaned back in the seat, closed his eyes for a moment, then opened them and gazed down again at the white boxes on the computer. "I'm not really surprised," he said to Broadbent. "Just disappointed. But that's silly of me. This whole thing was put together with a level of sophistication that shows this man knows his way around computers. He's not going to make any of this easy for us."

Now it was Broadbent's turn to lean back in his seat and close his eyes. In his mind he silently repeated Barr's curses.

Forty-Eight

SINCE THERE WAS NO surveillance equipment in Emma's apartment, Winslow decided to move down there to question Sarah and Emma about the workmen on the list she'd taken from Stevens. The apartment—a large L-shaped room containing a living room, a tiny kitchen, a dining area, and a bedroom nook—was more comfortable than Winslow had thought it would be. She sat on an easy chair, facing Sarah and Emma on the sofa. It soon became evident to Winslow that Sarah had been in charge of the work crew and that Emma knew nothing about the men at all. She just sat there, next to Sarah, tense, unhappy, and afraid while Sarah reviewed the names on the list.

"Ed Murrin's in his sixties, maybe even seventies, too old to match the physical description you gave us," Sarah said. "And Peter's twenty-four or twenty-five, so he's too young. I don't know the rest of the painters, but a few of them had dark hair and looked like they were in their midthirties. You'll have to ask Ed and Peter for the names. It's their painting company. The carpenters are in their fifties, and the electrician, Ivan, is older and weighs more than two hundred pounds."

She gave the list back to Winslow, who had already taken her cell phone from her purse and was now calling a number on automatic dial. "I've got something for you to check out, Broadbent," she said. "You're going to have to go back to the bureau and get another car."

Sarah was as tense as the E string on her violin. She couldn't hear what FBI Agent Broadbent said on the other end, but it wasn't much because Winslow continued almost immediately to tell him to come to the street entrance to Emma's apartment.

*

Kelly was standing with her crutches at the file cabinet, looking for the folders of the clients she'd seen in the last few days of her book tour, which had ended in Washington, DC. She remembered being pleased that so many people had signed up for consultations with her during the tour; now she wondered if even at that time one of them had already wanted to kill her and the other women that Agent Winslow had told her he had made his victims.

There was something different about how he was treating her, though, wasn't there? The other women had responded to an ad he'd placed; except for their interest in astrology, they seemed to have been selected at random. From what Agent Winslow had said, he hadn't called any of them and threatened them; he hadn't caused damage to their homes or caused them to have accidents before raping and murdering them; he hadn't spied on them.

Yet he had done all of this to her.

And something else was different, too. He had stolen her ephemeris and the term *intuitive astrologer*. It was horrible to think that he had used these words, her words, in the ads that had drawn his victims to him. And it was almost unfathomable to her that now he wanted to do to her what he'd done to them.

But what was reverberating in her mind was why, when she had done this dangerous man's chart five years before, had she not seen the potential for violence that lived in him?

In her consultation with him during the tour, it was possible that he'd put on a face that had fooled her. By the time she'd gotten to Washington, DC, she'd been traveling for two weeks, some days doing back-to-back interviews and then consultations, and she remembered being tired; when she'd met him, it was possible that she'd not seen through his mask. But when she'd gotten home to New York and done his chart based on his date, time, and place of birth, it should have been there in black-and-white—not the actual acts of violence, perhaps, not even that it was fated that he would do these monstrous things, but that he had the potential for hate to consume and destroy all his other feelings, the potential to want to hurt and kill.

How had she missed the possibility for him to be so violent? She'd started doing charts under her grandmother's tutelage when she was a young woman and had done them professionally since she'd finished her graduate work in psychology, and, to her knowledge, she had never missed anything so important. Had her desire to be positive rather than negative made her willfully blind to his potential for violence? Had she been so intent on finding a constructive interpretation for what the placement of his planets revealed that she had ignored the negative potential and just concentrated on giving him a positive perspective that she'd hoped would help him lead a good life?

As she brought the file folders she'd gathered to her desk, she told herself that besides looking at the men who'd had appointments with her around the date she'd noticed her ephemeris was missing and seeing if she'd taken any notes about the physical appearances of those in the right age range, she'd also review their charts to see what they told her now that she'd be looking at them with the benefit of hindsight.

She shouldn't need hindsight, of course. Astrology was a

science, and it was her job to practice it as a science. It disturbed her deeply to think that she might have avoided something so crucial because she'd been afraid to go into a place of potential evil. But if she'd made that mistake at the time, if she'd failed to live up to her job, this time, she vowed, she would not make the same mistake.

She heard a knock and looked up as Sarah opened the door.

"How are you doing?" Sarah asked quietly.

Kelly shrugged. "I don't know. How about you?"

"All right," Sarah said. "I came to see if I can help."

Kelly showed her the thirteen files she'd pulled from the cabinet. "Thanks. We're looking for a man who—"

"I know," Sarah said. "Agent Winslow told me. Late twenties or early thirties when you saw him five years ago, dark eyes, dark hair. She told me the psychological profile, too."

Kelly handed six of the files to Sarah. "Any men you find who match the description, bring me their files. I want to read their charts before I give their names to Agent Winslow."

Sarah nodded. Files in hand, she went into her office.

Alone again, Kelly suddenly felt anxious and dizzy, so much so that she found it hard to read the document in front of her. The words and numbers that she'd written on the page in the file before her appeared blurred; she had to concentrate for them to come into focus. She knew that in one of the thirteen folders was the information that Agent Winslow needed to find the man who had stolen her ephemeris and become a rapist and a murderer—if he hadn't already been one at the time that she'd seen him. The fact that he was going after her meant that her finding the information was a matter of life and death—her own life and death and the life and death of any other woman he might target in the future.

Forty-Nine

Stevens opened the door of his small, neat two-bedroom house in Jackson Heights and saw Diane sitting on the living room floor with Anthony, reading him a story. Usually, the sight of his wife and baby son enjoying each other filled him with such contentment that he was able to push aside thoughts about whatever case had been preoccupying him, but today the gloom he'd felt since leaving Kelly's brownstone was still with him and so was his preoccupation with the case.

He kept playing back in his mind the details Winslow had recounted about the serial killer's physical and psychological profile and wondering if it was possible that he'd actually seen the man as part of the work crew that had been in the brownstone when he'd first arrived there to interview Kelly. He also thought about what Winslow had told him about this man's skill in breaking into his victims' houses with no trace of his having been there except for the corpse of the victim that he left behind, and he wondered if Winslow was right, that the man might not have been part of the work crew, that he'd managed to break into Kelly's house and install the surveillance equipment without her knowing it as part of his methodical plan to terrorize her.

He was so immersed in mentally weighing the known and the unknown about this killer who was targeting Kelly that he hadn't even realized Diane had gotten up off the floor and come over to him until she gave him a kiss on the cheek.

"Why are you home so early?" she asked.

"I'll tell you later," he said, going back into his thoughts as he walked toward the kitchen.

Diane's eyes followed her husband. She knew he was working on Kelly York's case. She also knew she had to leave him alone with his thoughts so he could work through them.

"Do you want dinner?" she asked.

"I'll make it," he said, continuing to the kitchen. "It'll help me think."

Fifty

OF THE THREE FILES Kelly had looked at so far, one of them belonged to a man who had been twenty-nine when he'd had an appointment with her in Philadelphia, three days before she'd arrived in Washington, DC, and realized that her ephemeris was missing. His name was David Wheaton, he was a Taurus, and he was unmarried when she'd seen him. That meant that not only was he the right age to fit the description of Antiochus as in his midthirties today, but he'd been single, like the FBI profiler said Antiochus was.

The personal notes she'd taken on David Wheaton were scant, only that he was a pathologist who had been doing lab work in Philadelphia, where he'd grown up and gone to school, and that he wanted a change that would expand his life. She hadn't written anything about his eye or hair color, just that he had a friendly manner and seemed to be genuinely open. As she read the notes, she was disappointed to realize that nothing came back to her about what the man looked like.

She took out his chart and began to read it, looking for signs of the violence that would lead a man to become a rapist and killer. She noticed that his rising sign was Virgo, which meant that . . .

Her analysis stopped when Sarah came into her office with the file folders Kelly had given her.

"Sorry to interrupt," Sarah said, "but I've reviewed these and none of the men were in their late twenties or early thirties when they consulted with you."

As she put the files on Kelly's desk, the phone rang. Kelly looked across the desk at Sarah and saw in her eyes the same fear that she was feeling. Kelly hesitated a moment, letting the phone ring again. It was her office phone, and she'd heard it ring thousands of times before, but this time the ringing sounded louder and more shrill.

Sarah reached for the phone, but Kelly picked it up before Sarah could answer it.

"Kelly York," she said. She felt her throat constricting again; she hoped that if it was Antiochus, he did not hear the anxiety in her voice. "May I help you?"

Sarah watched Kelly's face, afraid that Kelly was talking with the man Agent Winslow was looking for. She reminded herself that the call was being traced, but even that didn't reassure her. All at once she saw Kelly's face relax into a smile.

"Of course," Kelly said, handing the phone to Sarah. "It's Connie."

Sarah took the phone, greeted Connie, and listened. "I don't think I can go," she said after a while. Then she cupped the phone. "Connie wants to call a rehearsal in forty-five minutes."

"Of course you can go," Kelly told her.

Sarah continued to cup the phone. "But don't you want me to help you—"

"There are only five files left from that part of the tour, and I can go over them myself," Kelly said adamantly.

Sarah didn't budge. "I think I should stay with you."

"There's no need," Kelly told her. "Agent Winslow is here, and she's going to have two men outside the house all night.

Nothing's going to happen to me."

Sarah still looked doubtful. "Are you sure it's okay?"

"I'm sure," Kelly said.

Sarah uncupped the phone and brought it back up to her ear. "I'll be there in half an hour." She hung up and looked at Kelly. "Thank you. But if you change your mind—"

"I'm not going to change my mind. I can read through the files, and I'm well taken care of. And Emma's here if I want company."

"Okay. Just as long as you know—"

Kelly stood up. "I know, Sarah. And I love you for it." She walked around her desk and gave Sarah a hug. "Now go and rehearse."

Sarah lingered a moment longer; then, seeing that the fear had gone from Kelly's face, she left Kelly's office and closed the door behind her.

Kelly returned to her desk and went back to David Wheaton's chart. Once more she began the task of looking for evidence in the location of his planets at the time of his birth that he might become the rapist and murderer who had killed four women and zeroed in on her. She was glad she'd made Sarah go to rehearse for her concert, that she'd been able to pretend to her that she wasn't scared; inside, as she stared at David Wheaton's chart, she was still shaking, and she had to work hard again to concentrate and make her eyes focus so she could read the words and symbols in front of her.

Fifty-One

His work space had just enough light for him to admire once again the precision of the two keys to her house that he'd made the week before. He'd had to file the zigzagged teeth on both keys several times to get them just right. He didn't enjoy filing; in fact, it was the one part of his job he didn't like. But it gave him pleasure to think about how he'd "borrowed" the keys to her house and made impressions of both of them in the soft wax without her knowing it.

Of course, that wasn't unusual. No woman he'd chosen ever knew what he was doing until he wanted them to. It was amazing how easy it was, providing you knew, as he did, how to create a situation that would get you into their lives without their realizing why you were there. Until it was too late, of course; then it didn't matter; then they were yours anyway.

He glanced at the leather cord next to him on the workbench. Seeing it, he started to grow hard in anticipation of what he was going to do with it. His next conquest was a proud, beautiful woman, a woman he particularly looked forward to bringing down. He'd been thinking about it and thinking about it, and now he was ready to do it.

Fifty-Two

KELLY OPENED THE LAST folder of the seven she'd been examining and found that it belonged to Arthur Jones, whom she'd seen in Baltimore, the day before she'd gone to Washington, DC, the last city on her book tour. Arthur Jones, an Aries, had been forty, married to Nona, a Scorpio, age thirty-nine, with one child, Niel, also an Aries, age three.

She closed the folder; Arthur Jones was outside the age group on which Agent Winslow had told her to concentrate.

Besides Wheaton, she'd found two other men who were in the right age range: Fred Nugent, a Virgo, who'd been thirty-three when he'd seen her in Philadelphia, and Scott Green, a Gemini, who'd been thirty-one when he'd seen her in Washington, DC, the morning she'd noticed that her ephemeris was missing. Like Wheaton, both men had been single and therefore fit the FBI profile. Also as with Wheaton, Kelly had taken few notes of her impressions of them. She'd written that Nugent had seemed lethargic and somewhat lost, and Green had seemed a classic type A personality. Not much to go on in either set of notes, but she also had their charts.

She pulled Fred Nugent's chart from the folder and began to look at the placement of the planets at the time of his birth. It showed that Saturn was in the first house, conjuncting his ascendant. Everything she saw pointed to the extreme lack of energy she'd observed during their consultation. She wondered if anyone who had been born with the challenge of finding enough vitality to live could possibly be taking the lives of others. She looked up from his chart and shook her head; it just wasn't possible.

Scott Green's chart showed Leo rising, which was in keeping with what she'd noted as his type A drive to achieve. But there was a softer side to him, too: his Venus in Pisces would give him a natural empathy and caring for women. He wouldn't want to hurt them.

Fifty-Three

BROADBENT HAD NEVER DRIVEN to Brooklyn before. Fortunately, the FBI garage was only a few blocks from the FDR Drive, which he took down to the Brooklyn Bridge. From there he proceeded onto the Brooklyn-Queens Expressway into Brooklyn, where the GPS led him to the house he was looking for at 1732 Cadbury Avenue. If it hadn't been for the traffic, the trip would have taken half an hour instead of an hour. He wasn't generally an impatient man, but waiting in heavy traffic always frayed his nerves. He consoled himself with the thought that Winslow had sent him on his own for what could turn out to be the key part of the investigation; if his mission bore fruit, he would be the first investigator to discover Antiochus's real identity.

As he drove up to the two-story light blue-shingled house, he saw two pickup trucks parked in the driveway. One truck was five or six years old, the other was older than that; both were beige in color except for a sign painted in black script on the driver's door that said Ace Painting with the phone number underneath and, below that, the words *homes & offices*.

Broadbent walked up to the white door of the light blue house and rang the bell. Before long, a woman he judged to be in her mid to late thirties opened the door and blew a cloud of cigarette smoke in his face.

"What do you want?" she asked. She was wearing tight jeans, a pink tank top, and a heart-shaped pendant on a chain. She looked too young for her voice to be as gravelly and ravaged as it was, but the cigarettes had already done their damage.

"I'm Eric Broadbent," he said, showing her his badge. "I'm with the FBI. I want to ask your painters some questions."

She finished another drag on her cigarette before she asked, "They do something wrong?"

This time he'd moved out of the way so he wouldn't get smothered by the smoke. "No. I just have some questions for them."

She moved out of the doorway. "Be my guest."

Broadbent walked into the house and found himself in a small foyer that opened onto a large living room, where he saw two painters. The living room was covered with drop cloths, and the painters were on ladders, painting the ceiling with rollers. One of them was in his sixties or seventies, with gray, almost white hair and hunched shoulders. The other was a gangly blond man in his early twenties. Broadbent had gotten the information Sarah had provided to Winslow about the painters. From the descriptions he'd been given of the men who ran Ace Painting, he recognized the older man as Ed Murrin and the younger man as Peter Heath.

He approached the older man and took out his badge. "FBI. Your wife told me you'd be here. I understand you painted Dr. York's brownstone."

Ed Murrin had stopped painting and was looking down at Broadbent, upset. "Why? Is there a problem with what we did?"

"No," Broadbent said, "but I want to ask you about the rest of your paint crew. Any of them in their midthirties, average height and build, brown eyes? Maybe brown or black hair."

"Yeah, I guess," Murrin said. "Ernie Guerrero, for one. Ernie's about, what—?" He turned to his younger partner.

Peter Heath thought a moment. "Thirty-five, thirty-six. I'll give you his number. You can ask him."

Broadbent frowned. "Does Mr. Guerrero have an accent?"

"Yeah," Heath told him. "Spanish. He's from the Dominican Republic."

"I'm looking for someone without an accent," Broadbent said, addressing both men.

Murrin laughed. "Then you've come to the wrong guys. Besides Guerrero, we got men from Puerto Rico, Albania, and Turkistan. They're not so great at English. We practically need a full-time translator to get the job done."

Broadbent was so disappointed by what he'd heard that he almost forgot his customary manners, but as he headed out of the living room, he remembered to turn around and say, "Thanks."

"What's this about?" Heath asked him.

Broadbent continued toward the front door. "Sorry. Can't discuss it."

"Good luck, whatever it is," Murrin called after him.

Broadbent was too discouraged to respond. The lady of the house was still standing in the entry, smoking. She'd heard everything that was said, and Broadbent could tell that she'd been intrigued by it. Before she could ask him anything, he thanked her and left the house. Once he was outside, he took out his cell phone and called Winslow.

"It's Broadbent," he told her. "None of the painters can be Antiochus. The guys who are the right age and physical description all have accents. The hotel clerk said Antiochus speaks without an accent."

"Okay," Winslow said. "But like I told Stevens, the son of a bitch we're looking for didn't need to block up the chimney to give himself an opportunity to get in. If Antiochus wants to get into a house, he gets in. Period. Good work. You've eliminated a futile lead."

It was rare that Winslow paid him a compliment, but it did little to lift Broadbent's spirits. "What next?" he asked with a sigh.

"Barr's still trying to trace his Web site, and Dr. York's going through her records from her book tour for men who fit our profile."

Broadbent didn't say anything.

"One of them is Antiochus," Winslow told him. "The same sick mind that set up the cameras and the microphones to watch her before he comes here for the kill. Kelly York is the prize, the one he's been working up to. He doesn't believe anybody's smart enough to see the link between the ephemeris getting stolen and him. You'll see. We're going to get him."

This time Broadbent spoke. "What do you want me to do now?"

"Go back to the office," Winslow said. "I'll call you as soon as something develops."

Broadbent waited until he clicked off the phone call before he sighed again. He was still disappointed that his trip to Brooklyn had yielded nothing, and now that it was late afternoon, he knew he'd be facing even heavier traffic on his return to Manhattan.

Fifty-Four

PLAYING JANÁČEK'S STRING QUARTET no. 1 in her tiny apartment with the other members of her quartet—another violin, a viola, and a cello—filled Sarah with exquisite sadness. Janáček, she knew, had found his inspiration for the piece in Tolstoy's novella, "The Kreutzer Sonata"; the music he wrote expressed the anguished life of the book's tragic heroine, a woman pianist whose jealous husband shoots her because he's convinced she's been having an affair with the violinist with whom she has been playing Beethoven's passionate *Kreutzer* sonata.

Sarah knew from her research that the married Janáček also had had another inspiration: his own unfulfilled love for a woman almost forty years younger than he. Janáček's music expressed such longing, such frenzy and mournful beauty that she wouldn't have had to know any of this to feel its elegiac power. As she played it, she thought about herself, and she mourned the end of her relationship with Kevin. She thought about Kelly being in danger; she prayed that Kelly would be safe, and her sadness and her prayers infused every note she played on the violin and made them more fervent and sorrowful. She hoped that the music, like a prayer, would rise to heaven, and God would hear it and make everything all right.

Fifty-Five

KEITH BARR WASN'T THE kind of man to give up, but he'd spent hours in the front seat of Winslow's car, working with his laptop and he was still stuck, unable to trace the broadcast from Kelly's house to the computer on which the killer was receiving it. He'd tried hundreds of user names and passwords, everything from Antiochus, followed by assorted numbers, to each of the astrological signs to various arrangements of the words and letters in *astrologer* and in the name *Kelly Elizabeth York*, to key words from the ad in *You and Your Sign*, and he'd gotten nowhere. He'd tried getting around the necessity for a user name and password, but that hadn't led him anywhere, either.

As he'd told Broadbent, the man who'd set up the mini-cams and microphones and transmitted the broadcast to Kelly York's computer was sophisticated; he knew his way around the technology.

Suddenly, Barr thought of another combination of user name and password that Antiochus might be employing. The cursor was in the "User Name" box, so all he had to do was type the possible user name: *Kelly Elizabeth York*. When he'd typed the last letter, he moved the cursor to the "Password" box and typed the word *dead*. Then he clicked to enter them to see if they worked.

The same message he'd read hundreds of times before appeared on the screen: *Invalid username or password*.

There was no one in the car with whom he could share his

frustration, but he cursed anyway. It didn't make him feel any better or any closer to tracing the broadcast back to the man they were looking for.

✳

As Kelly approached the door that led down to Emma's apartment, she felt apprehensive, and realized that since she'd become agoraphobic she'd never gone down there. She hadn't avoided it. She just hadn't needed to go to Emma's apartment, but now she did, because Mary Ann Winslow was there.

Kelly didn't understand why she should suddenly feel so nervous about going downstairs. Although she'd become terrified when faced with the prospect of leaving her house for the outside world, she'd never felt nervous about going into the garden, so why was her stomach upset as she walked toward the door to Emma's apartment? Was it because the garden's high walls made her feel protected? But Emma's apartment was just as much part of the brownstone as the garden, if not more so; and its walls and ceiling should have made her feel at least equally protected. So why was she feeling like this?

She walked slowly with her crutches down the hall toward the door, trying to build up her courage. In her right hand she was carrying the three men's files. When she reached the door, she switched the files to her left hand and opened the door with her right hand. Looking down the narrow staircase to the apartment below, she started breathing harder and sweating.

Emma appeared at the bottom of the staircase and looked up at her. For an instant, the older woman's face showed the strain under which they were all living; then Kelly saw Emma put on a smile, playing the charade that Mary Ann Winslow had asked them to play in case the camera and microphone in the first-floor hall was picking up their conversation.

"Do you need something, Kelly?" Emma asked.

"I was just looking for Mary Ann," Kelly said.

"She's down here, visiting with me," Emma responded pleasantly.

Winslow joined Emma at the bottom of the staircase and called up to Kelly. "I was just waiting until you finished your work," she said, keeping up the pretense that she and Kelly were friends. "If you're through for the day, why don't you come down here with us?"

In the doorway at the top of the stairs, Kelly felt dizzy; she leaned on the crutches to support herself so she wouldn't fall; she knew there was no way she could go down the steps. She tried to make her voice sound casual and cheerful. "Why don't we go back into the garden? It's so pretty this time of day."

Kelly saw Mary Ann Winslow's friendly expression turn to one of annoyance; then the FBI agent cleaned up her act. "Sure. I'll be right up."

"I'm too tired," Emma improvised. "If you two don't mind, I'll stay here and watch my television programs."

"You and your television programs!" Winslow said. She indicated to Emma with an approving nod that Emma had done the right thing in choosing not to join them; then she started climbing the steps toward Kelly.

By this time, Kelly could no longer bear standing at the top of the staircase. She moved away from the doorway into the hall so she would no longer have to look down the stairs.

*

Kelly preceded Winslow down the steps from the kitchen into the garden, but Winslow quickly caught up to her. Out of the range of the surveillance equipment, Winslow again dropped her imitation of friendship. She eyed the folders and said with an edge to her voice, "It took you long enough, but I see you've got something for me."

Kelly handed the folders to Winslow. "I found three men who would be the right age now. All of them were also single at the time. David Wheaton, Fred Nugent, and Scott Green. But my notes don't indicate that any of them showed particular interest in astrology except for how I could use it to help them make choices about their futures. Two of them discussed possible job changes. That's why a lot of people see me."

Winslow was already sitting on one of the benches and opening the first file. "What about build, eye color, hair color?"

Kelly remained standing, leaning on her crutches. "I didn't write anything down about what they looked like. But I reviewed their charts, and none of their charts show the potential for violence."

Winslow gave a tight laugh and looked up at Kelly. "You don't really take astrology seriously, do you?"

Kelly felt her face grow hot with anger. "Of course I do. Do you think I'm a fraud?"

"No. I just assumed you saw it as . . ." Winslow shrugged and thought a moment before she continued. "As some sort of game you engage in with other people. A superstition. Like you said, people come to you so you can predict their future. You don't really think you can predict their future, do you?"

"No, I don't," Kelly said, "and I never tell anybody that I can. But I do think I can help them see their unique strengths and the pitfalls they can fall into because of where their planets are." She focused her dark blue eyes on Winslow and spoke with intensity. "You said you wanted my impressions. I don't remember these men from my consultations with them, but who they are is in their charts. Their charts give us more than impressions of them. They tell us what they are like, what they are capable of. Their charts tell me that none of these men has the potential to be a rapist and a killer."

Winslow stood up. "The only thing you've told me of value is that these three men are now in their thirties, they were single, and they had appointments with you just before you realized your old ephemeris was missing." Holding the files, she walked toward the rear entrance of Emma's apartment. "Forget their charts," she told Kelly. "Leave the investigation to me. One of these men is Antiochus."

Despite the coolness in the afternoon breeze, Kelly's face was burning again. She didn't like Mary Ann Winslow, and she didn't like the fact that the FBI agent didn't respect her. But ego had no place here. What was important was finding the man who had raped and killed four women and had made Kelly's own life hell.

"What date were you born?" Kelly asked.

Winslow stopped walking and turned to face her. "February twenty-eighth."

Kelly stood there looking at the hard, attractive woman in front of her with blue eyes lighter than her own and filled with condescension. She was so taken aback that she didn't know what to say.

"What's wrong?" Winslow asked her.

"Nothing. It's just that you and I were born on the same day."

Winslow gave Kelly a triumphant little smile. "Then that proves it, doesn't it? We're nothing alike. I'm not afraid to leave my house. And I don't waste my time with superstition."

"Both of us being born on the same day means that we're both Pisces, but that doesn't mean we're the same. We were born in different years, at different times, in different places, so each of our charts is unique. But we do have some things in common. We're both creative problem solvers. We're both emotional, although obviously you think you can hide your feelings. And you're pretty good at it. Your intense emotions are all part of being a Pisces. But you can't hide how much you care, and in your own way, you care about helping people. Like me, one of the things you care about deeply is your work."

"You're right," Winslow said, doing nothing to hide her annoyance. "I do care deeply about my work. So let me start checking these men right away."

Kelly watched Mary Ann Winslow descend the steps to Emma's apartment and disappear inside; she had never met a woman as stubborn and prone to conflict with other people as Mary Ann Winslow. She would not be surprised if she had Leo rising and a moon in Scorpio. She hoped that the FBI agent's rigidity and need to be right would not stand in the way of her finding Antiochus before he raped and killed again.

✳

Walking into Emma's apartment, Winslow found herself resenting Kelly's attempt to analyze her character. How dare Kelly be so presumptuous, so personal, and so intrusive? And how off base to say that Winslow was emotional and hid her feelings. Everyone who knew her knew how she was, Winslow said to herself. Indeed, she'd often been criticized for being too frank.

Rather than continuing to think about it, she sat down at the table, called headquarters on East 57th Street, and asked for Gail Rothman, a junior agent. Once she got Gail on the phone, she read her the names and contact information of the three men Kelly had identified from her files as fitting the description.

Winslow had wanted to have Broadbent do the computer search on the men, but he was still in transit from Brooklyn, so she'd had to rely instead on Gail, whom she knew to be responsible and a fast worker.

Gail immediately began accessing all available information on the men and was now viewing David Wheaton's driver's license, which contained his age and physical description as well as a photograph of David Wheaton staring stiffly into the camera.

"David Wheaton," she said, "thirty-four years old. Five foot eight, brown hair, brown eyes. He doesn't live in Philadelphia anymore. He lives in Seattle." She called up Wheaton's most recent tax return to see what it had to tell her. "As of last April fifteenth, he was still single, and he was unemployed."

"Have the Seattle bureau see where Mr. Wheaton's been for the last week," Winslow told her.

"Got it," Rothman said. She tried getting Fred Nugent's driver's license, but nothing came up. The same happened with this year's income tax return. What finally came up instead was his death certificate. "Fred Nugent died three years ago," she told Winslow. She typed Scott Green's name into the government system and instantly saw his driver's license on the screen. "Scott Green, thirty-six, still lives in Baltimore. Five foot ten, black hair, brown eyes." It took her only three seconds to pull up his IRS return. "He's single. I guess you want me to call the Baltimore bureau."

"Right," Winslow said. "And tell Seattle and Baltimore to get back to me directly."

Winslow clicked off the call and sat back in her chair. With one suspect dead, that left only two men who could be Antiochus.

Fifty-Six

Two FBI AGENTS, BOTH male, stood at the door of the large wooden house in the Queen Anne Hill area of Seattle that David Wheaton listed on his driver's license and income tax return. It was one thirty p.m. Seattle time, and they hadn't expected that Wheaton would necessarily be home, but they saw a car in the driveway, which might well mean that he was. They already had their badges out just in case.

The door was opened by a woman in her thirties who had a round face, long brown hair, and inquisitive light brown eyes.

"We're here to see David Wheaton," the older agent said.

The woman's eyes changed from inquisitive to alarmed. "He's at work," she told him. "Can I help you?"

"Are you Mrs. Wheaton?" the younger agent asked.

"There is no Mrs. Wheaton. I'm Joan Morris. Mr. Wheaton is renting part of my house."

The older agent took over the role of questioner again. "Where is Mr. Wheaton employed?"

"He works in the lab at the Seattle Medical Center. Why?"

The agents ignored her question. The older one asked, "Is Mr. Wheaton at work today?"

"As far as I know. Why do you want to see him?" Joan Morris persisted.

The agents ignored her question again. "Thanks, Ms. Morris," the younger one said as they turned away and started down the broad wooden steps of the house.

Joan Morris walked onto the porch, crossing her arms over her chest as she watched the FBI agents head to their car. David Wheaton had been renting the top floor of her house for only seven months; he seemed like a nice man, but she realized that she didn't really know him. She hadn't needed to rent half her house to someone else; she'd done it because she felt she could use the company. Now she wondered if she'd made a mistake.

*

The FBI agents, one male, one female, who arrived at Scott Green's row house in Baltimore weren't as lucky as the Seattle agents. There was no car in the driveway or the garage, and no one was home to help them locate where Green might be. The three envelopes sticking out of the mailbox next to the front door were addressed to Green, however, and since they were bills and all were postmarked yesterday or the day before, the agents concluded that Green still lived there.

"Not much mail," the female agent remarked. "If Green's gone up to New York like they think he has, looks like he left yesterday or today."

"Could be, or could be he's been up in New Jersey and New York all week doing his dirty deeds, and he's got a post office box somewhere else where he's getting other mail," her partner proposed.

"Could be," the female agent said, "or could be he has someone picking up the mail for him while he's out of town."

"Or could be he just doesn't get a lot of mail."

This was a game the two agents played; they called it the *Hypothetical Game*. It made them see different possibilities that would explain the facts that they had in front of them, and it passed the time. Having run through the hypotheticals about the three pieces of mail, they put an APB out on Green's car. Running through the hypotheticals, they figured the car would be found on a street or in a parking lot in or just outside of New York or in the parking lot of Baltimore-Washington International Airport or of Baltimore's Penn North railroad station.

✳

The FBI agents in Seattle found the Seattle Medical Center downtown on East Pike Street. The three floors of the building were filled with doctors' offices, and the medical laboratory in which Joan Morris had told them David Wheaton worked was in the basement. The middle-aged woman who sat at the reception desk had the name *Pat Lister* on her identification badge. In response to the agents' questions, Ms. Lister confirmed Wheaton was working that day—she had seen him fifteen minutes before they arrived—and that he'd been working overtime for the past three weeks because they were short-handed. Just to be sure they were getting accurate information about the man they were looking for, one of the agents pulled up Wheaton's driver's license on his smartphone and showed it to her; she confirmed that yes, that was David Wheaton.

As they were talking, through the open doorway behind the receptionist's desk, the agents glimpsed Wheaton for themselves. Leaving the Seattle Medical Center, one of them called Winslow in New York and told her that Wheaton was not the man that she was looking for.

✳

After her argument with Mary Ann Winslow, Kelly walked slowly on her crutches toward her office. She was in a bad mood;

on one level it seemed ridiculous to her that arguing with the FBI agent should put her into such a funk when the woman was there to protect her and find the killer, but on another level it was a relief to feel the normal feeling of anger at having to deal with someone as disagreeable as Mary Ann Winslow instead of the fear that had been overwhelming her.

She let herself into Sarah's office and was about to close the door when King howled a greeting and ran in to join her. She wondered if he had to go out for a walk and remembered how much she used to like taking him for walks on Central Park West or on one of the paths that wound through Central Park. Now if he needed to go out, she could only let him into the garden and then clean up after him, or ask Emma or Sarah to walk him.

If the serial rapist and killer was caught before he made good on his threat to get even with her for whatever he blamed her for, was her life always going to be like this? Limited by the walls of the brownstone and the garden, trapped inside as if she were hiding to save her life?

"Do you want to go out, boy?" she asked King. "Do you want to go into the garden?"

The dog looked up at her and rubbed up against her, apparently just wanting to be with her and not needing to go out. Blocking the view of the mini-cam in the hall, she closed the door to Sarah's office and then went into her own office with King right behind her. He seemed to be looking at her crutches, trying to figure out why she suddenly had these long wooden appendages to her body.

"Don't worry, boy," she said. "They're just temporary."

She put her ephemeris on the desk and was about to go to her chair when she noticed that the files she'd eliminated because the men didn't match Agent Winslow's criteria were sitting in a pile and needed to be returned to the cabinet. Leaning on the crutches, she reached down and, with her right hand, tried to pick up all ten files at once. For a moment she thought she was successful, but one of the files fell out of her grasp and landed on the floor, spilling its contents.

She propped the crutches against the desk and, keeping her weight off her right foot as much as possible, bent down to pick up the manila folder and the papers it had contained. She picked up the initial information sheet and saw that the file was Arthur Jones's. She remembered reviewing it and seeing that five years ago, when she had seen him on the last leg of her book tour, Arthur Jones had been forty and married with one son.

She put the page back into the folder and her eyes fell on the chart she had drawn for him. It had fallen upside down, so that, from the angle at which she now viewed it, the astrological houses that should be at the bottom of the chart were at the top and those that should have been at the top were at the bottom. Instead of reaching for the chart, she just stared at this new configuration. Before, when she was reading through the files, she was so anxious that her eyes had blurred; now she was seeing perfectly clearly. She extended her hand, picked up the chart, and turned it right side up. Then she rose to her feet.

"Let's see what this has to tell us," she said to King.

✳

The FBI agents in Baltimore were alerted by the local cops who'd gotten the APB that Scott Green's car was parked in a lot at Baltimore-Washington International Airport. His parking ticket had been stamped at 10:17 a.m. yesterday morning. They decided to check the airline rosters to learn the destination to which Green had flown. While they waited for the airlines to give them the information, they played the Hypothetical Game and came up with different possibilities for why Green might have taken a plane to the New Jersey–New York area when the drive was just over three and a half hours.

Could be the man was in a rush. If he was the serial rapist and murderer, could be he'd targeted a woman he wanted to get to right away. Or could be he wasn't going to the New Jersey–New York area at all; could be he had a sense the FBI was closing in on him and he'd flown to a country that didn't have extradition.

✳

Kelly brought Arthur Jones's chart into the garden and waited for Agent Winslow. It was close to five o'clock and, knowing that the garden would be cooler than it had been an hour before, she had put on a heavier sweater. Standing by the steps that led to the rear door of Emma's apartment, she could hear Winslow ending a call by telling whoever was on the other end of the phone to check New York hotels, cabs, car rentals, and limousine companies.

When Winslow came up the steps from Emma's apartment into the garden, she was perturbed. She gave Kelly a look that told her whatever she had to say was a waste of time.

"It's Arthur Jones," Kelly said excitedly, ignoring the FBI agent's attitude. "He's Antiochus, the man who raped and murdered those women."

Winslow stared at her. "Who is Arthur Jones?"

Kelly gave her the file. "I did his chart in Baltimore, the day before I went to Washington, the day before I noticed my old ephemeris was missing."

Winslow opened the folder in the fading daylight and looked at the first page of the file. "Arthur Jones was forty when you saw him. He'd be forty-five now, and we know that—"

Kelly didn't let her finish. "You don't know how old the man who's calling himself Antiochus is. He could be forty-five and only have looked younger to the clerks at the hotels."

Winslow was still reading the information in the file. "Arthur Jones is married and he has a child. That doesn't fit our profile."

"That's only what he *told* me," Kelly said. "But he could have lied. If I'm right, he can't help lying. He—"

"I just got a call about Scott Green," Winslow told her. "He took a plane from Baltimore to Newark Airport yesterday. This is the fifth time he's made the trip this month. Four of those dates coincide with the dates on which victims were raped and murdered. Green fits our profile. We think he's our man."

"But it's not in his chart," Kelly said adamantly. Despite her effort to control herself, she was angry at Mary Ann Winslow all over again. "I told you that when I gave it to you!"

Winslow looked at Kelly levelly. "What suddenly makes you think it's Arthur Jones? Is there something in the notes you took about him that reminded you of the threats you've been getting on the phone?"

"No," Kelly said. "It's his chart. That's what tells me it's him."

Winslow didn't say anything; she just looked at Kelly with her usual reserve.

"I realized something about Arthur Jones's chart," Kelly continued. "It tells me he has the potential for cruelty and violence. At first I didn't even look at the chart I'd prepared for him, because I was doing what you said, only trying to find men who'd be in their midthirties now. Since I didn't look at his chart, I didn't ask myself what it would mean if he'd given me the correct birth date but the wrong birth time. But then his chart fell on the floor, and when I picked it up, I looked at it, and I realized . . ."

She stopped for a moment and started over again intently. "I think his real birth time was twelve hours later than the birth time he gave me. I've had it happen before, when clients inadvertently misread the time on their birth certificate or they wrote it down wrong, and they think it's a.m. when it was really p.m. Then they find out and call to tell me their mistake. But I don't think Arthur Jones made a mistake at all. I think he did it on purpose to test me."

She looked at Mary Ann Winslow to make sure that she was listening. "Antiochus is calling himself an *intuitive astrologer*, like me. I think he lied during our consultation and gave me the right birth date but told me his birth time was nine a.m. instead of nine p.m. because he wanted to see if I was intuitive enough to recognize what he'd done and to know who he really was and what his chart should show about him.

"He had to give me the right date, because he had to give at least one astrological clue to who he is, but the time—that's where the test was. He was daring me to know intuitively just from being in the room with him that he couldn't have been born at nine a.m. that morning. To be who he is, he had to be born twelve hours later.

"That kind of devious test would go along with everything you've told me about Antiochus. And it goes with what I see in Arthur Jones's revised chart. If he was born at nine p.m., everything would make sense."

"How?" Winslow asked, no longer quite as reserved.

"If he was born at nine p.m.," Kelly said, "the planets would have been in different houses than they would have been at nine a.m. So that means they paint an entirely different picture of him. If he was born at nine a.m., like he told me he was, his Mars would be in the fourth house and his Mars would have been squared to Pluto in the seventh house, which would make him the victim of angry people who lied to him. His challenge would be to learn to stand up for himself and commit to his capacity to heal, which he would've had in abundance. That's what I told him, because I believed his lies.

"But if he was really born at nine p.m., Mars would be in the tenth house, and if he gave in to his anger, he would be mad at the world. At nine p.m., Pluto is conjunct with his ascendant and his moon. He could be the *agent* of violence. He could want to get even with everybody, especially women, because of his mother. She would have been obsessive and controlling and cruel.

"Lying would be as easy for this man as breathing. He said he's married, but he told me his wife's name is Nona. Nona as in none, nonexistent. He said his son was named Niel, like the Latin word *nihil*, nothing. Arthur Jones's wife and son aren't real. He made them up, and he gave me the clues to know that if I'd been intuitive enough to realize he was lying. Arthur Jones could steal my ephemeris as a point of pride, and he could rape and kill without regret. That's not who Scott Green is."

"How do you know that?" Winslow asked. "How do you know Scott Green didn't test you by giving you the incorrect birth time, too?"

"Because I recalculated his chart and David Wheaton's by changing their birth times by twelve hours, too," Kelly told her, "and either way, the charts didn't show them having the slightest propensity to be murderers." She looked at Mary Ann Winslow and spoke as if her life depended on it. "I feel strongly that it's Arthur Jones. Please. Please just see if it's him."

Winslow closed the folder. Despite herself, she'd been thinking about what Kelly had said earlier about her being emotional but hiding her feelings, and she realized that it was true. She was emotional, and she hated letting other people see it. If Kelly was right about her, maybe Kelly was right about Arthur Jones. "All right," she said finally.

Fifty-Seven

FBI AGENT GAIL ROTHMAN learned that Scott Green had checked into the New York Skyway Hotel on 6th Avenue and 53rd Street that day just before one p.m. Now Rothman was standing in the hotel corridor, outside room 359, waiting for Green to answer the door. Winslow had wanted Broadbent to call on Green, but Broadbent was stuck in his car on the Brooklyn-Queens Expressway, so Rothman had to go in his place, and she took fellow agent Howard Gary with her as backup.

The door to the hotel room was opened by a dark-haired, dark-eyed man whom Rothman recognized as Scott Green. His shirt was half open, and even before they spoke, he looked at the two FBI agents anxiously.

"Scott Green," Rothman said, holding up her badge so she could see it. "We've got some questions for you."

Green ran his hand over his perspiring forehead. "Come in."

*

Stevens's fourteen-month-old son, Anthony, was sitting in his high chair as his father cut a piece of chicken for him. When Stevens finished cutting a small slice, he lifted it on a fork to Anthony's mouth. Anthony opened his mouth, took the chicken off the fork, and smiled proudly as he started chewing it. Usually, this expression of infant prowess tickled Stevens and made him laugh; tonight he was too absorbed in his thoughts to be pulled out of them, even by Anthony.

Diane was setting the table for dinner. She looked at her husband and saw that instead of sitting in his chair with his usual straight posture, he sat with his huge shoulders drooped, as if he were carrying a physical burden.

"What's the matter?" she asked.

Still holding Anthony's fork, he turned his tall frame toward her. "I'm worried about Dr. York."

"I thought you said the FBI was there."

"They are," Stevens told her. "But I'm still worried."

Diane continued looking at her husband. She expected him to say more, but he became silent again and returned to feeding his son.

*

By the time Winslow called into the office to check on Arthur Jones, Broadbent was back at his desk. Now he was looking at Arthur Jones's driver's license on the computer screen. Although the man was forty-five, his photograph showed that, as Kelly had suggested to Winslow, Arthur Jones had a youthful face.

"Arthur Jones is five nine, with brown eyes and brown hair," he told Winslow. "His address is Woodman Turnpike, Sienna, New Jersey."

"Sienna is just across the George Washington Bridge, isn't it?" Winslow asked him. "Not very far from any of the victims."

"Yes, and that's not all," Broadbent told her.

He'd googled Jones's address to see if there was a photo of the place where Jones lived. When he described what showed up in the photo, Winslow's attention was riveted.

✳

Scott Green sat on the sofa in his hotel room, drinking a glass of water. He seemed nervous, which Rothman and Gary both took as a sign that Green had something to hide.

"I'm a business consultant," he told them. "The reason I've flown up to New York so often in the last week is because I have a client here, but I have other clients in Baltimore that I need to service, too."

Rothman decided to focus on his activities during the time the most recent victim was raped and killed in Tarrytown. "What were you doing last night?" she asked.

"Last night? I was having dinner with a vice president of RMA Bank."

"After dinner," Gary said, picking up where Rothman had left off, "say three or four in the morning?"

Green looked away embarrassedly. When he faced the FBI agents again, he said, "Actually, I was sleeping with her. We've been having an affair. She works for the client, so I shouldn't be doing it, and if this comes out, I'll be fired. But it's the truth. I can give you her phone number if I need to prove it."

"You do," Rothman told him.

"I should know it by heart, but it's programmed into my phone," Green said, "so I never learned it." He got up from the sofa and went over to his jacket, which was hanging on the back of a chair.

Rothman's cell phone rang. She opened it and saw that it was Winslow. As she watched Green looking up his lover's phone number on his smartphone, she told Winslow that it looked like a dead end with Green. At first Rothman was surprised that Winslow seemed to take the news in stride; then Rothman listened to what Winslow had to tell her. When Winslow was done, Rothman hung up, turned to Gary, and told him to stay with Green and check out his alibi.

"Where are you going?" Gary asked her as she headed out the door.

"Broadbent's coming to pick me up."

That was all she said. In the meantime, Green had gotten his lover's number from his phone and written it on a piece of the hotel's notepaper. When he handed the number to Gary, Gary was so involved in wondering about what Rothman and Broadbent were doing that he had to remind himself why they'd wanted the number in the first place.

*

Kelly had sat on one of the stone benches and listened in silence as Winslow had made the phone calls. She knew that Winslow was excited by what her first phone call had revealed about Arthur Jones, excited enough to make the second phone call and send FBI agents to question him. But so far, the FBI agent had said nothing to Kelly; she'd made her calls and acted as if Kelly weren't even there.

Finally, she turned to Kelly and spoke. "You may be right. Arthur Jones matches the physical description and he lives within an hour's drive from all four victims and from the locations where the calls were placed to you. But it's not just what he looks like and where he lives that makes it possible he's Antiochus. It's what was in the photo of his property."

Winslow's pretty face became animated, as if the knowledge she was about to impart were an aphrodisiac. "Jones has horses. And the women were strangled with a leather cord, like the kind used for horse reins."

Fifty-Eight

IT WAS EARLY EVENING when two agents from the Newark office of the FBI pulled onto the shoulder of Woodman Turnpike, opposite the horse farm. The agents, both men in their thirties, drew their guns as they got out of the car. They closed their car doors, but not all the way, because if Arthur Jones was home, they didn't want him to hear the sound of metal against metal in the quiet evening.

The moon lit their way in the darkness as they walked across the asphalt road to the farm, climbed over the white wooden fence, and lowered themselves onto the grass. The meadow in which they found themselves was bordered by a forest. They ran over to the trees and used them as a cover as they proceeded swiftly toward the house and barn about four hundred yards away. The one-story house had lights on inside; the barn was dark.

Inside the barn, a five-foot-nine, youthful-looking man of forty-five with brown hair and brown eyes, wearing a black sweater and black jeans, was sitting at his worktable. Earlier, he'd closed the shutters of the window in the workroom he'd built for himself, and now he was working by the light of the architect's lamp that he found so helpful when he hypnotized women who responded to his ads for an appointment with Antiochus. The man was Arthur Jones. In his left hand he was holding a new set of horse reins that he'd bought; in his right, a pair of scissors. He opened the scissors and put one side of the rein between the two blades; then he cut off a piece of the leather, making a cord of the size he liked to use to strangle the women he conquered.

After cutting off the cord, he returned the scissors to a drawer under the worktable. In the drawer was an ephemeris, the one he'd bought to replace the ephemeris he'd taken from Kelly York—Dr. Kelly Elizabeth York—which had recently been stolen from him in one of the hotels. Next to his new ephemeris was the mirrored disk he used for hypnosis, a box of surgical gloves, and the sharp-pointed tool he'd made from the alidade of an astrolabe so he could mark the corpses of his conquests with the astrological sign that they had been born with.

Beside the surgical gloves were some of the needles he'd gotten from his mother's house after she died. The needles she had inserted under his fingernails when she'd caught him playing with himself. That's what she had called it when she'd come into his bedroom in the middle of the night to check him. It had been the first time he'd done what he'd heard other boys in school talking about, and it had felt good, until she'd pulled the covers back and, when she saw what he'd been doing, slapped him and screamed at him, made him pull up his pajamas; then, while he was crying, humiliated, she had gone to get sewing needles and stuck them, one at a time, under each fingernail and watched the blood trickle from his fingertips onto his bed.

For years before that night, she had locked him in the closet because she'd found him wetting his bed; now the closet seemed like a haven to him. He'd never had needles under his fingernails in the closet; he'd just sat on the floor, in the dark, holding his knees, alone and safe from her for a few hours.

From the night that she found him playing with himself, he was afraid to do it again, and he never did, but she put the needles under his fingernails anyway, to make sure, she said, that he didn't. And she told him, as she'd told him since the earliest time that he could remember, that he was bad because he'd been born with ill-disposed planets and that it was he who made her stick the needles under his fingernails, because he was bad and would do bad things if he wasn't punished.

When he was a child, the needles had been shiny; he remembered how they had sparkled after he had cleaned them—as his mother had always made him do—of the blood that he'd gotten on them when she'd stuck them into the flesh beneath his fingernails. Now the needles he held in his hand were tarnished.

Kelly Elizabeth York was tarnished, too. She wasn't the intuitive astrologer she claimed to be; otherwise when he'd met her in Washington, DC, despite the lies he'd told her, she would've known who he really was, wouldn't she?

It gave him pleasure to think of how he'd fooled her and how he'd surpassed her. He'd told her he wanted her help in finding a career, but he'd found the career he'd been searching for on his own. It had taken him time to plan for the work he was now doing, but he had practiced along the way, without having all the details in place, of course. Now that he'd worked out his plan and what he thought of as his trademark, there was no limit to what he could do. No limit at all.

He'd surpassed Kelly Elizabeth York as an intuitive astrologer in other ways, too; he could use his intuition to insinuate himself into people's lives, and he could tell them not only about their lives but about their deaths, too.

Looking at the needles, he thought about the morning four months earlier that he'd discovered his mother's body, dead and cold, in her bed. In that moment it had come to him, clearly—as clearly as if someone had spoken to him—that this was the job, the vocation, he was born for. He would stop battling what his mother called his ill-disposed planets and stop trying to hold back the rage and violence that he had inside him; he would use it to fulfill his destiny and empower his work. He'd accomplished so much in the three months since his mother died.

And tonight he'd be working again.

He heard the horses neighing in the stalls outside the workroom and wondered what was troubling them. He had three of them, and one was particularly skittish. Maybe an animal was on the property; foxes were common in the area, and wolves were not unheard of. But the sudden roiling in his gut told him it could be something else. He turned off the lamp, leaving the workroom in utter darkness, opened one of the shutters a few inches, and peered out. In the moonlight, two men were walking from the woods toward the house and barn. They were both carrying guns. There was no way he could get past them without being seen.

He opened a second drawer under the worktable and grabbed his gun. Taking aim through the open space between the shutter and window frame, he shot at the man nearest him and watched him fall to the ground.

The second agent turned toward the barn and fired in the direction from which Arthur Jones had fired his shot, but the barn was dark, and the agent had no idea where the shooter had fired from.

It wouldn't have mattered anyway; Arthur Jones, gun in hand, had already fled the workroom and was running out the rear door of the barn and toward the woods. As he picked up speed, he heard a man shouting at him.

"FBI! Drop your gun, Jones, or I'll shoot!"

Still running, Jones looked over his shoulder and saw that the man who had fallen to the ground wasn't dead but was running after him, gun raised. He was the one shouting.

"Do you hear me, Jones? Drop your gun!"

Jones turned around, took aim, and missed.

Broadbent and Rothman were climbing over the fence onto Jones's property when they heard shots. They looked and in the moonlight saw Jones running across the field to the trees and the two New Jersey FBI agents shooting at him. It was evident that one of their bullets hit Jones's shoulder, because Jones broke his gait, stumbled before he regained his balance, and put his hand up to his shoulder. Suddenly, he stopped running and pointed his gun at the men behind him.

"Fuck you!" he screamed, and shot at the agent he thought he'd killed before. The man collapsed and dropped onto the lawn.

By now Broadbent and Rothman had their guns out. The sharp sounds made by the firing of the two guns overlapped. It was impossible to know whose bullet hit Jones or if both bullets did, but Jones fell down just before he reached the trees. Broadbent and Rothman kept their guns raised as they ran over to Jones's still body, not knowing if he was alive or dead.

As they neared him, Jones didn't move; his hand was clenching the handle of his gun, but his arm was outstretched on the grass, and his eyes stared without consciousness at the full moon. Broadbent, his gun still ready, knelt down next to Jones and saw the reflection of the moonlight in the puddle of blood that had collected on his chest. He knew there was no reason to check Jones's pulse, but he put his fingers to Jones's neck. Nothing.

Broadbent glanced up at Rothman and got to his feet. Together they walked toward where the New Jersey FBI agent had fallen to the earth. The man's partner was already approaching them. He was shaking his head and walking slowly. He didn't have to say a word to let them know the state of his partner.

Minutes later, Broadbent and Rothman were in Arthur Jones's cell-sized workroom. Broadbent stood at Jones's worktable, looking at the leather cord that had been cut from the set of reins and the open drawer that held the ephemeris, the box of surgical gloves, the mirrored disk, the piece of old brass that had been honed to a point almost as sharp as a needle, and four discolored needles, the kind used for sewing. He could see how Arthur Jones could have used the mirrored disk to hypnotize potential victims, but he wondered what the old needles had been used for. Still thinking about it, he took out his phone and called Winslow.

"Jones's dead," Broadbent told her. "He got one of our men first. But he's the one, all right."

Winslow answered immediately, "I'll be right there."

✳

When she hung up with Broadbent, Mary Ann Winslow turned to Kelly. "You were right. It was Jones." She realized that she admired Kelly, but she showed her no sign of approval.

"They killed him?" Kelly asked.

"Yes. You've got nothing to worry about anymore."

Kelly soberly absorbed the news. She'd been correct about Arthur Jones; he'd been the man who had raped and killed the four women, who had covertly entered her house, pulled up the runner on her staircase, and put in surveillance equipment so he could see the effects of the accident he'd caused and her fear when he'd called and threatened her. And now he was no more.

She felt as if she'd been facing a black void that would swallow her up and make her disappear, and now all at once the blackness was gone. But nevertheless, she felt she was still facing the void, the void of incomprehension. She knew from Arthur Jones's chart that he had been filled with hatred, that he'd been capable of conscienceless rape and murder, but that didn't mean that she understood it. And the four women he had raped and murdered were still dead.

She looked at Mary Ann Winslow. "Those poor women . . ."

"At least we got him before he got you," Winslow said.

Kelly nodded gratefully.

"Thank you," Winslow said finally. With a strain in her voice, she added, "If it weren't for you, we wouldn't have gotten him."

Before Kelly could say anything, Winslow turned away from her and made a call on her cell phone. "Barr, it's Winslow," she said. "Forget about trying to trace the broadcast back to the SOB's computer. And tell them to take the monitor off Kelly York's phone. We got him, and he's dead."

Fifty-Nine

EMMA WAS IN THE kitchen when Kelly told her the news. She was so jubilant, she threw her arms around Kelly, crutches and all. "Thank God!" Emma said.

Kelly looked into the soft gray eyes of the woman she'd known longer than anyone else in the world. Emma's relief and happiness were so powerful that Kelly finally allowed herself to feel relieved and happy, too.

"Yes," Kelly said. "Thank God."

"We've got to tell Sarah," Emma told her.

Kelly watched Emma hurry to the phone on the counter and make the call.

"Sarah, it's me, Emma. They shot the bastard. He was one of Kelly's clients from her book tour."

As she talked to Emma on her cell phone, Sarah was walking toward her parents' house in Bensonhurst. After the rehearsal, she'd taken the subway from Manhattan and had gotten off at 18th Avenue, four blocks away. She was carrying her violin case in her other hand as she held the phone to her ear. What she'd heard from Emma made her so joyous she started to cry.

"It's what I prayed for!" she said.

"Me, too!" Emma told her.

"I'm so happy," Sarah said, still crying. As she continued walking, she listened to Emma's account of what had transpired.

When Emma finished telling her all the fine points, Sarah asked her to send Kelly her love and to tell her she'd see her in the morning. Then she put her phone in her coat pocket and dried her eyes. Her spirits lifted for the first time in days. Not even thinking of Kevin for the moment, she started whistling Brahms's Hungarian Dance no. 5, a melody so rapturous that it always elated her to play it. Whistling it as she walked down the street, she felt she was serenading the whole neighborhood with her joy. In the light of the street lamp, she saw the truck with the Ace Painting sign on the door in the driveway of the Heaths' house, five houses up the block from her parents'. Peter, still wearing his painting coveralls, came out of the garage and waved to her.

"Hi, Sarah," he said. "If you're looking for your father, I just saw him drive away."

Sarah stopped walking as Peter reached into the back of the truck and took out a ladder.

"I guess I should've called him first," she said, "but I thought I'd catch him at the house and we could go to see my mother together."

Peter put the ladder down on the driveway and ran his hand through his messy blond hair. "Sorry you missed him."

Sarah smiled. "That's okay. Nothing could ruin my mood at the moment."

Peter smiled, too. "Why not?"

"The FBI found the man who was threatening Kelly."

"Someone was threatening her?"

Sarah saw the surprise in the face of the young man in front of her and realized that the threat had become so pervasive in Kelly's, hers, and Emma's lives that she'd assumed Peter knew about it, too, because he'd been painting Kelly's house.

"I forgot you didn't know," she said to him. "We were told not to talk about it."

"So that's why the FBI came to talk to Ed and me today about the guys we hired to paint the brownstone with us. They thought it might be one of them."

Sarah nodded. "But it wasn't. It was someone else. And now it's over. I can't wait to tell my parents the good news."

Peter picked up the ladder. "Say hi for me, all right?"

"I will." Sarah was about to start back to the subway station when she turned to Peter again. "How's your Dad?"

"He's doing okay. Thanks for asking."

"Say hello to him."

"Sure thing."

Peter lifted the ladder onto his shoulder and headed toward the garage. Sarah began whistling Brahms again as she started her walk back to the subway station. She'd forgotten what it felt like not to be scared; what it felt like was a miracle.

✳

Emma opened the refrigerator and surveyed the contents of the shelves. "What should I make for dinner to celebrate?" she asked Kelly.

"I don't want you to make anything," Kelly said, leaning on her crutches and putting cat food in Meow's bowl while Meow and King were jumping up on her, waiting to be fed. "I want you to go out with Donald."

"But—" Emma protested.

"I mean it, Emma," Kelly said, overriding Emma's objection before she could make it. "There's no reason to stay home with me. I'm perfectly fine."

Emma looked at her and considered. "Well, Donald did call

and—"

Kelly interrupted her again. "Then it's settled."

Emma closed the refrigerator and watched as Kelly propped the crutches against the counter and put her weight on her left foot so she could bend down to put the animals' bowls of food on the floor. "I'll be home by midnight," she said to Kelly.

Kelly stood up and placed the crutches under her arms again. "You don't have a curfew. You don't have to be home by midnight."

"You know what my mother said," Emma said with a mischievous smile. "There's nothing you can do after midnight that you can't do before midnight if you want."

Kelly laughed and so did Emma. It felt good to laugh together again.

✳

Winslow stood with Broadbent over Arthur Jones's body. She stared at the undistinguished face of the serial rapist and killer and wondered as she had in the past when she'd encountered evil in its human form why this man had lived as he'd lived and devoted himself to inflicting suffering on others and then taking their lives. She knew that psychologically there were reasons for it. There always were. Although in Jones's case she might never learn what they were. Kelly York had seen it in his chart. If you believed in astrology as Kelly did, the arrangement of the planets at the time of Jones's birth reflected the existence of conditions that had made him who he was, psychologically, emotionally, intellectually; they had shown his potential to succumb to darkness or to seek healing, and he had succumbed to darkness.

But even if the planets reflected the conditions that had created Jones's potential for darkness or light, there was another *why* that Winslow could not answer: Why had Jones been born

on that particular date at that particular time? If she believed in
God, Winslow might have said that God had chosen that time
for Jones. But she knew from her Sunday school classes that God
also had given man free will, and that meant that Jones had chosen between light and darkness for himself, and that still left her
with the question. Why?

She saw that men from the local coroner's office were bringing stretchers to take away Jones and the felled FBI agent. For
a moment, she mourned the loss of a colleague; then, her wall
of reserve up again, she turned to Broadbent. "Did you call
Detective Stevens to tell him about Jones?"

Broadbent shook his head.

Winslow took out her cell phone. "Might as well call him and
let him know we've done our job."

✳

Kelly finished trimming the fat off a piece of lamb that she
was going to broil for her dinner. She was about to chop the
broccoli she'd washed when the phone rang. She was so used to
reacting to the sound with apprehension that she felt her body
tense up, and she had to remind herself that it was over and she
could relax. He wasn't calling anymore; he was dead.

Picking up the phone and hearing her son saying, "Hi, Mom,"
she laughed, and once she started, she found it hard to stop.

"What's so funny?" Jeff asked her.

"Myself," Kelly said. "I just . . . " She took a deep breath to
calm herself down. "I just scare myself sometimes over nothing.
How are you, darling?"

"I'm okay. What were you scared of?"

Kelly could hear the distress in her son's voice. "I told you,
honey," she assured him, "it's nothing. I'm fine. Just fine."

"Okay," he said, sounding better. "I just want to make sure you are."

"You don't have to take care of me," Kelly told him. "I'm a grown-up. I can take care of myself. You have enough to do taking care of yourself."

Jeff laughed. "That's true," he said, "especially taking five courses this semester."

Kelly smiled; she loved knowing how hardworking and responsible an adult her son was becoming.

"Love you, Mom," he said.

"Love you, too, honey."

"Only a few more weeks until Thanksgiving and Julie and I come home."

"Can't wait," Kelly told him.

Hanging up the phone, she felt that things were finally back to normal. Then she looked into the hall outside the kitchen, saw the front door, and felt her body tense up again. She was still afraid to leave her house. And that meant that even though her life was no longer in danger, things might never really be normal again.

Sixty

Sarah sat next to her mother's bed, filling in her parents on the events of the last few days and their victorious outcome.

"He told Kelly on the phone he was going to get even with her because she made a woman leave him," she said. "But it turned out he didn't have a wife or girlfriend, so Kelly never consulted with a woman who was thinking of leaving him. He must've just said that so she wouldn't be able to figure out who he was."

Sarah was about to tell her parents what Emma had recounted to her about Kelly realizing who the man was from reworking his chart when she noticed that her mother was staring at her. Not staring with fascination or relief or confusion but with alarm. Sarah wondered if something had happened to her mother related to the stroke; then she saw that Rose's lips were parting and she was trying to speak, but no sound was coming out of her mouth.

"What is it, Mom?" Sarah asked.

Sam pulled his chair over to his wife's bed, too. "What is it, doll?"

Rose closed her lips and tried again; this time a word came out. "Helen," she said.

"Helen?" Sarah asked.

With great effort, Rose nodded.

Sam turned to his daughter. "She must mean Helen Heath."

He faced his wife again. "Helen Heath?"

For a moment, Rose just stared at him, her lips moving noiselessly. Then she said, "Yes."

Sixty-One

KELLY STOOD IN THE greenhouse with her crutches, picking herbs to go with the lamb she was making for dinner. It had been a long day, and so much had happened that she was still in the process of absorbing it all. The moon shone through the greenhouse roof, illuminating the plants with a white glow, making the night seem magical. She gathered a handful of sage and rosemary, left the greenhouse, and walked up the slate steps. As she opened the rear door to the kitchen, she heard the phone ring, and for the first time in days didn't feel frightened. She locked the door and walked with her crutches to the phone, wondering if Jeff was calling back or if it was Julie or Michelle and Mark.

The phone was still ringing when she picked up the receiver. She was about to say hello when she heard a man's whispered voice, the same voice that she'd heard before.

"So you don't have a monitor on your phone anymore," he whispered.

At the sound of his voice, Kelly stopped breathing and felt herself growing faint. Only the crutches were holding her up. "I thought you were—"

"It doesn't matter what you thought I was," he whispered, venom in every word. "What matters is that I know what you did. You told her to leave. You didn't care about me. You didn't care about what my life would become."

Kelly's mind was whirling in confusion. She didn't know how he could still be alive, and she didn't know what he was accusing her of, but whatever it was, she knew he was wrong. She struggled against blacking out as she cried, "That's not true. I—"

He continued as if she weren't speaking. "Just like now I don't care about your life," he said.

She couldn't listen to him anymore; she just couldn't, not if she wanted to keep her sanity. She slammed the phone down and looked around the kitchen at the familiar things that she lived with every day and tried to remind herself that she was safe. She told herself she would call Detective Stevens.

The sharp crack of shattering glass broke the silence like a gunshot. She turned and saw a man letting himself into the kitchen through the garden door. His hand was reaching through the broken pane of glass to unlock the door. She stared at him, transfixed and frozen.

"Guess I don't need this anymore," he said, opening the door and slipping his iPhone into his pocket.

He was in his early twenties, tall and thin, with a tangle of blond hair, and he was wearing coveralls stained with paint. She'd seen him that morning and the day before when he was painting her house.

She continued staring at him, barely breathing. It was hard for her to speak, but she did. "I know you . . ."

"No, you don't know me," he said. "You just know I painted your house. You don't even know my name, do you?"

As he looked at Kelly, his light brown eyes were as cold as his whispered voice had been on the phone. She could see how much he hated her. And he was right; she didn't know his name.

"Peter," he said. "Peter Heath. Does the name *Heath* ring a bell?"

Still staring at him, Kelly wished she could give him the right answer; she knew that her life depended on it; but she couldn't. His name meant nothing to her.

King ran into the kitchen, carrying his new bone. He looked at Kelly and Peter. Kelly waited anxiously as the dog looked from her to the man who had invaded her house. She expected King to pick up her fear and to attack Peter, but the dog, the bone in his teeth, walked over to Peter, wagging his tail.

Peter petted King's nose and spoke to him calmly in a manner that King would interpret as affectionate. "So you like my little present," he said.

The dog nuzzled against Peter.

"Let's play a game," Peter said. He gently pried the bone from King's mouth and tossed it into the front hall. King immediately ran after the bone. When the dog was in the hall, Peter closed the door, leaving King on the other side of it and him and Kelly alone in the kitchen.

"You gave him the bone," Kelly said, meeting his gaze.

Peter smiled. "I figured it would make this easier." He reached into his pocket and took out a wood scraper with a blade as sharp as a knife and held it up for Kelly.

"I could've killed him," he said, "but I've always liked dogs. And besides, I was saving this for you. It's got a beautiful blade, don't you think?" He glanced admiringly at the thin, pointed blade. "Look at the power of it, Kelly."

She felt her helplessness as she stood there on her crutches, gazing into eyes that despised her and that wanted to see her dead. The knife she'd been using to cut the lamb and vegetables for her dinner was on the other counter, out of her reach; all she had to fight him with was what she knew about people.

"Don't let it control you, Peter," she said. "You're bigger than that blade. You have the power to put it aside."

"Don't try to mind fuck me!" he shouted at her, his face reddening with rage.

Kelly heard King jumping up and scratching the other side of the kitchen door. She turned toward the door, hoping to find that he'd been able to open it, but Peter had closed the door tightly and King's attempts did nothing but produce futile noise.

"Poor King," Peter said to her with mock sympathy. "He can't protect you."

He looked as if he was going to say something else, but before he did, the phone started to ring.

"Don't answer that!" he shouted.

As the phone continued ringing, he came closer to Kelly with the razor-sharp wood scraper. On the fourth ring, the answering machine picked up, and Kelly heard her recorded voice answering as it had so many thousands of times before. "This is Kelly York. Sorry I can't get to the phone. Please leave a message."

There was a brief pause and then a beep before Sarah's voice came through the answering machine.

"Hi, Kelly. It's Sarah. It's probably not important anymore, but I thought you should know. Peter Heath's father, Joe, he's a drinker, and he used to be Ed's partner in Ace Painting. Joe's wife, Helen, came to you for her chart just before she left him. It must've been twenty years ago. I know the FBI says it's the man they shot who was calling you, but I thought you should know about Helen leaving Joe after she saw you, since the man on the phone kept blaming you for making a woman leave him. I'm sure it doesn't matter. See you tomorrow."

Kelly heard a *click* as Sarah ended the phone call. Then she heard the tape with her greeting rewind. All the while she silently repeated to herself the name *Helen Heath*. Desperately, she searched her memories to find the woman who matched the name, going back twenty years to when she'd been twenty-one years old and her grandmother had been alive. She and Jack had been living in Kings Point, and she'd been pregnant with Jeff. She hadn't started doing charts professionally then; she'd done only one or two of them because her grandmother had asked her to.

She remembered doing the first chart . . . Then she remembered Helen Heath.

She looked at Peter and saw that his face had turned white, but his eyes were filled with no less rage and his hand still held the blade steadily as he pointed it at her chest from two feet away.

"I remember your mother," she said quietly. "My grandmother asked me to do a chart for Sarah's mother, Rose. Rose was my grandmother's nurse. Your mother was Rose's friend. Rose asked me to do her chart."

Peter said nothing; he just looked at her, and she could see that beneath his rage was a deep hurt, a hurt that she knew could be just as deadly as the anger it had turned into. But she felt that if she could make him hear her . . . if only she could make him hear her . . .

"I never told your mother to leave," she said. "And she wouldn't have left, even if I had. She loved you too much to leave. I remember her talking about you. It touched me how much she loved you."

"Liar!" he screamed. "You made her leave!"

"Peter, please listen to me—" she begged.

He advanced on her with the blade. "I didn't even know what happened till my father got so sick I had to give up my job in California to fucking come home and take care of him! That's when he told me that she saw you, and that the next day she walked out! That's why I asked Ed if I could take over for my father on his painting crew, so if your house needed painting, I could get in here. And it did need painting, didn't it? And then you had your 'accident' on the stairs."

He looked at her, not with satisfaction about the success of his plans, but with anger so great that it consumed him. It made his body rigid with hate, and Kelly knew that if she could not stop him, it would lead him to end her life.

"I told you, Peter, I—"

He stopped her again. "You made him suffer, and I wanted him to see you suffer. And we did. Both of us. That's why I put the surveillance equipment in here, so we could both see you suffer!"

"Your father made your mother suffer," Kelly said, trembling. "I remember, because she cried the whole time she was talking to me. She—"

"Shut up!" he screamed.

"Your mother was scared of him," she continued, "but she wanted to stay because of you. She wanted to know what she should do to get him to stop drinking, so he wouldn't beat her. She asked me to do his chart for her, and I did. And I tried to—"

Before Kelly knew it, Peter grabbed her, knocking one of her crutches to the floor as he pulled her around and held the blade to her throat. "My whole life would be different if it wasn't for you and your fucking astrology!" he shouted.

She could feel the blade's edge against the skin of her neck. All at once something came to her, not something she remembered from her talk with Helen Heath, but something that she *felt.* "You tried to protect her from him, didn't you? You were only four or five. There was nothing you could do—"

"I said shut up!" This time his voice wavered.

Terrified, she forced herself to continue. "Then he turned his anger on you."

"Because you made him!" he shouted. "Because you made her leave! It all happened because of you."

She heard him start to cry, and she could feel that although he was still holding the blade to her neck, his hand was shaking and the blade was no longer pressing against her throat. A surge of adrenaline shot through her, and she reached up, took hold of the wood scraper, and pulled it down and away from her with all her strength. It came loose from his hand and fell to the kitchen floor. Instantly, she swooped down and picked it up, and as he bent down to take it from her, a primal violence rose within her. She picked up the crutch that had fallen to the floor and started beating him over the head with it until he slumped to the floor, unconscious, his head bleeding.

With the blade in her hand, she moved on her crutches as rapidly as she could to the kitchen door where King was scratching and howling. She opened the door and hurried down the hall toward the front door, unlocked both locks, opened the door, and faced the street. Standing on the threshold, looking out onto 85th Street, she was breathing hard and her body was drenched with sweat. She gripped the doorjamb, scared to leave and scared to stay.

She heard a sound behind her and turned to see Peter coming out of the kitchen, getting his bearings. In his hand was the large knife that she'd used to prepare her dinner.

King had been with Kelly; now he ran toward Peter as Peter started unsteadily down the hall toward the front door.

"Get out of here, you fucking dog!" Peter shouted at him as King ran through his legs. He pushed King out of the way and continued toward Kelly.

Kelly turned toward the street again. Her heart was beating

so fast she felt it would burst. Death was only a few steps behind her, but looking out on the street it felt like death was in front of her, too, that she would literally die if she went outside onto the tree-lined street that she had known all her life.

In that instant, she knew only one thing: She wanted to live, not only for herself, but for her children. Closing her eyes, she let go of the doorjamb, crossed the threshold onto the stoop, and, opening her eyes, descended the steps on her crutches, ignoring the pain in her ankle. Reaching the sidewalk, she realized that she was still alive, and she kept going.

Knife in hand, Peter ran onto the stoop. Enraged by what Kelly had done to him, he was determined to kill her even if it meant stabbing her in the street in front of anybody who might be walking by. He was so intent on catching up to her that he didn't notice King until the dog ran between his legs, and Peter felt himself stumbling over the husky's strong, muscular body and falling onto the cement steps.

Kelly was across the street before she allowed herself to glance back over her shoulder. She was startled to see Peter Heath sprawled headfirst down the steps of the brownstone. He wasn't moving. King was sniffing him.

She stood where she was and started to catch her breath, full of wonder that she had escaped death by daring to do something that had seemed impossible to her for so long. She was outside the brownstone; she was like everybody else who could leave their houses. It was what people did; it was what she had done her whole life until the day after Julie had left for college.

But that wasn't exactly true, was it?

She *hadn't* done it for her whole life; there was another time that she'd been afraid to leave the brownstone. It was a long time ago, when her grandmother was alive. It was when she'd first come to live with her grandmother after her parents died.

For several months she'd been afraid to leave her grandmother's side. That had meant that the only place she'd go besides the three floors of the house was the garden, where her grandmother would come with her. Her parents had left so suddenly that she'd been terrified of being abandoned again by the only family she had left.

Little by little her grandmother had taught her about astrology and had increased her trust in the world, and eventually she had gone out of the house again. But late this past summer, with Jeff already away at school, Julie's leaving for college, too, had triggered her fear of abandonment all over again. That was why she'd been afraid to leave the brownstone. But she was no longer afraid.

She'd known that Pluto's conjuncting her Mars and Mars's squaring her Pluto would bring up the past, secrets, things that had been hidden. She had been right: the reason she'd been agoraphobic had been hidden in her past all along. And so was the reason that Peter Heath had wanted to kill her. She had found the key.

She heard the shrill sound of brakes and turned to see that a black car had sped to the curb in the middle of the street. A man well over six feet tall jumped out of the car, and she recognized that it was Detective Stevens.

"Are you okay?" he asked, running up to her.

"Yes." She looked at Peter Heath again. He was still not moving.

Stevens took out his gun and ran up to Peter's body. Kneeling down, he could see that Peter had fallen onto a knife and that the cement beneath where the knife had entered his chest was covered with blood. He also saw that Peter was still breathing, and as he listened, he heard him faintly crying. He kept his gun on Peter, took out his cell phone, and made a call.

"Get me an ambulance," he said into his phone.

Slowly, Kelly walked on her crutches toward her house. She stood on the sidewalk and looked up at Stevens.

"How did you know?" she asked Stevens.

"I can't explain," he told her. "I just kept thinking, what if Winslow was wrong? What if it wasn't the same man?"

Kelly looked at Peter Heath's body on the steps and heard his whimpering. "He kept saying I made his mother leave his father," she said to Stevens. "I don't believe his mother left. I don't believe she could. I believe his father would've killed her if she tried. I was very young, and I remember how frightened I was for her. I think you should look for her body."

*

Joe Heath's hands shook as he stood in the basement of his house, watching two men from the police department digging a hole in the earth beneath the cement he'd poured twenty years before. Behind him was the worktable where he'd sat drinking his beer and watching Kelly York, thanks to the cameras and microphones his son had planted in her house. His hands weren't shaking because he was afraid. He *was* afraid, but his hands always shook when he hadn't had a drink for a while, and he'd had to stand there with two detectives for an hour, at least, without a beer or anything stronger to give him courage while the other policemen had jackhammered through the cement and then used crowbars to lift the broken chunks off to the side so they could shovel into the dirt.

He knew the policemen were getting close. He brought a hand to his face and felt it shaking as he touched his cheek, trying to comfort himself, telling himself that it didn't matter anyway. His eyes stayed on the cop who was digging nearest him. The cop had already dug out three shovelfuls of dirt. Now he was digging a fourth shovelful. The cop threw the fourth shovelful of earth onto the cement and was about to dig into the ground again when he stopped and stared down into the hole. Joe Heath saw what the cop saw: the bones of a rib cage. He started sobbing, his whole body shaking; he knew it did matter. He had killed his wife, and for all these years, he had hidden it from everybody, including his son; there was no hiding it anymore.

Detective Stevens looked at the bloated old man with the dull eyes and red, blotchy face, body and soul ruined by alcohol. As Stevens watched the detective from the Bensonhurst division put the cuffs on Joe Heath, he thought of Heath's son in the hospital and wondered if Peter would survive the wound in his abdomen that he'd gotten from falling on the knife. Then Stevens thought about Kelly; he had to call her to tell her that she'd been right again. Helen Heath had never left her husband; she'd been there all the time. Hidden. A dark secret of the past.

Epilogue

It was the Saturday after Thanksgiving, and Kelly was at Merkin Hall for Sarah's concert. She loved being there to hear Sarah play, and she loved wearing the red dress she'd bought for the occasion. The dress symbolized her sense of freedom: freedom to come and go from her house as she chose, freedom to enjoy her life. She liked being able to go to an event that she cared about and wear a special dress just for the hell of it. She liked being able to enjoy the way the dress looked on her, the way the vivid red contrasted with her blond hair and her dark blue eyes and the way its cut accentuated her height and her trim figure. She was no longer afraid to be herself.

She loved that Jeff and Julie were there with her to hear Sarah. They sat on either side of Kelly, holding her hands. Looking at them, she recognized once again that they were handsome, vital young adults, even though they were and always would be her children.

Emma was there, too, sitting between Jeff and Sarah's parents, Rose and Sam. Rose had been home for three weeks and was able to get around with a cane; she was rehabilitating more quickly than the doctors had first predicted. Kelly saw the pride in Rose's and Sam's eyes as they waited for the curtain to rise on their daughter's quartet. The aisle seat next to Sam was empty, and Sam had placed his coat on it. Every now and then he'd glance over his shoulder as if he was expecting someone.

Kelly leaned over Jeff and Emma. "Who's the seat for?" she asked Sam.

"Our future son-in-law," Sam told her. He smiled at Kelly mysteriously, and she noticed that Rose was smiling, too.

The house lights began to dim, and Kelly turned her attention to the front of the concert hall. A moment later she felt Jeff moving beside her and, looking in his direction, saw Kevin taking the empty seat next to his future parents-in-law. Kevin met her eyes and smiled warmly, and then all of them sat back in their seats and focused on the stage.

Under the brilliant stage lights, Sarah's quartet started walking onto the stage. Sarah was first to enter. She looked radiant in her long black dress, carrying her violin, her back straight, her black hair shining like onyx. She walked to her chair and gracefully sat down. As the other members of the group took their seats, Kelly reflected that, since the time of danger was over now, it was the time for second chances and adventure. That's what she'd seen in the stars, and it was already happening around her. Kevin had broken up with his fiancée, Sarah had given him another chance, and they were starting over; maybe it was time for Kelly to call Chris Palmer and apologize to him and hope that he would give her another chance, too. And if he wouldn't, then, for the first time in a long time, she knew that she was open to meeting someone.

Sarah applied her bow to her violin and, with the other members of her group, played the haunting first notes of Janáček's String Quartet no. 1. As the rich melancholy music filled the hall, Kelly lost herself in its beauty.

About the Author

GEORGIA FRONTIERE WAS AN author, a businesswoman, a performer, and a philanthropist—a woman who lived life to the fullest.

Frontiere was born in St. Louis, Missouri, to Lucia Pamela Irwin, Miss St. Louis of 1926, KMOX radio's "gal about town," and the leader of America's first all-girl orchestra, and Reginald Irwin, an insurance salesman and businessman.

Frontiere had early aspirations to work as an opera singer, eventually travelling to Milan to train with the Milan Opera. By the age of ten, she was performing along with her mother and brother in the singing group the Pamela Trio. The group traveled the state and entertained at ballrooms and state fairs. A few years later, the family moved to Fresno, California, where Frontiere performed at dinner theatres alongside her mother in a duo, the Pamela Sisters.

In the late 1950s, Frontiere moved to Miami and had her own television interview show. Later, she made appearances as part of NBC's *Today* show cast. She also performed as a night-club singer in Miami.

While living in Miami, Frontiere was introduced to the then Baltimore Colts owner, Carroll Rosenbloom, at a party hosted by Joseph Kennedy at his Palm Beach estate in 1957. Frontiere married Rosenbloom, who became her fifth husband, in 1960.

In 1972, Rosenbloom traded ownership of the Baltimore Colts for ownership of the Los Angeles Rams. During this time, the couple resided in Bel Air, California, and Frontiere became a part of the Los Angeles social scene, hosting numerous parties and philanthropic events. Tragically, Rosenbloom died in 1979 in Golden Beach, Florida.

Upon her husband's passing, Frontiere inherited a majority ownership stake in the Los Angeles Rams. She was often dubbed the first female owner of a National Football League franchise, although the NFL reported that she was actually the second female majority owner. However, during Frontiere's tenure, she was the only active female majority owner in the NFL.

During her years as owner, Frontiere moved the Rams twice. In 1980 she relocated them from the Los Angeles Memorial Coliseum to Anaheim (a deal Rosenbloom made in 1978). Then she moved the team to St. Louis in 1995.

Throughout her career, Frontiere was devoted to a range of philanthropic causes. In 1991, she made a $1 million donation to the Fulfillment Fund, which provides support systems to help underprivileged students pursue higher education. She was also an outspoken supporter of the NFL Alumni Association. In 1997, she spearheaded the formation of the St. Louis Rams Foundation, which has contributed more than $7 million to charities in the St. Louis area.

Always a patron of the arts, in 2000, Frontiere donated $1 million to help build a 5,500-seat amphitheater, the Frontiere Performing Arts Pavilion, located in the Sedona Cultural Park in Arizona. She also produced the Tony-nominated August Wilson play *Radio Golf* and Richard Dresser's *Below the Belt*.

Frontiere also sat on numerous boards and was awarded an honorary doctor of philanthropy from Pepperdine University.

Preview of:

Horoscope: Murder in Mercury Retrograde

KELLY WAS SITTING AT the desk in her office on the first floor of her brownstone, thinking about the two women she had interviewed to take the place of her assistant, Sarah, when the doorbell rang. It was Sunday, and Kelly knew she had no appointments with clients coming to see her so she could do their astrological charts. She heard the doorbell ring again and then an insistent knock. She looked out her office window and saw, standing on the stoop at the front door, a young woman in her early twenties. She had dark hair midway to her shoulders and was wearing earmuffs, an expensively tailored brown woolen coat, a brown scarf gathered around her neck and chin to protect her from the frigid January wind, and a very troubled expression on her pretty face.

Thinking she might be a friend of Jeff or Julie, her children, who were away at college, Kelly got up from her chair and walked toward the front door.

"Who is it?" she asked loudly enough to be heard over another knock.

"Amber Moretti," an emotional voice called through the door.

"My father, Lionel Moretti, came to see you about his company, Moretti Fashion."

"Yes," Kelly said. "But today is Sunday, and—"

"My father is dead, Dr. York!" the voice shouted. "Murdered!"

Kelly stood there for a moment and then opened the door. The freezing wind that blew into the house was less of a shock to her system than what the young woman had just told her.

"I'm so sorry," she said. "Come in. I had no idea. I just saw him yesterday."

Amber Moretti walked into the long, narrow entrance hall. Her face was red from the cold, her eyes red from crying.

"He died this morning. The medics who came in the ambulance said he had a heart attack, but if he did, it didn't happen naturally. He was only fifty-eight, and he was healthy. He was obsessed with his health. He never drank, he never smoked, he never ate anything bad, and there was no heart disease in his family. Last week he went to have his heart checked, and the cardiologist said it was like a thirty-year-old's. It may have looked like a heart attack, but I know he was murdered. And I know who killed him: Chelsea Nelson, the president of his company. He was having an affair with her."

All at once she started crying.

"Let's go into the living room and sit down," Kelly said. Gently, she put her arm around the young woman's shoulder and led her down the hall, toward the rear of the brownstone.

Amber wiped her eyes with her gloved hand as Kelly showed her into the gracefully furnished living room and gestured to a chair at the dining table near the French doors that looked out at the garden.

"Would you like some tea? Or hot chocolate?" Kelly asked.

"No, thank you." Although it was warm inside the room and

she was still wearing her coat, earmuffs, scarf, and gloves, Amber shivered. She glanced at Kelly and then looked down at her lap. After a while, she looked up at Kelly again. She took off her earmuffs and gloves before speaking. "I apologize, Dr. York. It hits me in waves, the reality that my father is really dead."

"I understand." Kelly's clear, dark blue eyes looked at Amber with the compassion and sensitivity of a woman who really did understand.

Amber dried her eyes again, this time with the back of her hand, before continuing. "My father said you told him not to sell part of his company . . . that he should retain full ownership himself."

Kelly felt Amber's anguish and didn't want to contradict her, but what Amber had just said didn't coincide with the facts. She wondered how much she should tell Amber about her talk with her father. Lionel Moretti hadn't seen Kelly as a psychotherapist—indeed, although she had a PhD in psychology, she didn't practice as a therapist—so she had no obligation for confidentiality, but she wasn't in the habit of discussing her astrological consultations with people other than her clients.

Another look at the sorrowful young woman decided the matter.

"Your father told me he was entertaining an offer from someone who wants to buy forty percent of Moretti Fashion, and he asked what the astrological aspects indicated he should do. I explained to him that Mercury is retrograde now—it went retrograde four days ago, on January twenty-second, and will stay retrograde until February twelfth. During that time, it's not a good idea to make any major decisions. But I didn't tell him not to sell part of the company. All I told him was that, obviously, selling part of a privately held business, especially one as successful as

Moretti Fashion, is a major decision, and I suggested that he wait until after February twelfth to decide."

Amber looked at Kelly a moment more and then started crying again.

"I know how you're feeling, losing your father so suddenly," Kelly said. "My parents died in an accident when I was nine, and I—"

Amber cut her off. "Didn't you see in his chart that he was going to die? That someone was going to kill him?"

Kelly's heart went out to the young woman across the table from her. She wanted to comfort her, but she didn't see that she had any comfort to offer.

"Didn't you see it in his chart?" Amber demanded, half accusingly, half pleadingly.

Her desperation made Kelly feel even more like comforting her and more acutely aware that she didn't have the means to do so.

"I didn't do his chart," she said. "Your father was a friend of my ex-husband, Jack York. He mentioned he wanted to consult an astrologer and Jack recommended me. The day your father saw me, he was in a rush. He stopped in for just a few minutes between appointments. When I told him Mercury is retrograde and it's not a good time for important decisions, he told me that was all he needed for now, and he'd have me prepare his chart later. He was supposed to call me with his birth information, but he hadn't called yet."

"Was Chelsea with him when he saw you?"

"Yes."

"Did she say anything when you told him to wait?"

Kelly's first instinct was to say that Chelsea Nelson had said nothing. Then she thought about the beautiful woman, who had been introduced as the president of the company, sitting with Lionel Moretti, her boss, who had designed the women's and men's clothing lines that had made Moretti Fashion one of the most famous fashion houses in the world. Kelly remembered Lionel: he'd been handsome and vital, with thick, graying blond hair, lively hazel eyes, and a ready smile. She pictured the woman sitting next to him. She'd had long red hair and pale, smooth white skin, looking as lovely and striking at forty as she had twenty years before when Kelly had seen her on the covers of *Vogue, Harper's Bazaar*, and *Elle*.

Chelsea Nelson's sable coat and multicolored Moretti cashmere scarf, with the initial *M* embroidered near the fringe, had been folded on her lap, and she had listened attentively as Kelly explained that Mercury is the planet that governs communication, and that was why when Mercury is retrograde—literally going backward—there are bound to be glitches in communication; business agreements negotiated or signed during that time are likely to have problems. For that reason, it would be wise for Lionel to postpone crucial decisions about the company. Kelly remembered that after she'd said this, Chelsea Nelson had turned to Lionel, parted her perfectly shaped red lips, and given her opinion in a calm, even voice.

"Yes, she did," Kelly said. "She told your father that he knew she thought he should sell a share of the company but that just in case Mercury retrograde really meant something, he might as well wait three weeks and see how he felt after February twelfth."

"Of course she wanted him to sell part of the company!" Amber said, upset. "It would mean a lot of money for her. All she ever wants is money! That's the reason she was having an affair with him! She got him to put it in her contract that if he sold the company, or even a piece of it, she'd get millions. Then she found this Russian investor who made the offer! I don't know how she did it, but she killed him. She wasn't going to wait three weeks. She didn't want to take the chance that he'd decide not to do it!"

Amber took a moment to get her anger under control. "My father was weak to be taken in by Chelsea, but he was a wonderful man, and he loved my stepmother. If he lived, he would've realized that. He didn't deserve to die just because he was foolish."

"Have you told the police what you think?" Kelly asked.

"Yes, but I don't think they believed me. That's why I need your help."

Kelly felt her body tense. "I don't understand. How can I help you?"

"You can help me prove Chelsea murdered him like you helped the FBI find that serial killer."

Kelly shook her head. "That was different. That was because—"

"I know about how you got involved in finding the serial killer. I saw stories about it in the paper and on TV and on the Internet. I know a man was threatening you, too. That he tried to kill you. But you helped the FBI find a murderer they never would've found without you. You're an astrologer and a psychologist, and you used what you know to find the killer. I want you to use what you know to help me prove that Chelsea killed my father."

Kelly looked at the grieving young woman. Amber's brown eyes were wet from crying, and she shivered again. Kelly felt for her, but the last thing she wanted to do was get involved again in finding a murderer—if in Lionel Moretti's case there even was a murderer.

"I'm going to call someone I know in the police department. I'll talk to him about it."

Amber stood up. "I don't care what it costs for you to help

me. I have a trust fund. I can pay you any amount you want. Just tell me."

Kelly rose, too. "It's not a question of money. Just let me speak to the police detective. I'll call you after I reach him."

Amber looked plaintively at her. "No matter what he says, will you at least think about helping me?"

The desperation in the young woman's eyes was so deep that Kelly felt she had no choice. "Yes, I will think about it."

Amber held Kelly's gaze long enough to make sure that Kelly really meant what she'd said, that she would think about it. Then quietly, and with a gratitude that moved Kelly, she said, "Thank you."

Amber put on her earmuffs and gloves and walked into the hall. Kelly followed behind her. Just before reaching the front door, Amber turned to her, took a card from her coat pocket, and handed it to her.

"Here's my contact information. Call me day or night. Thank you again."

Kelly opened the door and watched Amber walk out into the cold, like a somnambulant. She seemed oblivious to the freezing temperature, oblivious to everything but her father's death and her conviction that Chelsea Nelson had murdered him.

Kelly closed the door and looked at the card with Amber's name and phone number on it, along with the words "Pro Bono Family Law." Kelly was surprised that Amber was a lawyer; she didn't look old enough. And she was impressed that Amber was a pro bono family lawyer; instead of practicing law for a lucrative income, Amber was donating her services to families and children that couldn't afford a lawyer.

Suddenly Kelly saw Amber in a different light—not as a rich young woman who fell into the category of hating her father's mistress, but as a young woman with a strong purpose in life. Kelly didn't know Amber's birth and rising signs, or where any of her other planets were located, but clearly she cared about children and families. Amber had grown up with wealth, but she was spending her days in courtrooms with poor parents and children plagued by problems that could affect their lives forever, and she served as their lawyer with the hope that she could help make their lives better in the future than they had been in the past.

Finding out that Amber Moretti was a lawyer told Kelly something else, too. It told her that what Amber had said about Chelsea Nelson's contract with Moretti Fashion was coming from someone with the legal training to understand contracts.

Besides wanting to comfort this young woman, Kelly felt she needed to take her seriously.

Holding Amber's card, she walked into her office and called a number she remembered from two and a half months before, when she'd called it more than once in a panic, afraid for her life. Now she called it with a different urgency, the urgency to help a young woman in emotional pain.

An officer answered and told her she'd reached the 20th Precinct. Kelly asked for Detective Stevens. While she waited for him to come on the line, she made up her mind: if there was any way she could help Amber Moretti, she would. Maybe Lionel Moretti really had been murdered.